Praise for WYNNE'S WAR

"The book's pacing is cinematic, and it echoes adrenalized silver-screen war stories like *Three Kings* and *The Hurt Locker,* as well as the gentler cross-species concerns of *The Horse Whisperer.*"

—John Williams, *New York Times*

"A hard-eyed depiction of modern warfare leavened slightly by its Western spirit, Gwyn's novel is rich in equestrian and military detail . . . It'd take wild horses to pull you away."

—*Entertainment Weekly*

"Gwyn depicts the eventful mission with tight dramatic control and a flair for suspenseful twists. His cleverest touch is to transplant the vintage conventions of the Western into his battle pieces . . . *Wynne's War* evokes John Ford's *The Searchers,* and the same ambiguities that surround John Wayne's ruthlessly single-minded Ethan Edwards come to define Wynne."

—*Wall Street Journal*

"A work of narrative alchemy . . . A prose smelter brimming with horses, soldiers, heroism, villainy, horrific violence, and unexpected tenderness . . . It's also a page-turning romp . . . There's entertainment aplenty and characters whose lives are real enough to have been lived."

—Bruce Machart, *Houston Chronicle*

"Gwyn controls the plot and its mounting suspense tightly . . . A straightforward, tautly written soldier's tale where military goal, leadership, character, battlefield friendship, and the degree of acceptable human sacrifice are the main concerns."

—Katherine A. Powers, *Chicago Tribune*

"A gripping tale of men at war in the desolate snow-capped mountains of eastern Afghanistan [that] captures the essence of close combat—the terror, excitement, chaos, tension, and cruelty, as well as the harsh decisions men make under stress . . . Its gritty realism is part of the strength."

—*Publishers Weekly,* starred review

"Pulsates with a verisimilitude that places readers in the war-torn mountains of Afghanistan . . . Many folks have wondered when American authors would begin producing memorable fiction about the Iraq-Afghanistan wars; with this well-researched, heart-pounding novel, Gwyn stakes his claim." —*Library Journal*

"Gwyn's combat scenes are realistic, meticulous, and passionate." —*Booklist*

"This novel feels like Cormac McCarthy meets Tim O'Brien. I could not stop reading it." —Philipp Meyer, author of *The Son*

"*Wynne's War* is a deep and beautifully written story of men, war, and madness, told by a young American master. A page-turner of poetic and savage grace, of our time but transcending it, this novel takes its rightful place among the great American literature of war."
—Nic Pizzolatto, author of *Galveston,* creator of *True Detective*

"I haven't had this much fun as a reader in a long time. *Wynne's War* is a great adventure story, impeccably researched, masterfully plotted, with chapters that blur by like a hail of bullets."
—Benjamin Percy, author of *Red Moon*

"*Wynne's War* combines two of America's great literary genres, the Western and the war story, brilliantly. This taut, elegant, beautiful novel takes us straight to the tension at the heart of combat decision-making: mission or men."
—Nathaniel Fick, author of *One Bullet Away*

"Propellant storytelling in the tradition of McCarthy and Conrad. A gripping morality tale told with bristling exactitude."
—Paul Lynch, author of *Red Sky in Morning*

WYNNE'S WAR

Books by Aaron Gwyn

Dog on the Cross

The World Beneath

Wynne's War

WYNNE'S WAR

Aaron Gwyn

An Eamon Dolan Book

MARINER BOOKS

HOUGHTON MIFFLIN HARCOURT

BOSTON • NEW YORK

For the men in tan berets—

MALA MALIS FACIMUS

First Mariner Books edition 2015

www.hmhco.com

Library of Congress Cataloging-in-Publication Data
Gwyn, Aaron.
Wynne's war / Aaron Gwyn.
pages cm
"An Eamon Dolan Book."
ISBN 978-0-544-23027-9 (hardback) ISBN 978-0-544-48404-7 (pbk.)
1. Afghan War, 2001- —Fiction. I. Title.
PS3607.W96W98 2014
813'.6—dc23
2013048434

Design by Chrissy Kurpeski
Typeset in Plantin and Grotesque

Printed in the United States of America
DOC 10 9 8 7 6 5 4 3 2

He spoke of his campaigns in the deserts of Mexico and he told them of horses killed under him and he said that the souls of horses mirror the souls of men more closely than men suppose and that horses also love war. Men say they only learn this but he said that no creature can learn that which his heart has no shape to hold. His own father said that no man who has not gone to war horseback can ever truly understand the horse and he said that he supposed he wished that this were not so but that it was so.

— Cormac McCarthy, *All the Pretty Horses*

HE SAW THE horse before the rest of his team and thumbed the selector on his rifle to SAFE. There were eight of them hunkered behind the row of HESCOs, eight Rangers in digital camo, black kneepads, and vests. Rifle rounds from the insurgents snapped against the wire mesh of the barricades, and he'd been watching, through a crack, the quadrangle of marketplace between him and the hostiles—sandstone, pottery, a dry concrete fountain—and then the horse emerged from behind the burnt husk of a Toyota and walked toward the center of the square. Left hind leg, left front leg. Right hind leg, right front leg. No hurry in its gait. No saddle or blanket. Just a bridle and a set of split leather reins. Russell had seen plenty of mules in this country, a disheveled pony, but never a creature such as this. It was a varnish roan, dark brown on its cheekbones, elbows, and hocks, and if it was startled by the noise of gunfire, it certainly didn't show. The horse walked to the center of the quad and stopped. A hush descended over the square, and for several moments they didn't take any fire. The men behind him were peeking over the barriers and examining the animal through their scopes. Fifty meters away, the horse snorted and stamped. It took a few more steps, ears pivoting left and right. Russell got his feet under him and rose to a crouch. His squad leader was a Texan named Cairns, and the man clapped a hand to Russell's shoulder and gestured.

"They'll shoot that thing," he told him. "You see if they don't."

Russell shook his head. The sun sat on the edge of the horizon, and the sky was suffused with a warm crimson light. Stars were beginning to show. He couldn't see a single cloud. It would have been a lovely evening but for the half-dozen men trying to kill them. He looked at the ground a moment and then he raised his rifle and stared through the scope. Caught in the center of his reticle, the horse looked to be about sixteen hands, and its conformation was very fine. He studied the horse's face and then walked the gunsight down its neck and across its shoulders and back. It wasn't a horse yet, just a year-and-a-half colt. How it got here and who it belonged to and why it had walked toward the shooting instead of away from it, Russell had no idea. He lowered the weapon slightly, blinked the dust out of his eyes, and then raised it to look again. He'd not gotten the scope to his eye when he heard the first shot.

Just to the left of the crosshairs was a puff of gray talc where the round had struck, and he thought he could see the small cavity it had made, but he wasn't really sure. The horse took several steps and then stopped and turned to look in his direction. Russell felt his pulse quicken. The scope mounted on his rifle was a Trijicon ACOG with a magnification level of four, and through it he could see the horse's eyes. He could see its lashes. The horse seemed to be staring straight at him, and before he'd lowered his weapon he knew what he was going do, and if it didn't get him killed, he couldn't imagine what would.

He glanced at Cairns.

"What'd I tell you?" said the sergeant. "That's how dumb they think we are."

Russell nodded. He slipped a hand in his pocket and touched the silver dollar, then unslung his rifle and propped it against the barrier. He had two grenades in the pouches of his chest rig, and he took these out and laid them alongside the rifle's stock. He double-knotted the laces of his boots and then he unsnapped his chinstrap, took off the helmet, and set it on the ground upside down, placing the grenades inside. Cairns watched in confusion and then vague comprehension and then horror. The first words out of his mouth were, "Don't you even think about it," but it was already too late. Russell was around from behind the HESCOs, moving at a sprint.

Later, he'd not remember the gunfire. There'd be plenty of it, but he'd never recall a single round. There would be the feel of dead September air on his cheeks, the packed earth against the soles of his boots: it seemed to muffle your footsteps as you ran. He'd remember the shouts of his teammates at the barricades behind him, Sergeant Cairns's voice deeper and slightly louder than the rest. Russell had only lowered his head. The blank odor of desert surrounded him, and then, of a sudden, there was the scent of horseflesh, and the moment he smelled it, there was no team screaming for him to get down or insurgents firing their rifles on automatic. There was only him and the colt.

The animal had turned to watch his approach and then shuffled sideways a few steps. Russell slowed several feet from the horse, wanting to hunker but knowing how the colt would respond. He stood straight as he could, face to face with the animal, and they began to rotate, the horse stepping to its right and Russell likewise stepping, like wrestlers circling for advantage. He extended a hand as slowly as he could, presented his palm, and began to make the clucking noises he'd first heard from his grandfather. "Whoa there," Russell said, then gave the series of clucks, and the horse released a whinny and shook its head. The ground beneath their feet was a steel-colored powder, a few broken bits of sandstone, a few rusted metal shards. A half-demolished building stood two dozen meters away—ancient stone walls, baroque wooden shutters, a minaret. The horse backed toward it. Russell thought if he could back it completely behind the walls, he might get them out of the lane of fire.

But he couldn't get them out of the lane of fire. The horse continued to turn, angling them toward the square's center, back into the open, and the sand popped at either side, craters erupting in the ground as the bullets struck and caromed back behind him. He reached for one of the reins and missed it, and he reached again and caught hold of the leather, doubled it around his left hand, and drew himself against the animal's face. He figured the colt would try to jerk loose from his grip, but the colt just continued to circle, Russell tethered to the animal now, and he could see for the first time the terror swirling in the horse's eye and he himself reflected, distorted as in a funhouse mirror.

They kept turning, Russell trying to seize hold of the other rein so he could lead the animal down a side street, get it far enough from the fighting that it wouldn't return. He was seventy-five meters from the nearest hostile, and he thought if the men who'd been firing at them were better marksmen, he and the colt would be dead already. He'd decided to release his grip on the rein and try to swat the animal to get it moving, when something exploded behind him and he was lifted on a warm cushion of air and slammed against the horse's side.

When he came to, he was being dragged across the ground and his left arm felt like it had been jerked out of its socket and was numb to the shoulder. His vision was blurred and there was a loud ringing in his ears, and his entire body had the jangled sensation you get when you knock your elbow against a wall. There was the strong metallic taste of explosives in his mouth. His teeth hurt. He spat several times and then craned his neck to look behind him. The horse was walking sideways, its head cocked and its body crooked. It would take a few steps, tugging at Russell, and then stop and try to shake free of the rein. Russell could see the white of the animal's teeth, lips pulled away from the bit and working furiously. He was dimly aware of shouting, and when he brought his palm to his face, it came away wet.

The horse took another step, jerked its head, and a sharp electric pain traveled the length of Russell's spine. He scrambled to his feet before he even had time to consider the action, and the horse immediately straightened itself and took off at a trot, Russell shuffling as quickly as he could, turning to run alongside the colt with his left arm still tethered to the rein. There was a stabbing behind his shoulder blade, and he reached with his right hand, grabbed a palmful of the animal's mane, and heaved himself onto its back. He forgot the pain momentarily and let the astonishment of what he'd just done wash over him. He was in northern Iraq, seated on a magnificent roan, and when his vision cleared and the world righted itself, he saw he was moving toward the enemy at a gallop. He fumbled his right hand down and took hold of the bridle and began tugging, trying to turn the horse. He'd never ridden with body armor, and he had no pommel to lean against, no stirrups to keep himself upright. He thought at any moment he'd be thrown.

But he wasn't thrown. The horse sped slightly, and Russell flattened himself against the colt's neck and held fast to the bridle. He began to hear the gunfire now—the only he'd ever recall from the incident—and the horse dropped to a canter and turned down an alley between two partially destroyed buildings, ancient and massive. They went to the next street over and across that to another alley and then to another beyond. They emerged into a courtyard where several Humvees sat, U.S. soldiers with rifles at the ready, and the horse slowed to a walk, brought them into the center of the convoy, and then came to a stop. Russell eased himself upright on the animal's back. Stunned American faces stared at him from beneath their helmets. Iraqi interpreters watched cautiously, Iraqi policemen shaking their heads. Then a man walked toward him with a second-lieutenant's patch on the Velcro strip above his sternum. He came to the horse's left side and looked up at Russell.

"Corporal," he said.

The ringing in his ears had receded to a low whine, and the word echoed twice. Russell cleared his throat to respond, but the rush of something came from down inside him. His last memory was the nicker of the animal as he collapsed against its neck.

When Russell was released from the aid station ten days later, he dressed in the clean uniform laid out on a folding chair beside his bed, gathered his belongings into a small plastic bag, and made his way across base to his squad's barracks, stepping carefully along the gravel walkways, his boots untied and the laces tucked behind the tongues. It hurt too much to bend over. His torso was an enormous bruise.

He reached the Quonset hut, and when he stepped up the short cinder-block flight and into the building, the men were waiting for him in a semicircle around the door. Someone threw on the lights and a cheer went up, and there were hands slapping his back and sides. Russell tucked his elbows to try to protect his ribs, but the men left off, took him by either arm, and ushered him to his bunk. They fetched a laptop and placed it on his thighs. Cairns was standing there over him.

"Man of the hour," said the sergeant.

"Yeah," Russell said.

A soldier they called Wheels—Russell's battle-buddy and a Texan like Cairns—lifted his hand to quiet everyone. He was very short with a scar that went up his forehead, and pupils that quivered perpetually back and forth. Pale skin sunburned a bright red. Hair bleached almost white.

"Let's see," he said, "if he'll tell us how it feels."

Russell looked around at the expectant faces. He asked what was going on.

Wheels bent over, palmed his knees, and stared at Russell. Then his brow went slack and he began to nod.

"He doesn't know," Wheels told them, glancing at the others, then back at Russell. "You don't even know."

"Know what?"

Several of the men chuckled. Watching someone return from the infirmary with a concussion and bruised ribs was apparently very funny. He wondered where they'd gotten their hands on liquor.

Wheels clutched him by the shoulders. "You're famous, son."

"You're drunk," Russell said.

The men had crowded behind him on the bed, positioning themselves so as to see the computer screen. YouTube was open on the browser, a rectangle of video and below it the caption "Soldier Rescues Arabian." Wheels reached down and clicked a button, and the footage began to play—a man running along a street, the distorted chatter of gunfire. The camera followed the man until a horse appeared in the frame, and it took Russell a few moments to realize the person in the video was him.

He sat there shaking his head. He asked where it was from.

"Film crew on a balcony across the street," Wheels told him. "BBC."

Russell watched as his image took one of the horse's reins and then as he and the animal began to turn. He could see the puffs of dust kicked up by the insurgents' rounds. He hadn't recognized how close he'd come to getting shot.

And then the blast of the RPG—the rocket's vapor trail and the explosion that sent him crashing into the animal's side—and then, briefly, a shot of him being dragged beside the horse. This was obscured by a building, and the camera searched left and right, and you could hear the cameraman asking where he'd gone. When the horse reemerged, Russell was on its back, and the camera tracked him until he went out of frame. There the video stopped.

Wheels said, "Been playing it on the news every fifteen minutes."

"They did a thing on your granddad," said a specialist named Bowen. "Guy on CNN."

"CNN," said Wheels with contempt.

"Talked about his being a Ranger, your granddad. World War Two. Talked about his training horses."

"Communist News Network," said Wheels. "Fuck they know about horses?"

Bowen studied the floor a moment. He was a goliath from South Boston and had dominated the New England Golden Gloves circuit before joining the army.

"They had pictures," he said, shrugging.

"Everyone's got pictures," Wheels said.

Russell ignored them. He clicked the button to replay the video, and when it was over he just sat.

"That's not an Arabian," he finally said.

"What's that?" Wheels asked.

"It's not an Arabian," Russell told him. "The caption says 'Arabian.' 'Soldier Rescues Arabian.' It's an Appaloosa."

"Jesus," said Wheels, "I want you to listen at him."

Cairns shook his head. He turned and made for the other end of the barracks.

When the men tired of discussing the incident and went back to their evening routine—poker, e-mail, a few of them reading a series of novels in which the dead became animate and rose to feed on human flesh—Cairns came back around. He had very blue eyes, jet black hair, and his Texas accent gave his voice a strange authority. He pointed at the edge of Russell's bunk.

"You mind?"

Russell was lying on his back with his hands at his sides, trying to breathe as shallowly as possible. He opened one eye and squinted up at the man. He told him to be his guest.

Cairns hitched his pants and seated himself, turned toward Russell, crossed his left leg over his right, and sat with his fingers interlaced, cupping his knee.

"You feeling good, Corporal? You feeling satisfied?"

"I feel all right."

"Lord knows," said Cairns, "we want our Rangers happy."

Russell stared at the man. He asked if there was something wrong.

"*Wrong?*" said Cairns, affecting a theatrical look. "Why would anything be wrong?"

The blood in Russell's body seemed to slow. He'd known he was going to have to listen to this at some point, he just wasn't sure when that point would be.

"Let me ask you something," said Cairns.

Russell nodded.

"What do you think the proceeds of your little stunt would've been if that grenade had gone off about ten meters closer?"

"I don't reckon I'd be laying here," said Russell.

"No, I don't reckon you would, either. Fact, I reckon you'd be laying someplace else. Maybe half a dozen places." Cairn's face had gone red, and veins stood out on his neck. "Am I boring you, Corporal?"

It wasn't a question and Russell didn't answer it.

"You pull another maneuver like that, you'll wish you'd deserted."

"Roger, Sergeant."

"I'll see you charged with insubordination. I'll see you in Leavenworth."

Russell lay very still. He could feel the headache coming on.

"Are you a Section Eight?" Cairns asked. "If you're a Section Eight, just tell me."

"I'm not a Section Eight, Sergeant."

"Why'd you do it? Don't tell me you don't know."

Russell came up onto his left elbow, but that was as far as he got. The headache was very sharp, and the pain in his side was like needles and pins. He took a few moments and then he said, "I couldn't watch them shoot the horse."

Cairns just stared.

"Corporal," he said, "why are we here?"

Russell shifted his weight, repositioned his hips, and lowered himself back against the mattress. "'To provide overwatch,'" he quoted, "'for our operators and support assets in direct contact with hostiles.'"

"Anything in there about rescuing horses or kittens or whatever the fuck else?"

"No, Sergeant."

"Are you a Section Eight?"

"Negative, Sergeant."

"Are you going to pull any more ridiculous shit?"

"Sergeant, that's the first horse I've seen since I left home. I doubt I'll see another."

Cairns scooted closer.

"Corporal, are you going to fuck up my squad with any more of this dumbass behavior?"

Russell took a short breath and released it.

"Negative, Sergeant. I think that I'm done."

Russell laced his boots in the half-light and the cold of the barracks and stood from the narrow aluminum cot. The lieutenant was waiting at the end of the building, her silhouette in the doorway, black against the purpling sky. He glanced at Wheels in his rack—the man's face slack now and blank as a child's—took the tan beret and the jacket from his footlocker, and went up the aisle. The woman nodded to him when he reached the door, and he followed her into the courtyard and then along the sandstone corridor that went curving against the inner wall. The air prickled the skin on his arms, and he threaded his hands through the sleeves of his jacket—left and right—shrugged into it, zipping as he walked. The lieutenant went on before him, her steps almost soundless and the hair at the nape of her neck in an intricate bun.

The mosque at Qara Serai was calling worshipers to prayer, the sounds traveling in the predawn chill with their own peculiar lilt, alien to his ears and yet familiar in the way of dreamspeech, the way of song. They reached the colonel's quarters at the end of the passage, and Russell closed the storm flap up the front of his jacket, smoothing a hand across the Velcro fasteners. The woman motioned him through the doorway and took up a post outside. As he passed, he peeled the beret from his head and tucked it beneath an arm. He forced a smile at the woman, and she gave him just the slightest one back.

The hallway looked to have been carved from granite. He passed two doors on his right and three on his left, and at the next door he paused, straightened his jacket, and knocked lightly on the wooden jamb.

A voice told him to come in.

The room was small with very high ceilings, and there was a west-facing window that had been cut into the wall by hammer and chisel a hundred, maybe two hundred, years before. Stars were visible in the sky just beyond. The colonel sat at a mahogany desk, and when Russell entered, the man pushed his chair back and rose. He was in his early sixties, hair gone silver, the flesh beneath his chin just beginning to sag. He wore a precisely trimmed mustache whose bottom had been clipped so it didn't touch his upper lip or extend beyond the edges of his mouth. He returned Russell's salute and motioned him to one of the chairs in front of the desk, which was too large, Russell decided, to fit through the doorway. It would have been taken apart and reassembled, piece by piece.

Russell lowered himself onto the thin metal seat. His heart had begun to race. He tried to slow it, but that only made it faster. He focused on his posture: feet together, back straight, hands resting palm down on his thighs.

The colonel seated himself and scooted closer to his desk, glancing through his reading glasses at a sheet of paper, which he fingered briefly and set aside.

"Morning," he said.

Russell told him good morning.

"Lieutenant Wilkins get you up?"

"No, sir," said Russell. "I was awake."

"Watch how you sit in that thing," the man told him. "Leg wobbles. We had it taken over to supply; they sent it back with the same exact problem."

Russell said he'd be careful.

The colonel nodded, brought a fist to his mouth, and cleared his throat.

"Dr. Halpern tells me you're recovering."

"Getting there," Russell said.

"He tells me there was a concussion?"

"Yessir."

"But you're feeling better?"

"Much better. Yessir."

The colonel rubbed his palm along his jaw and repositioned himself in his chair.

"That was a hell of a hit you took."

Russell nodded.

"Watched the video on Fox. You've seen it?"

"Yessir. Just last night."

The colonel leaned back in his chair and regarded him a moment.

"Kind of crazy, aren't you, Corporal?"

"I don't know, sir."

The colonel stared at him. "You don't know?"

"No, sir."

"You were that Ranger in the video riding an unsaddled horse through a firefight?"

Russell shifted in his chair. He glanced at his hands on either knee, the knuckles white.

"Yessir," he told the colonel, "that was me."

"And you won't own up to being crazy?"

Russell looked down at his hands again and then back up at the desk. He tried to speak but nothing came.

"Corporal?"

Russell closed his eyes briefly. When he opened them, he said, "Sir, I never done anything like that before."

"Never done anything like that?"

"No, sir."

"So your position is this craziness is kind of new to you?"

"Yessir," Russell told him. "Pretty much."

The colonel wiped the crease of a smile from the left side of his mouth. He reached and took up the sheet of paper he'd set on a stack of manila folders and held it at arm's length, squinting.

"Message came through last night," he began, his voice shifting into a formal cadence. "You been attached to us six months now, so you're acquainted with the protocol."

Russell nodded.

"You know about our sister company in Afghanistan?"

"I know we have one," he said.

The colonel blinked several times. He glanced at the paper in his hand and then seemed to study a spot on the wall just behind Russell's head.

"You also have to know that there are officers in this task force way up the food chain above me."

"I assume so, yessir."

The colonel opened his mouth to continue and then closed it. He exhaled a deep breath and tossed the paper back onto the stack of folders.

"Let me be as direct as I can."

Russell nodded.

"I have received an order to release you from my command next Tuesday at nineteen hundred hours and put you on an overflight to Bagram. You'll be reassigned to a Special Forces element operating in Nuristan Province, mountains of eastern Afghanistan. Captain by the name of Wynne. I assume you've heard of the man."

"No, sir."

"Haven't heard of him?"

Russell shook his head.

"Do you know the region? Nuristan?"

"Sir, I do not."

"There are loud voices," said the colonel, "who don't believe we should be anywhere near this area, and to be frank with you, Corporal, it chaps my ass to send one of my men on some Green Beret bullshit, but I have protested your transfer and have been kindly advised to fuck myself." He stopped and shook his head. "I fought it hard as I could."

Russell sat there a moment. His home was seven thousand miles away in northeastern Oklahoma, and for the first time in months, he wanted to be there very badly.

"May I ask a question, sir?"

"Ask it."

"Do you have any idea why they want me?"

The colonel's mouth tightened. He tapped the desk three times with the knuckles of his right hand. He said, "Captain Wynne's made a bit of a name for himself. He's the one got those marine snipers out during that clusterfuck in Fallujah. Almost died doing it, but he's got balls, and he's not afraid to stand up to the Agency."

"Which agency?"

"CIA."

"How's he get away with that?"

"He gets away with it," said the colonel, "the way anyone gets away with it: he gets himself a different idea than the spooks and then he convinces the head-shed that it's right."

"Where do I fit in to all this?" Russell asked.

"Hard to say," the colonel told him. "My guess would be that our captain got a look at your highlight reel and figured out a way to make use of it. Has himself some slick friends in higher." The man shook his head. "Can't say I envy your position."

"No, sir," said Russell. "I'm not all that envious myself."

"Your grandfather was Second Rangers?"

"Yessir."

"Normandy?"

"Yessir."

The colonel nodded.

"And he trained horses for a living?"

"Yessir, he did."

"That's where you learned it?"

"That's where I learned everything," Russell said.

The colonel watched him a moment. Then he said, "I've been able to get your battle-buddy attached."

"Sir?"

"Corporal Grimes. He'll be coming with."

"Wheels?"

The colonel nodded. "I got them to agree to that much. Kind of solves two problems at once." The man cast Russell a knowing look, but whatever he'd meant to convey was lost on Russell entirely.

"You'll have about a week to rest up," said the colonel. "I assume you'd like some downtime."

"Yessir. I'd appreciate it."

The colonel looked down at his papers a moment and then back up at Russell. The smile creased the left side of his mouth again, but he didn't bother to wipe it away.

"Can I ask *you* something?" he said.

"Of course."

"Why in the name of God did you take your Kevlar off?"

"Sir?"

"In the video. You aren't wearing your helmet. What possessed you to remove it?"

Russell took a moment to think about this. He said, "I guess I was afraid it'd scare the horse."

The colonel's eyes widened momentarily and then they narrowed. "Scare the horse."

"Yessir," Russell said.

Russell would say that his grandfather had taught him to ride, but his grandfather always said he hadn't taught the boy a thing. At stock shows and county fairs, at rodeos and clinics, men would tell Leroy Crider how well he'd instructed his grandson.

"I didn't instruct nothing," Crider would say. "Just the way he was born."

The men would nod and smile and sip from their Styrofoam cups of coffee, small cups, six ounces. They thought the old man was being modest, but Crider never numbered modesty among his sins. Stubbornness, yes. Ignorance. He'd admit, at times, to outright lunacy. But he was not a modest man, and he'd taught his grandson nothing about horses he didn't already know.

Elijah, for his part, had no sense of when he'd learned what he knew, and he couldn't even recall the first time he sat a horse. They seemed to inhabit his memories in much the same way as sunlight or wind or his grandmother's voice: they were inexplicably and undeniably there.

His first word was the name of his Welsh Mountain pony, a palomino named Cream. He had the white face and stockings, and he was only thirteen hands—a very gentle little horse. His grandfather would saddle him and lead him around the corral with Elijah on his back and still in diapers, Elijah's grandmother standing in one corner of the pen with her arms cradled against her and her elbows in her palms.

"You get that baby off him," she'd say.

"He ain't hurting nothing," Crider would tell her, and she'd respond it wasn't the pony she was worried about.

"That thing could buck," she'd say. "You don't know what it could do."

Crider ignored her. He led the pony very slowly by a leather halter, Elijah seated against the pommel with both hands on the horn, his toddler's legs bouncing.

By the age of five he could ride this animal unsupervised to the barbed-wire fence at the end of the south pasture. By seven, he could saddle and cinch and push the horse to a canter. He was performing in children's rodeos before his tenth birthday, and when he was thirteen he was employed by Lee Brothers Horse and Cattle Auction outside Skiatook, riding show ponies through the cast-iron chute and then down a short concrete tunnel, emerging into the half-acre expanse of loose powdered dirt skirted on four sides by an eight-foot wall, atop which bleachers ascended toward the fluorescent lights hanging high above. From the arena's floor he could only see the first few rows of horse and cattle buyers, their stone faces and cowboy hats, many in ball caps advertising feed stores, barbeque joints and rib shacks, farm-equipment suppliers, and Tinker Air Force Base, where more and more would commute as the farms went bankrupt and the ranches sold to oil companies. He'd walk the animals in a slow circle while the auctioneer's voice boomed from the speakers in its sharp, staccato twang and men in the audience lifted a hand or gestured their bids with the touch of a hat brim.

"Going four, four, four. Who'll give me four? Got four. Now four and a quarter, four and a quarter, now five, five, five. Got five. Five and a half, five and a half, five and a half. Thank you, sir. Now six, six, six."

He'd circle the arena floor at a slow trot, with the auctioneer singing in his ears and the smell of horse and dust and manure and the clean scent of straw still in his nostrils, turning the pony with a squeeze of his thighs and just the slightest pull of the reins, bringing the animal to a halt, turning it once more and then again at the auctioneer's command—"Got seven, got seven, got seven, now eight, now eight, who'll give me eight?"—gestures now from all over the stands, and the price is pushed to nine, nine-fifty, a thousand, sold for a thousand dollars to the man in the silver Stetson. And Elijah turns and rides back down the concrete tunnel past the owners and handlers, dismounts the horse, and quickly mounts the next, a nervous bay he must lean and speak to, and he feels her gentle and soften between his legs—"Now that's a good girl, that is very good."

Afterward, lying in bed with hair damp from his shower, Elijah would stare at the ceiling with his heart pounding high in his chest, still feeling their pulse in his legs and the articulated working of their spines, and he is in absolute love, this boy of thirteen years, father dead, abandoned by his mother, you'd certainly never know. His grandfather is a war hero and his grandmother devoted and doting, and the horse beneath him is every horse that ever was, eyes like stars and a coat like shining brass, galloping up, up, up, out onto the pastures of the night.

He went up the short flight of steps, past the guards, and into the aluminum-sided building that rested off the ground on concrete slabs. He'd grown up in a double-wide of similar manufacture, but this prefab had been built to military specifications and its roof was rigged with a satellite antenna and radar and electronic senders and receivers for which he knew neither the names nor purpose. The temperature outside was 107 degrees when he'd checked it after lunch, but this building was kept a consistent 63. All of the soldiers wore jackets, and a few of the women had stocking caps pulled over their headsets. He dug his ID out of his pants pocket, showed it to a sergeant seated behind the sign-in desk, and was directed to a row of what looked like the carrels in his high school library. There were four of them, and each was equipped with a computer and telephone. He went to the first nook, pulled out the chair, and sat. He spent a few moments collecting himself and then reached for the phone.

He heard the metallic click of the satellite hookup and then the sound of the digital ring. When she picked up and said hello, her voice was surprisingly crisp and he had to steady himself all over again.

"Teresa," he said.

"Hello?"

"Aunt Teresa? Can you hear me?"

"Elijah?" she said. "Hello?"

"It's me," he told her.

She said, "Hold on a second, hon," and he could hear static. "Let me get to this other phone."

He brushed a hand across his face and leaned against the desktop, propping himself on his elbows. There was another click, and he heard her ask her husband to hang up the extension.

"Elijah?" she said. "You there?"

"Yes, ma'am. You hear me all right?"

"I hear you good. Can you hear me?"

"Loud and clear."

She laughed nervously. "We're building a room onto the south end of the house, and that phone in the den—you can't hear anything on it. Are you home? Did they send you back home?"

"No, no. I'm still over here. I—"

"Oh, Lord Jesus. Are you hurt? You're hurt, aren't you?"

"No," said Russell, "I'm fine."

"No, you're not, either. I can hear it in your voice. You better tell me what happened."

"It's nothing," he said. "I yanked out my shoulder a little. That's not even why I called."

"You're not hurt?"

"No, ma'am."

"You wouldn't story to me?"

"No, ma'am. You know I wouldn't. They're just assigning me to another post."

"Did you get the shirts we sent?"

"I did."

"Do they fit?"

"They fit real good."

"I was worried they wouldn't fit."

"No," he told her. "They're perfect."

"And you promise you're not hurt?"

"I'm absolutely fine," he said. "I just got a chance to call you, is all."

"You said they were moving you?"

"Yes, ma'am."

"Don't suppose you could tell me where?"

"No, ma'am."

"Better or worse?" she asked.

He moved the receiver away from his mouth and coughed into his shoulder. "Reckon it'll be about the same."

"Well," she said.

"How's everyone? How's Buddy?"

"He's fine," she said. "We're all fine. I had a cold all summer. I keep thinking I'll get over it, but I don't."

"And Duncan," he asked, bracing himself. "He doing all right?"

"What's that, hon?"

"Duncan," he said, more forcefully than he intended.

"*Duncan,*" she said. "He's fine. We fed him this morning, and Buddy rode him night before last."

"His leg about healed?"

"It's healed real good. Dr. Keppel, when he looked at the x-rays, said he hadn't seen anything like it. Especially not in a ten-year-old."

"Is he favoring it?"

"A little. You've been on him a while, you'll notice on the way back up to the barn. But not like it was. We rub all down the fetlock with that liniment. Buddy took the dressing off three weeks ago."

"He put on weight?"

"Duncan or Buddy?"

"Duncan."

"Oh, I think he maybe could've. Not bad, though."

The two of them went quiet several moments. Then she asked when they'd let him come home.

"I don't know," Russell said. He tried to lean back in the office chair, but it wasn't the kind that leaned. "I just got the new assignment. And I still got half a year left."

"Can they keep you after that? I mean for longer?"

"They can if they get a mind to," he told her, and was sorry as soon as he said it. He tried to think of something to soften it, but she was already talking.

"When do you leave on your new deal? Can you tell me?"

"I can say soon."

"Soon?"

"Yes, ma'am."

"Well," she said.

Then there was silence and Russell knew she'd pressed her palm against the receiver and started crying.

"Teresa?" he said.

He heard her clear her throat.

"Sweetie?" he said, and he felt as he often felt when he called home—that he was toxic somehow. He could infect.

"I'm sorry," she told him, and there was a snuffling sound. "I promised I wouldn't do you this way."

"It's okay," he said.

"I don't know what my problem is," she said brokenly. "You're the one over there fighting." He heard her blow her nose. "I'd swap places with you if I could. Don't think that I wouldn't."

"I know you would," he said. "And then I'd be the one blubbering."

She released a short, tearful laugh.

"Yeah," she said. "I s'pose there's no getting round it."

"No, ma'am," he told her.

There wasn't.

They turned in their rifles to the armory and were issued carbines with the shorter 11.5-inch barrel—commercial rifles from Bushmaster Arms. Wheels eyed his carbine from stock to muzzle and then lifted it off the foam-pillared lining of its case, racked the charging handle, and checked the chamber. He shouldered the weapon and drew a bead on an imaginary target against the cinder-block wall, sighting through the red dot with great intensity. He puffed his cheeks, pouted his lips, and made a short, plosive sound.

He glanced over at Russell, smiling crazily, and then his face quickly clouded and he looked back to the specialist working behind the armory's plywood counter. The specialist was a fat, balding man whose pale eyes pointed in slightly different directions. Russell had been in here several times and he was never sure which eye to look at.

"These are ours?" Wheels asked him. "Just to take?"

The specialist gave a noncommittal shrug and pointed to a yellow sheet of paper where something had been itemized. He reached below the counter, hefted a cardboard box, sat it on the plywood surface, and pushed it toward the Rangers.

Two pairs of Merrell hiking boots were inside, one sized for Russell, the other for Wheels. Four pairs of North Face pants in a color the tags called "dune beige." North Face fleece in gray and black. North Face thermal jackets. Long-sleeved T-shirts from REI. Nylon duty belts from a company that made equipment for firefighters and police. Cotton watch caps with the Nike logo in army green. Under Armour boxers and compression shirts and pairs of stay-dry socks.

They stood there pulling out the gear and measuring items of clothing against arms and legs, surprised by how accurate the fit.

Wheels looked at Russell. "People are going to think we're Greenies," he said.

"Delta Force," said Russell.

"CIA," Wheels said.

He took one of the caps and pulled it over his head.

"You're going to need to sign," the specialist said.

The Rangers looked at him. He'd pulled out another sheet of paper, bright green in color, and laid it on top of the yellow one. "I can't do it for you."

Russell stepped over and took up the pen, scrawled his signature on the line next to the man's index finger, and then handed the pen to Wheels. Behind the counter were rows of two-by-four shelves that extended to the back of the building, shelves of rifles and ammunition and body armor, pinewood crates of C-4, pinewood boxes of grenades. Russell looked at the specialist—whose eyes were pointed one at him, one at Wheels—and he looked back to the shelves toward a lumber-board crate containing two dozen Claymore mines. They could propel steel balls into enemy soldiers out to one hundred meters. He picked up his new gear and turned toward the exit.

That evening they ate dinner in the mess tent—spaghetti and meatballs—and then walked along the compound's outer walls, where they sat on the battlements that looked east toward the Tigris. Here, Russell listened to Wheels recite the details of his latest conspiracy and they made plans for if they were captured. Wheels had a dotted line tattooed around his neck, clavicle to clavicle, above which the crooked words *CUT HERE* had been inked in caps. He said he didn't want his parents seeing him beheaded on Aljazeera, and Russell agreed it'd make for sorry programming.

"You'd shoot me, right?" Wheels asked. "If we got taken?"

"Might shoot you anyways," Russell told him.

"Yeah, yeah," Wheels said.

Then he said, "But seriously."

"Seriously," said Russell. "I'm thinking about shooting you now."

This evening there was no such discussion. They watched the light reflect off the river's surface and casual flocks of doves scatter and bunch. Cranes standing in the shoals. Wheels pulled a pack of Marlboros out of the chest pocket of his jacket, offered one to Russell like he always did, then placed the refused cigarette between his lips and thumbed open his Zippo. They'd been talking about Captain Wynne.

"When we were in Ramadi those first couple weeks—what was it: July of 'five?"

"June."

"June," Wheels said. "Medic there at the Rifles Base I got to be friends with—he'd treated him after his team was ambushed in Fallujah."

Russell said, "The captain?"

"Yeah," Wheels said.

"Where was I when you were making friends with medics?"

"Medic's name was Walton," said Wheels. "This ambush would've been during Second Fallujah, fall of 'four. Wynne's team got in a bad way when they went in to help the marines."

"Colonel mentioned this."

Wheels nodded. "These scout snipers got boxed up, called for air support, but they got Special Forces instead. 'Parently, when the cavalry came, insurgents were waiting. Twelve guys in Wynne's ODA, and they took six causalities. Wynne was one of them—shot through the chest—and he nearly bled out in the Black Hawk on the way back to base. This medic I'm telling you about, he was on that ride, helped Wynne's medic who was trying to—"

"Wait," said Russell. "Which medic?"

"There's Walton," said Wheels, pointing the thumb of his right hand, "and then there's Wynne's medic"—pointing his index finger—"don't know his name, his team's medic—"

"Special Forces medic."

"Correct. Special Forces medic."

"Gotcha," said Russell.

"Anyway, Walton said Wynne was circling the drain, and they were about to land at Blue Diamond when the chopper got strafed by machine-gun fire and they had to put down.

"So they get everyone off the helo and call for another. Pilot had them set up a casualty collection point, and they started to triage. This friend of mine—"

"Walton," said Russell.

"Right—Walton—checks Wynne's vitals and he can't find a pulse. Figures the captain's fucked the monkey and tries to move to the next guy, but captain's medic won't let him, says his man is still alive, so Walton goes back, checks the pulse, listens for a heartbeat, tells Wynne's medic he's sorry, Captain's gone. Gets up to go to work on the next poor bastard."

"Standard procedure," said Russell.

"Standard," Wheels said. "But when Walton stands up to move

down the row, Captain's medic grabs Walton, gets him in a chokehold. They start to tussle, and the pilot comes over and wants to know what the hell's going on. 'He's trying to make me treat a dead man,' Walton tells him, and Wynne's medic says that he isn't dead, and the two of them start going at it. Pilot gets them separated, squats down over Wynne, and puts his ear to the man's chest. He looks up at both the medics, shakes his head, then turns back to close the captain's eyes. That's when Wynne spits in his face."

"Damn," said Russell.

"Damn is right," Wheels said. "So they go to work on the captain, other Black Hawk comes in, gets him aboard, and six months later, he's back in the field."

Russell nodded. He squinted at the darkening sky.

"Good story," he said.

"True story," said Wheels. "Wynne got a Bronze Star and, according to what Walton told me, he starts catching the eye of the shot-callers back at Bragg."

"That makes sense."

"Well," said Wheels, "up to then, he hadn't. They just thought he was a test-taker. College boy. Supposibly, he'd been some sort of entrepreneur. Before he'd joined the army."

"What kind of entrepreneur?"

"Don't know what kind. Managed head funds or something."

"*Hedge* funds."

"Whatever," Wheels said. "'Parently, when 9/11 happened, he goes into the army and joins SF. So, now they're impressed with the man, is my point, and—this is all from Walton, you understand—they start giving him freer rein."

"What's that mean?"

"Means he starts doing whatever the fuck he wants, is what it means, taking his ODA up in the mountains, tear-assing around."

"Afghanistan?"

"Afghanistan," said Wheels. "Gets the ass-puckerers no one wants, out there in the boonies hunting Talibs."

Russell thought about all this for several moments. He exhaled slowly through his nose.

"This is the sumbitch they've chopped us to?"

"Yeah," Wheels said.

Russell stared out at the river. Then he glanced back over at Wheels.

"You heard all this from a medic?"

"Yeah," the man told him. "Walton."

"How'd he know it? All the stuff after the helicopter."

"I asked him the same question."

"What'd he say?"

"Said in his line of work, he hears things."

"Hears things."

"Yeah."

Russell considered it. "You believe him?"

Wheels said he believed the medic believed it.

Russell crossed his hands behind his head and leaned back against the sandstone wall. Then he shook his head and stood.

"We need to get you out of this," he said.

"Get me out of what?" Wheels asked.

"This," said Russell. "This mission."

"You're out of your cotton-pickin' mind," Wheels told him.

"You don't want any part of it," Russell said.

"Why don't you let me decide what I don't want any part of?"

"I not going to sit down at Mama Grimes's dinner table and tell her how I got her son killed. Sit there sipping coffee: 'Oh, I'm sorry, ma'am, he followed me off to Afghanistan because of a YouTube video.'"

Wheels sat smoking for several moments. Then he flicked away his cigarette, rose, and dusted the seat of his pants.

"My mom doesn't even drink coffee," he said.

He lay there after lights out, staring at the ceiling. He couldn't sleep on his left side because of his shoulder, and he'd slept on his right so much that his arm had gone numb and started to prickle, electric sensations in the tips of his fingers. After a while, he rolled to the edge of the cot and sat with his head in his hands and his elbows braced against his knees. He couldn't quit thinking about what Wheels had told him. Wynne's former occupation. Wynne's recovery. Wynne spitting into a pilot's face to prove he was still alive.

He pulled on his new pants and slipped his feet into a pair of running shoes, tugged on a sweatshirt, fetched his pack from the head of his cot, and then went down the hall and into the room where the team kept its gear. He closed the door behind him, found the light switch, and set his pack on the bare concrete floor.

When he and Wheels had come in that evening, two warrant officers without nametapes or sleeve insignia were waiting. They confiscated the Rangers' uniforms, their military-issue boots. They took Wheels's cell phone and Russell's GPS, then took their shaving kits and razors.

"How we supposed to shave?" Wheels asked.

"You aren't," said the taller of the two. "You're both of you growing beards."

"I've never been able to grow a beard," Wheels told him.

"Work on it," the man said.

This was fine with Russell, but when they were ordered to hand over their wallets and dog tags, he just stood there staring.

"C'mon," said the shorter man. "You don't need a driver's license where you're going. You can write your blood type on your boots."

"You have tattoos?" asked the tall one. "Either of you?"

Russell didn't, but Wheels had several—the dotted line around his neck, a Punisher skull on his shoulder—and the warrant officers made them strip to their Skivvies. The short man stepped up, gave Russell a once-over, and then unsnapped the ball chain from around his neck, took his dog tags, stepped over and began to study Wheels. When he saw the skull on Wheels's shoulder, he motioned to his partner. The tall man came up and examined the tattoo, frowning.

"What do you think?" asked the short man.

"No unit marker," said the tall one. He seemed to consider it for a moment, then looked at Wheels and shrugged.

"We'll let you keep it."

"I appreciate that," Wheels said.

Lastly, the men took their rucks, handed them to a specialist waiting beside the barracks door, and set down two Maxpedition assault packs in their place.

Russell unzipped the front pouch and checked the water reservoir. He felt violated, but the pack was expensive-looking and filled almost to bulging.

He began, now, to go through it. Two quarts of water in his canteen and two bottles of iodine tablets. An E-tool on the right-hand side. A poncho in the middle outside pouch and a wet-weather top in the pouch on his left. Three pairs of socks and two brown T-shirts in the right outside pouch, and in the top, two range cards, a protractor, and a mosquito headnet. One hundred feet of paracord, another Nike watch cap, two wet-weather bags, a poncho, and an extra pair of gloves. He filled his CamelBak, fastened it in place, ran the hydration tube out of the hole in the fabric, and snapped it onto his shoulder strap. He discovered three snap links, a safety line, three more pairs of socks. He checked the CLS bag: an IV, Kerlix, surgical scissors, Israeli dressing, a roll of surgical tape, J-tube, scalpel, and three cravats. There were 360 rounds of 5.56 ammo in the ammo pouches he'd been given, twelve 30-round clips. An anglehead flashlight. Four DD batteries. He opened the cleaning kit for his new rifle—barrel rods, scraper tool, wrench, bore brushes, and CLP—and located a strobe light, four MREs, and lastly, four ChemLights—two red, two green. When he was finished, he secured the straps and buckles and then lifted the pack with one arm to weigh it. About fifty pounds, but a day's march would make it feel twice that.

He reached down into his right pants pocket and pulled out the coin. It was an 1899 Liberty-head silver dollar, and it had belonged to his grandfather. Russell had found it just after the man's death, attached to a belt buckle. He'd pried the coin from the buckle with the carbon scraper on his MultiTool, polished it with toothpaste, carried it through Jump School and Ranger School and now across the ocean. He had a game he played. Or you could call it a game. Before going into battle, Russell would pull the coin and flip it. Heads meant he would live, tails he wouldn't, and if he got tails, he'd go three out of five. The most tails he'd ever flipped was two and he considered flipping the coin now but decided against it. He held it in his palm for several moments. Then he slid it back into his pocket and stepped outside.

There was a half-moon tonight, and he went along the gravel walkway between the aluminum trailers, turned the corner, and passed several more. He went back up the concrete steps of the call center, opened the door, and stepped inside.

The chairs in front of the computer terminals were now empty, but the same staff sergeant sat behind the sign-in desk reading the same fantasy novel. He glanced up at Russell, then nodded and went back to his book.

Russell walked over to the carrel where he'd spoken with his aunt earlier that afternoon. The computer was on, and he logged in and brought up a browser. He had an e-mail account he almost never checked and a Facebook page that a cousin had set up for him. He'd been on it exactly twice. He checked baseball scores, read through a horse blog he kept up with, then went to YouTube and typed in the words *ranger horse*. His video was the first to come up, and he muted the sound and watched it play through. Then he watched again, expanding the player to take up the whole screen. When the camera zoomed in on the colt, Russell paused the clip. The angle or the light or the distance had caused its coat to take a darker sheen, turned the browns to rust-colored splotches. The animal was stunning. It didn't matter how many times he saw.

He sat a moment. Then he opened Google in a separate window. In the search box he typed *carson wynne* and then the word *captain*. Before clicking the search button, he added *special forces*. He stared at the blinking cursor. Then he began to scan the results.

He'd half expected this to be another one of Wheels's conspiracy theories, but it was true. Or the details were true. They were factual, at least. The captain had been born and raised in Rhinebeck, New York, a few hours north of Manhattan, and he'd graduated from Princeton, class of '94—double major in religious studies and finance. After that, he'd become an associate at an investment firm; it looked as though he had started in the fall of '96. Back in high school, he'd been the football team's quarterback and had led them to state championships in his junior and senior years. Russell pulled up a news clipping along with a grainy black and white photo of an athletic young man with a football chambered above his shoulder. You couldn't see much of what was beneath the helmet, but his eyes were two gleaming points in the pixelated image.

Russell read and clicked and scrolled. He found another photo of the man, color this time, likely taken with his unit at Bragg. Shot in three-quarter profile. The Special Forces and Ranger tabs on his left shoulder, the twin bars of a captain pinned to his beret. High cheekbones. Square jaw. Blond hair and blond eyebrows and very blue eyes. Women would have thought him handsome, and it occurred to Russell this image would've made a fair recruiting poster—ideal, in fact. Why you would put this man in the field, he couldn't imagine. Ivy League education. Experience in business. This wasn't an operator; he was an enlistment campaign.

Russell stared at the screen a few minutes and then he minimized the window and sat. The generator outside the building produced a loud, steady hum, and in the black background of the monitor, Russell could see himself reflected, his ghost image caught there in the glass. He had the creep of something very cold inching up his spine, and it wasn't just the AC. He closed his eyes and imagined the horse, and he could recall, very distinctly, its odor—musty and rich and still so vivid it might have been in the room. He thought that all of this had started because of his choice to come from behind the barricades and help the animal, and he knew if he'd not made that decision, he wouldn't be sitting where he was. He thought that it was a foolish decision, a foolish choice.

Then he opened his eyes and brought up the video, the horse frozen in mid stride.

"What choice?" he said.

A WEEK LATER THEY watched the sun set from the starboard side of the C-130 that transported them from Mosul to Bagram Airfield in the Parwan Province of Afghanistan. Russell had thought he'd nap on the flight, but the cabin was cold and he couldn't sleep. He turned sideways in his seat and pressed his forehead against the padded insulation beside his window to study the sun's descent as it dropped below a cloud bank; the air turned from plum to purple and the vapor trailing beneath the aircraft's wing caught the day's last light and sparkled briefly and then tarnished against the sky. He put a hand inside his jacket and ran his fingers very lightly across his ribs.

"Lithium," said Wheels.

"What's that?" asked Russell.

"Lithium."

"The hell are you talking about?"

"Afghanistan," Wheels told him. "Why we invaded this dump in the first place." He turned and looked out the window. "Bin Laden, my ass."

Russell stared at the man for several moments.

"Where you getting this?" he asked.

"Cell phones," said Wheels.

"What?"

"What do you think all those BlackBerries run on? All those iPods and laptops? This place has the largest lithium reserves on the planet. You think we're here because of Al-Qaeda?" Wheels gave a snort and a shake of his head. "We need their lithium."

"You need lithium," Russell said.

They landed at Bagram just after dark, and an air force tech sergeant named Hollis came aboard to escort them off the runway. The man conveyed them to a cinder-block building beside one of the hangars where they would spend the night, and then he was back for them at dawn, walking them across the tarmac and up to a buglike helicopter that had been in service since the sixties. The chopper was a CH-47, a troop carrier with four windows along each side of the cabin, circular, like the portholes on a sea vessel, larger windows on the doors behind the cockpit, where machine guns were mounted.

"This is you," said Hollis, gesturing toward the craft. "There's a surgical team on its way out. Hope you don't mind the company."

Russell said they didn't.

Hollis had been carrying a manila envelope under one arm, and now he passed it to Russell. The envelope was sealed with transparent tape and the words DO NOT BEND stamped in red on both sides, but there were no other markings. The sergeant made no mention of the packet, just handed it across.

"Guys need anything else?" Hollis asked. "Coffee or anything?"

Russell glanced briefly at the envelope. He told Hollis they were good.

The man wished them a safe flight, turned, and started back across the runway. Russell watched him for several moments. The air was cool and the breeze prickled the skin on the back of his neck. He looked at Wheels in his cargo pants and polar fleece. He looked once more at the envelope in his hand.

"You think he had any idea who we were?"

"Don't be speaking for me," said Wheels.

"What?"

"I said don't be speaking for me."

"Speaking for you?" said Russell.

Wheels turned to watch the tech sergeant recede into the shadows.

"I might've liked a coffee," he said.

They shouldered their packs and started for the chopper, Wheels in front, Russell following.

"If you wanted coffee, why didn't you say something?"

Wheels didn't respond.

"I'm sure we can find someone onboard with a thermos."

"Let's just drop it," Wheels told him.

They went past members of the flight crew busy at the rear of the helicopter, men who looked up and nodded to them and then fell back to work, some momentary judgment flickering across their faces. You'd see this kind of thing on cargo craft from time to time: men out of uniform with hair past their collars. Beards and ball caps and pistols strapped to their thighs. You didn't make eye contact. You didn't dare address them. You didn't know what agency they worked for and you didn't want to know. Better just to treat them like ghosts.

Russell and Wheels walked up the loading ramp, went stooping past the rear gunner and then up the aisle between the red canvas bench seats on either side of the cabin. There were several older men wearing glasses, surgeons, Russell assumed, a number of support staff, and some empty space toward the helo's front. Wheels shucked out of his pack and let it hang from one shoulder, turned sideways to move past the surgical team's techs and medics, and Russell did likewise, eyes adjusting to the near dark of the cabin, shuffling around the rucksacks and duffles, trying not to step on ankles or feet. He switched his rifle from left hand to right, checked a cargo pocket for his sunglasses, and then a voice said, "Excuse you, asshole," and Russell turned to look.

A woman was sitting there in digicam jacket and trousers. A young woman, petite and very short. She had a vaguely exotic look, eastern European, and her skin was pale and smooth, almost porcelain, her thick, coal black hair pinned in an intricate bun. She pointed toward Wheels and said, "Tell your friend to watch it."

There'd been a low mumbling inside the fuselage, and now it stopped. Russell knew the men were staring at him.

"Sorry," he said.

"What happened?" asked Wheels.

The woman told him that he'd just about knocked her over with his bag. She was addressing Wheels but looked at Russell as she spoke.

"He's sorry," Russell said.

"Hey," said Wheels. "I'm standing right here."

The woman continued to stare up at Russell. Her eyes were a pale shade of green. He couldn't make out her nametape, but she wore the inverted teardrop of a specialist on her chest. A voice from the rear of the helicopter told her to stow it.

Russell stood there blinking a few moments. Then he apologized a third time and started for the front of the craft.

When they'd gotten themselves seated and their gear snapped in, Wheels turned to Russell and said, "Listen: I don't need you apologizing for me. I don't need you deciding about my coffee. I can decide about my own coffee. I can apologize for myself. We're the same rank, Russ. You didn't take me to raise."

Russell nodded. He said his friend had a point.

Wheels raised his hands in a gesture of conciliation and leaned back against his seat.

"See," he said, "that's all I'm saying."

But Russell didn't see what he was saying.

He was looking toward the woman at the cabin's rear.

Firebase Dodge had been constructed atop the ruins of a redoubt built by the British in the nineteenth century. In the photos Russell pulled from the envelope, it looked like a castle. Or the ruins of a castle. The American outpost had been built on top of it: high, sturdy walls constructed from old stone masonry, a good deal of granite, it looked like. There was a large tower in the compound's center, octagonal, maybe fifty, sixty feet in height, thin slits in the upper stories from which defenders could observe and snipe. The whole fortress perched on a mountaintop overlooking valleys of terraced green.

He sat on the rumbling seat, thumbing through the photographs. Six of them. Seven. Five color and two black and white.

He realized that they'd yet to be briefed on the details of their mission. They'd yet to be given any sort of objective. He knew this helo would take them to Firebase Dodge, but he didn't know where the Special Forces camp was in relation to this outpost. He didn't know if they'd be put aboard another helicopter and flown to a second location or perhaps be required to ruck up and march out into the hills. The best thing he could say about any of it was the new clothes and gear. He glanced at Wheels sleeping there beside him, slid the photos inside the envelope, leaned his head back against the quilted insulation, and closed his eyes.

He'd not been asleep for long when the copilot's voice came through their headsets, informing them that the outpost was taking mortar fire. Then, five minutes later, they were notified that shelling had ceased and their helicopter was cleared to land. By the time the Chinook circled the firebase and started to put down, mortars were falling once again, detonating fifty meters north of the sandbag perimeter. Russell watched out the Plexiglas window as rounds came in and sent up clouds of gray dust in the morning sky. Panic inched its way up his spine, vertebra by vertebra. He didn't think the pilot would land under these conditions. He thought they'd be ferried back to Bagram. Then he felt the chopper rapidly descend and the wheels touch earth, and he heard the engines shift pitch and begin to wind down.

A mortar landed closer and shook them in their seats. The panic reached the back of his skull, and his jaw seemed to go cold. He lifted his headset's left earpiece and leaned over to Wheels, shouting to be heard over the whine of the rotors: "How'd you feel about getting the hell off this thing?"

Wheels told him he was for it.

They unfastened their gear and began moving through the kerosene-scented air. The helicopter seemed to rest at a peculiar angle, and Russell had the sensation they were going downhill. When they reached the rear of the cabin, the members of the surgical team were standing there bunched against one another. Russell raised himself on the tips of his toes and saw that the M-240 gunner on the loading ramp was shaking his head and motioning the passengers back toward the front, one hand in the air making chopping motions, furiously mouthing words Russell couldn't hear. They turned, went back up the aisle, scrambled through the narrow crew door, and then ran hunching across the gravel toward the row of HESCOs that marked the nearest bunker. They'd not gone farther than twenty meters when Russell felt the wind from the rotors kick up and saw the helicopter's shadow grow smaller across the ground. The breeze was out of the north and there was a sharp edge to it, and they reached the bunker's opening and started down a flight of cinder-block steps, at the bottom of which squatted a burly man, naked to the waist and wearing flip-flops. He had a headset to one ear and a walkie-talkie to the other. He nodded and told them to keep moving. Russell turned to look up the steps he'd just descended and saw the helicopter moving off to the south. He couldn't believe they'd just been dropped off like this, and then another mortar struck and rattled the thought from his head. The surgical team came down the stairs dragging their duffle bags and equipment, squeezing by the Rangers and traveling along the corridor. He and Wheels waited until they'd passed and then fell in behind them.

They went down an earthen hallway, sandbag antechambers to their left and right. Russell could hear mortar rounds hammering somewhere in the world above. Grains of sand dislodged from the ceiling and sprinkled down the collar of his jacket, strangely cool. The corridor turned and turned again, and they started going up. When they ascended the incline at the far end of the bunker, the surgical team was gathered at the top of the steps, some kneeling, some seated against the wall with palms over their ears. The woman was standing in the entryway, silhouetted against the bright blue sky. Wheels and Russell watched her for several moments. Wheels asked him what she was doing.

"Beats me," said Russell. "Maybe she's curious."

"Maybe she's fucking nuts," Wheels said.

Russell looked at him. A voice said, "Behind you," and they turned to see the shirtless man coming up the passage. His shoulders were wide enough to touch the tunnel walls, but he twisted sideways, snaked past Wheels and Russell, and went up the steps. He had blond hair buzzed down to stubble, coated with a thin layer of talc, and tattooed in an arc across his back was the word INFIDEL. He wore the headset around his neck now, but the walkie-talkie was still in hand. He gestured with it.

"We're good," he said. "They're done for now."

Members of the surgical team began to ascend the last few steps and exit the bunker. Wheels and Russell followed, blinking in the sunlight.

They stood for several moments, all bunched together. Then Wheels asked the shirtless man how he knew the attack was over.

"Prophet just gave the all clear." The man pointed his radio's rubber antenna at the sky and described a small circle: "Our intel network." The surgical team had formed up around him as he spoke, and he gave them a quick once-over and said, "If you're ready, we got you set up over here." He set off walking, and the team began to follow him across the camp. Wheels and Russell just stood.

"I don't think he means us," said Wheels.

"I don't think he does, either," Russell said.

He glanced around the firebase. At the trenches snaking between the sandbag walls. At the cinder-block bunkers, the canvas tents of various sizes. At the HESCOs surrounding the base's perimeter, stacked on top of the sandstone walls, the machine-gun emplacements every twenty meters. Concertina wire sparkling in the sunlight. And everywhere the bustle of men—most of them shirtless, pants legs cut off at the knee, many wearing tennis shoes or no shoes at all. One soldier passed in front of them with a bright red mohawk, tattoos sleeving both arms to the wrist.

Another soldier, this one in uniform, approached the shirtless man and the column of techs and surgeons. They conferred together a few moments, the shirtless man turning to point back at the Rangers. The uniformed man nodded and then started in their direction.

Russell saw, as the man drew closer, that he wore the rank of a first lieutenant on his chest, and the sleeve insignia of the 82nd

Airborne on his left shoulder. He was tall and thin with dark hair buzzed in a crewcut. He came up, shook Russell's hand and then Wheels's. He introduced himself as Kent, but his nametape read KELLAM.

"Weren't expecting you guys till tomorrow," he told them.

Russell didn't know how to respond to this. He just nodded.

"You want the tour?" Kent asked. "We can get you chow if you're hungry."

He turned and pointed to the mess tent, which squatted at their right, long and low-slung, canvas flapping idly in the breeze and exuding a faint odor of grease.

"Hell," said Wheels, "give us the tour. We can eat anytime."

He hadn't addressed the officer as "sir," but the lieutenant didn't seem to notice. He escorted them down a trail worn smooth by a thousand boot heels. There was the armory bunker, he told them. Over there, supply. Russell asked where they could find the commanding officer, but the man seemed not to hear. They went along the wall of HESCOs at the camp's western edge—cutouts in the shape of soldiers, plywood decoys propped above the barriers—and there was a gap in the barricades; they were granted a view of the valley beneath: the mountain falling sheer for several hundred meters and then descending in green terraced slopes. In the distance, more mountains, dotted with pine trees, thick in the morning haze.

He asked the lieutenant if they got sniper fire at this altitude.

Kent pointed to one of the plywood silhouettes to their left, and Russell glanced over to see the nickel-sized holes perforating its torso.

"Anyone ever get hit?" Wheels asked.

"They get hit," Kent said.

He walked them toward the north end of camp and the camp's main entrance—steel gates protected by gunners and razor wire. Kent told them about the trail that ascended the face of the mountain in switchbacks and then he led them down another path by the latrines, lengths of PVC pipe hammered into the ground, damp ground and the swarm of flies, plywood outhouses a little farther down. It was the job of some unfortunate private to burn their contents every day with diesel.

Down another trail—more bunkers, more trenches, an alcove where the platoon had set up their 120-millimeter mortar, lethal out to 7200 meters. Then along a short passageway that went underground, its walls braced by cinder block and two-by-fours, and out again into the noonday light, where they saw the valley on the other side of the mountain, this one to the east.

Kent said, "The captain has his camp down there. They'll send someone to get you in the next couple days. We're not allowed to go down there uninvited."

"Captain Wynne?" asked Russell.

Kent nodded. He explained that the chief purpose of Firebase Dodge was to provide security for the Special Forces camp below.

As the lieutenant spoke, Wheels climbed up onto the sandstone wall and was standing on tiptoe, trying to see over the HESCO barriers and down into the valley. When Kent saw what he was doing, he said, "You're not going to be able to see much. Not from up here."

Wheels turned and looked back at him. "We can't just walk on down?"

"Not without authorization, you can't. They'll send someone up. We've got a bunker you can use in the meantime."

Wheels seemed to be considering all of this.

"That's kind of fucked up," he concluded.

The lieutenant shrugged. He said it was the way it was.

Russell cleared his throat. He asked if they got many women in camp.

Kent stared at him several moments with his brow furrowed. Then his face relaxed and he started nodding.

"Right," he said. "The surgical team."

"Yeah," Russell said.

"We get a new team choppered in every few months. They'll have female medics sometimes. RNs or whatever. Way we're situated, we get casualties all the way from Bargi Matal. They'll stabilize them here before shipping them out to Bagram. Or try to stabilize them, anyway."

"I didn't know if it was a regular thing," said Russell.

"Wouldn't call it 'regular.' It happens."

They turned and looked over at Wheels. He was up on his tiptoes again, trying to see down into the valley.

They watched him several moments.

"I don't see why we can't just walk on down there," he said.

They filled the days playing cards—poker mostly. They'd been assigned quarters in a cinder-block bunker that housed three other soldiers, and they spent their nights here, listening to wolves howl on the slopes about, Russell lying on the low canvas cot, each of its legs in coffee cans filled with kerosene as a defense against scorpions. He'd awaken before dawn each morning to find clusters of them floating in the thick amber liquid, some still alive and wriggling. You had to empty the cans every few days or they'd fill with the skeletons of the creatures. He'd heard men compare their sting to being stabbed with a carving fork. Only the pain didn't diminish once the tines left your flesh. Like everything else in this country, it got worse with time.

This firebase, for instance. Aside from members of the surgical team and the handful of Afghan militia, Lieutenant Kent seemed to be the only soldier still in uniform. The only soldier in boots for that matter. The Green Berets remained in their camp on the other side of the mountain, and the Airborne platoon had been told, apparently, to pretend they didn't exist. Russell had yet to set eyes on one. The angle was too steep to see into their camp from this hilltop fortress, and he figured that was precisely how the Green Berets wanted it. Or planned it, rather. Nothing Special Forces did happened by accident.

Up here it was all accident. Mishap. Confusion. In place of actual uniforms, these soldiers fought in shorts and sandals and sleeveless T-shirts, and the patches on their body armor—when they bothered to wear it—didn't indicate blood type but asked "What Jesus would shoot?" or told you to "Rock out with your cock out" or broadcasted half a dozen other slogans that would get you written up on outposts farther west.

He was discussing it with Wheels over a game of pitch when he glanced up to see a man in tan fatigues come down the steps of their bunker. He had a khaki ball cap that he wore backward, and there was a bleached strip around his eyes in the shape of the sunglasses he'd just pushed onto his forehead. He had a great bushy growth of beard—brown and silver—and his hair touched his collar in back. There were no patches on his uniform other than blood type—O POS—no rank or unit insignia, no skill tabs or badges. He stood for a silent moment.

"I help you?" Wheels asked.

"I'm Billings," the man said. "Assistant commander for Wynne's team." He gestured to their cots and told them to grab their gear.

Russell and Wheels fell to lacing their boots and filling their packs, but Billings had already turned and gone back up the steps. The two of them scrambled around, stowing their equipment, harnessing up.

"What would he be," Wheels whispered, "warrant officer?"

"I believe so," Russell said.

When they made it outside, Billings was leaning against a row of sandbags, surveying the camp with a thinly veiled disgust. Then he looked at the Rangers with a similar expression.

"Ready?" he asked.

"Yessir," they said in unison.

"Don't 'sir' me," he told them. "I apologize for not coming up to collect you sooner. We had half the team on recon."

He turned, held shut one nostril with an index finger, and ejected a spray of mucus onto the dirt. He wiped his nose with the side of his hand and turned back to study the two of them. He asked if they were healthy, and Wheels told him they were.

"Well," said Billings, turning to give the camp a last look, "there's that."

The camp below was a collection of beehive huts and adobe structures, and seen from a distance of several hundred meters it resembled a nineteenth-century pueblo from a movie set. It was nestled in these remote hills and sheltered by a trick of geography, cut off from roads and indigenous settlements, protected by the outpost on the mountain above. There were no HESCOs or trenches, no rolls of concertina wire. Russell didn't see so much as a sandbag or defensive berm.

Hiking down the hillside, all he could make out were several of the larger buildings. But the next morning, he woke to a familiar smell in the predawn air, and he knew before he could confirm it with his eyes. He hurried into his clothes and then out of the adobe shelter, made his way across the compound in the early chill, and there on the camp's northern side was the half-acre corral of split-rail fencing and a dozen or so horses waiting to be curried and fed.

He came forward like a man testing a new pair of eyes. Five of the horses were standing with heads over the corral's top rail, four watching his approach, the other staring at something in the distance. Two roans, two paints, and a magnificent Arabian whose coat glistened in the faint morning light. Fog had settled several feet above the ground, and Russell waded through it, a luminous, waist-high mist that parted and twirled behind him as he passed. The horses watched. One of the paints lifted its nose to test the air. Russell could see the leather nostrils expand slightly and contract, and the animal gave a low whinny from deep inside its chest. A little two-year gelding. He reached out his palm and the horse stretched its neck to him, and Russell brushed his fingers through the rough hair beneath the horse's jaw.

"Hey, fella," he said.

The horse nuzzled his hand and snorted. Russell ran his palm down the horse's neck. He could see, now, it wasn't a gelding at all. She was a little filly.

"That's a good horse," he said.

He backed a few feet, climbed the fence, and threw a leg over the top rail, straddling it. He sat watching the horses on the other side of the corral, stepping about the bare-dirt enclosure. Several more paints, another roan. The mists were rising and evaporating in the gathering light. He turned and glanced toward the low building that served as a stable and felt something against his shoulder, a warm sweet breath moving across his arm.

Russell ran a hand over the filly's neck.

"You going to follow me around?" he asked the horse. "Is that how it's going to be?"

The filly raised her nose. She blinked and Russell watched the long lashes flutter up and down.

"How long since you been rode?" he said. He braced his boots against the lowest rail of the fence and stood precariously, both hands on the horse's neck, and then gradually leaning against her, seeing how much weight she would accept. The horse lifted her left front hoof and then lowered it.

Russell swung over the fence and stepped into the corral with the horse. He brushed his hands down the filly's neck and spoke to her and then slid a palm over her back. The hide trembled slightly under his touch, that loose feel of flesh, then the muscles relaxing. He could feel the massive bellows of the horse's lungs inflating and deflating, and he knew whoever had broken her had done a poor job of it. She'd likely have to be broken all over again if she was to accept a saddle. He placed both arms over the animal and, bouncing, heaved himself onto her back.

He had expected the animal to step about anxiously, but the only recognition she gave of bearing a rider was a brief snort and a slight toss of her head. Russell eased himself erect and sat there a moment watching the other horses in the corral, watching the day compose itself out of the scattering mists. He ran a hand back and forth across the filly's neck and then squeezed his thighs and took a gentle grip of the mane, turned the horse, and began to walk her toward the center of the bare-dirt corral. The horse stepped smartly, responsive, and Russell talked to her and told her she was a good horse, she was doing very good. He pushed the animal up to a trot and circled the pen, the other horses beginning to shy, several moving back under the stable's overhang. He made two circuits and then slowed the filly, tugging firmly on the mane, and walked her over to the fence. When he had her stopped, he reached down and patted the horse several times on the shoulder and then, shifting his weight, slung his right leg back over and dropped to the ground.

He stood there stroking the horse's neck and talking to her. He'd forgotten for several moments exactly where he was.

When he walked through the doorway the first thing he saw was Wheels crouched on his cot like a surfboard and both hands out in front of him, palms uplifted as though he was motioning someone to stop. Russell stared at his friend a few moments. He asked him what was going on.

"Tarantula," said Wheels.

"What?" asked Russell.

"Tarantula," Wheels said.

Russell leaned against the doorjamb. An enormous black and brown spider was crossing the hut a few feet from their cots, making its way forward in a strange and unsettling rhythm. They'd had tarantulas on the ranch where he was raised, but those were barely the size of a coffee cup and cautious to the point of invisibility. Their survival depended on remaining unseen. Whatever this creature's existence relied on, it clearly wasn't concerned with being detected. Something about its movements appeared to even welcome attention. Russell watched it travel the packed-dirt floor of their quarters, trying to think of something to reassure his friend. He cleared his throat, but just as he did, the spider reached the adobe wall, squeezed itself into a crevice Russell had yet to notice, and was gone.

Wheels pointed toward the doorway.

"Yonder comes another," he said.

Russell turned. A second spider, this one smaller than the first, was just entering the Quonset, making its way out of the morning light.

"I'll be damned," Russell said.

"It's been that way for the last fifteen minutes," Wheels told him.

Russell glanced at the man. He was still squatting atop the metal-and-canvas cot. Russell gestured at it.

"You're going to split that thing wide open," he said.

"Ain't the cot I'm worried about."

"It'll be your head you're worried about. Fall off and crack your damn skull."

Wheels pointed back at the spider. It seemed to be following the other's path, crawling across the dirt floor, then reaching the wall and pressing its fat body down into the crevice.

"They been coming in through the door and then down into that hole." He pointed one hand toward the entrance and the other toward the crevice. "Come right in through there, go down right over there."

"How many?" Russell asked.

"Fourteen," said Wheels. "Counting that one."

"Reckon there's a nest in there?"

"I don't know," said Wheels, "and I don't want to know."

Russell cleared his throat. "Well," he said, "you want to get down off your rack and get something hot to eat, or you want to stay in here counting spiders?"

"Quicker, the better," Wheels said.

They sat on Russell's cot lacing up their boots. Two more tarantulas came in and disappeared under the cinder block. One of them Wheels didn't notice, but when the second made its way into the hooch, he stood from the cot with one boot on and the other in a hand, his socked foot in the dirt. The corporal balanced on one leg and slipped his foot into the boot. Then he squared his cap on his head and stomped out of the bunker, trailing laces.

That afternoon, Russell followed Billings over to the stables, and the two of them stood with their arms crossed and a boot on the bottom rail of the corral. Ten horses were bunched on the other side, blowing and stamping, and two circled the pen at a slow trot. Several more were backed under the overhang of the aluminum-sided barn, staring out at them broodingly. The lieutenant glanced over at Russell and then back to the animals. He said they needed these horses broken before the spring thaw. He said they needed Russell to do it.

For a moment, Russell didn't say anything. The last month of his life swirled and then began to sift neatly into place. He understood why he'd been brought here. Or part of it, anyway. A sick feeling entered his stomach, but it was quickly absorbed by something else. Elation. He felt drunk.

"You need the horses to ride?"

"We need to be able to ride them, and we need to be able to shoot around them without getting thrown."

Russell turned and stared at the lieutenant for several seconds.

"You want them gunbroke?"

"If that's what you call it," the lieutenant said. "We don't want them going crazy."

"Gunbroke," said Russell contemplatively.

"Can you not do that?"

"I can do it," said Russell. "You mind if I ask you why?"

"Why what?"

"Why you'd want them that way."

"You're getting ahead of yourself," the lieutenant told him. He gestured to the corral with his chin. "We have nineteen horses here. We need fifteen our men can ride and that aren't going to break their necks if they have to fire a rifle in the saddle. That clear enough?"

"It's plenty clear, Lieutenant. It's just—some of those horses you could put a saddle on right now and do pretty much whatever you want with, and some won't ever be able to do much of anything. It'd help to know exactly what you're wanting out of them."

"Corporal."

"Yes, Lieutenant."

"This isn't a mission briefing."

"Yessir."

"Don't 'sir' me. All you need to worry about is getting these horses to where we can ride them. Shoot off them if we need to. Nothing fancy. Turn left and right. Back up. Stop. This isn't a rodeo."

"What about your men?" Russell asked. "Have any of them even been in a saddle?"

"Ahead of yourself again, Corporal."

"Roger that," Russell said.

He stood for a moment. Then he asked the lieutenant how they'd managed to bring the horses into camp.

"Helicopter," Billings said. "Flew them down from Camp Blessing. I don't know where they were before that."

"What," Russell asked, "—on a Chinook?"

Billings nodded.

"I'd liked to've seen that," said Russell.

"No, you wouldn't," Billings said.

When Wheels walked out to the corral sipping coffee, Russell had his elbows over the top rail of the pen, studying the horses. Wheels had seen Russell talking with the lieutenant, and he leaned against the corral there beside him.

"What was that about?" he asked.

"He wants these horses to where they can ride them."

"Are any of them even saddlebroke?"

"Some," Russell said. "He wants them gunbroke too."

Wheels had been staring out at the horses. Now he stared at Russell.

"What in the hell for?"

"Wouldn't tell me," Russell said.

"You ever gunbreak a horse?"

"'Course not."

"Can you do it?"

"I can do it."

Wheels considered this for a few moments. He sipped his coffee and then tossed the remains on the dirt. Russell turned to him.

"What kind of rider are you?" he asked.

Wheels shrugged. "I ain't Craig Cameron."

"You said you had horses, right? On your farm?"

"Yeah," Wheels told him, holding up the index and middle fingers of his right hand, "we had two horses. When they died, Papaw wouldn't buy no more. I don't think he could take seeing another one put down."

Russell nodded. "But you can ride?" he said.

"'Course," said Wheels. He gestured at the horse now rounding the pen—a chestnut with white stockings. "How many of them have been rode before?"

"No idea," said Russell.

"Any?"

"We're fixing to see."

He started with Fella, the filly he'd ridden bareback that morning. He had the Afghan groom who looked after the animals take the other horses to the square pen on the other side of the stable and then he sat straddling the split-rail corral, studying the filly where she stood looking at the horses who'd been led away. He thought that at least they were halterbroke. That was something. They'd allow themselves to be led, which meant someone had worked with them at some point. That was good and bad, depending on who it was, depending on how and how much. His grandfather was always leery of working a horse someone else had started, but that was the way it was.

They went into the tack room inside the stable, where brand-new saddles sat over sawhorses, brand-new bridles and leads and good leather reins. Wheels carried out a blanket and folded it over the rail next to Russell and carried out one of the smaller saddles, so new it creaked. He balanced this on the top rail next to the blanket and then stood there, waiting on Russell.

"How you want to do this?" he asked.

Russell didn't answer. He was watching Fella with great intensity. She looked remarkable in the afternoon light—chocolate splotches over white, white stockings, a brown and white tail. Her face was brown with a strip of white that traveled between her eyes and on down her nose. She wore a Gatsby leather stable halter with a brass snap and buckles and a brass tie ring on the underside of the noseband. He heard Wheels clear his throat behind him.

"Russ," he said.

"Yeah."

"Where you want to start?"

"At the beginning would be nice," said Russell, and he threw his left leg over the rail and dropped down into the corral. The filly had turned to face him, and when his boots touched the dirt floor of the pen she raised a front hoof. One ear twitched away a fly. Russell had on his Oakleys, but as he approached, he slid the sunglasses up and seated them on his head so the horse could see his eyes. He had the ten-foot lead rope gripped loosely in his left hand, and he came up with his right palm raised, talking to the horse. He was saying, "Hey there," and "Hey now," and the horse lowered her head, then raised it, and he clipped one end of the lead rope to the tie ring and then ran his hand along the horse's jaw, back toward her neck. She felt loose beneath his palm; she hadn't started to tighten on him, but she was alert now, watchful.

He slipped two fingers under the halter's throatlatch and pulled the filly's head gingerly to his chest. The halter had been cinched a notch too tight, and whenever he tugged on it, a tremor ran across the horse's ribs: you could see it start in her shoulder and shimmer like ripples on a pond.

"How long you been wearing this?" he asked the horse.

He unbuckled the crownpiece, backed the strap a notch, and rebuckled it. He gave another tug and watched the horse and then he unbuckled and backed the strap another notch. He looked into the horse's eye.

"That's better, isn't it?"

The filly's breath was hot against his forearm. Russell turned and looked at Wheels leaning against the corral.

Wheels said, "What—it was chafing her?"

"Yeah," said Russell, turning back to the horse. He ran his hand back and forth across her neck, then stepped alongside and ran his hand across her shoulder and down her side. She didn't as much as twitch, but when he paid the rope from left hand to right and brushed it over her brown hindquarters, she stepped quickly away from him and shook her head.

"You see that?" said Russell.

"I saw it," Wheels said.

Russell coiled the rope back over his left hand and stood there breathing. She was tensing on him now, the muscles flexing under her coat.

"Yeah," he told her, "I don't blame you."

He gave her slack and stepped back a few feet. The horse stared at him several moments, perfectly motionless. Then she blinked and raised her head slightly, nostrils testing the air. She took a step toward Russell and then she took another. She stood there, tentative. Then she came forward on cautious hooves and nosed Russell's hand.

"I'll be goddamned," Wheels said.

Russell turned and gave him a smile. He turned back to the horse, paid rope into his right hand, about six feet of rope, started spinning the long line so that one end touched the filly's hindquarters. The horse immediately backed away and turned counterclockwise, and Russell followed her, still swinging the rope, just brushing its end over her stifle, always aiming for the stifle, though it would sometimes land on her point of hip or gaskin. As much as the horse relaxed when Russell would pet her, she quivered at the slightest touch of the rope. She circled and Russell followed, swinging the long line, just touching her, touching her, touching her, the rope's end describing an arc through the air, brushing that same area on her rear left leg.

When he stopped swinging the rope, the horse stopped also—stopped and stood with her ears twitching, swishing her tail. She wasn't irritated yet, just a little unsure, and Russell took the time then to step over and begin to rub his right hand down her neck and shoulder, across her flank. The horse exhaled and gave a brief shake of her head. He turned after a few minutes of this and looked at Wheels.

"You've done this before," Wheels said.

Russell nodded. He asked Wheels if he'd seen the corral panels in the stable.

"Yeah," said Wheels. "There's a bunch of them. Four-by-fives. Doesn't look like they've even been used."

"Let's start dragging them out," Russell said.

Wheels looked over toward the stable.

"What," he said, "—you want to build a round corral?"

"Round corral," Russell said.

They spent the remaining daylight dragging the galvanized panels from the stable and leaning them against the wooden pen. Each of the panels weighed about fifteen pounds and were bound to each other by paracord in bundles of eight. At first they cut the cord and carried them out by twos, but then Wheels began to hug entire bundles and lug them out, and Russell followed suit. When they had all of them outside, they cut the cords and separated the panels and then began to link them to one another, lining up the connector tubes and dropping in the foot-long pin, moving to the next section and then the next. By dark, they'd connected three-quarters of the panels and had built a round corral next to the split-rail pen, about fifty meters in diameter. They stood there surveying their work and then they went down to the mess tent for supper.

He was up again before dawn, in the tack room sorting through leads and ropes—stirrups, bits, and bridles—negotiating the dark of the stable with a small flashlight between his teeth. He threw a saddle over his shoulder, picked up the stack of blankets and ropes, carried the equipment out to the round corral, and stacked it to one side. Then he went for Fella.

When Wheels came over to the corral half an hour later, Russell already had the filly tethered to the lead and was back to twirling the rope. The filly still turned counterclockwise, but she no longer quivered at the rope's touch and Russell had taken the fear out of her eyes. Wheels stood quietly, sipping his coffee, watching his friend move the horse several turns and then pet her, move the horse and pet her. He continued this until he'd swing the rope to brush her flank and she'd just stand there, blinking. Russell dropped the lead and began rubbing her all over, and when he took up the lead again, he'd changed directions and begun to work the other side, turning the horse to the right, clockwise this time, the horse fidgety again, as startled by the rope as though she'd never felt it.

By the time the sun had crested the eastern ridges, Russell had the filly where the twirling rope would only move her, never make her quiver or flinch. He rubbed her down again and spoke to her, and when he turned he saw one of the Green Berets from Wynne's team standing beside Wheels at the edge of the corral. He nodded to the man and the man nodded back, and then Russell looked over at Wheels.

"I need something red," he told him. "I need a stick about yay long." He held his palm a little higher than his head to indicate the length.

"Red?" said Wheels.

"Yeah."

"That'll likely be a problem," Wheels told him, but the man standing there spoke up.

"Can it be fabric?" he asked.

"It can be pretty much anything," Russell said.

"I have a red shirt," the man told him, his lips curling toward the left side of his face. He had a long brown beard like Billings, and like Billings his hair touched the collar of his jacket and he wore a ball cap to keep his bangs out of his eyes.

"You wouldn't mind me cutting it up?" asked Russell.

The man shook his head. "Give me a minute and I'll grab it."

Russell unsnapped the lead from the horse's halter, brushed his hand along her jaw, and then walked over and climbed up and over one of the corral panels. He headed down to a small grove of willows that grew beside the creek on the north end of camp, selected a long limb about half an inch in diameter, removed his knife from his pocket, thumbed it open, and cut the branch from the trunk. He walked back toward the corral, stripping the smaller branches from the limb, whittling himself a seven-foot switch. The bearded soldier was back with the T-shirt, and Russell thanked the man and began to rip the shirt to shreds. The man said his name was Pike, and the three of them shook hands. When you spoke to him, he turned his head slightly and put his left ear forward, as though he might be deaf in the other. Russell cut a pennant-shaped strip of cloth from Pike's shirt, and splitting the narrower end of the switch, wedged the fabric into the stick. He cut another piece of the shirt and used it to secure the makeshift flag, then took the switch by its thicker end and popped it in the air. He swiped it back and forth several more times and, nodding, approached the corral.

He took his time with her. Anyone could see. How he'd talk to the filly and stop to rub his hand down her neck, how she'd gentle at his touch. He never seemed like he was in a hurry about any of it. He never seemed to get mad. If the horse did what he wanted her to do, he'd pet and rub on her, and if the horse didn't, he'd work her until she could do it. He was using the switch and flag now, jerking the red scrap of fabric back and forth until the horse began to circle away from it—counterclockwise again—touching the horse's flank with the end of the switch, just the slightest touch, holding the lead in his other hand. He'd bring her a full revolution and then he'd bring her another, and right when her ears began to twitch, he'd stop and pet the horse and tell her she was doing good. Then back to work with the flag, jerking it back and forth until she started stepping, petting her down afterward, taking the fear out of her, until the horse just stood while he moved the flag and he could touch and pet her with it. Then he'd swap the lead and switch to opposite hands and work the other side: everything you did on one side you had to do with the other.

When he turned back to look at Wheels and Pike, two more Green Berets were standing alongside them, arms crossed to their chests, watching. Russell walked over, leaned the switch against one of the corral panels, and approached the horse with just the lead.

He began by looping the rope around the filly's left front leg, taking the rope in both hands and running it along the inside of the heel and pastern, up past the chestnut and forearm, and then back down. The horse watched all of this as though curious. She leaned her head down and sniffed his jacket and then nuzzled his neck. Russell pushed her away very gently, swung the lead line over her back, and caught it under her barrel, then tightened the rope around her, right where the saddle's cinch would be, snugging the rope against her coat, then flipped the lead farther down the horse's loin to where the back cinch would tighten, all the way to her flank, then down her rear legs. At this the horse sprung suddenly forward, and she began to circle counterclockwise, faster than she'd done before. Russell allowed her to trot and then he pulled up on the lead and straightened her back out.

"Found your trouble spot, didn't you?" Wheels said.

"Yeah," said Russell, and then went right back to it. He flipped the rope over her back, caught it underneath, worked down to her flank, and then once again down her hind legs. This time, when the filly began to move, he kept a hold on her with the loop of lead around her croup and barrel, the left hand still close to her nose where the line attached to her halter. He turned with her, one hand gripping the lead under her nose and the other gripping the loop he'd made at her flank, as though swinging the horse on the end of the rope as a father swings his child by the arms. He let her carry the rope, controlling her with his left hand at the halter, and they went round and round: once, twice, three times, a fourth. He began to whoa her, and she continued circling, and he whoaed her again and told her she was all right. When she came to a stop, she stood blowing with her neck craned back to watch him. He wasn't going to hurt her, but the horse didn't necessarily believe that and, like all creatures, only knew what she knew.

He worked the same technique again, then once more, then he changed directions and began to work the filly to the left, getting her soft, getting her to accept the rope against her flank and elbow, her tail swishing the entire time, agitated now, impatient. When he was done with this, he paid out the lead to its full length, walked back over, and picked up the switch and flag. He turned and, touching the flag to the horse's hindquarters, sent her forward, trotting around the outermost edge of the corral, circling it with him in the exact center, switching the flag behind the horse whenever she started to slow. Then he whoaed her and brought her to a halt and took a knee a few feet away from her, caught his breath, and allowed her to recompose herself.

After a few minutes, he looked over at Wheels.

"Can you bring me that blanket?"

Wheels nodded. "You want the saddle too?"

"Just the blanket right now," Russell said.

One of the newer spectators cleared his throat.

"You going to ride her?" the man asked.

"Depends," said Russell. "Want to see how she does with the blanket. I don't know that she's ever been saddled. She might not even take it."

"She kicked Sergeant Boyle when they were bringing them into camp," the man informed him.

"Yeah?" said Russell. "What was Sergeant Boyle doing?"

"He was behind her, trying to get her into the pen. He clapped his hands to kind of get her moving, and she kicked."

"That'll happen," Russell said.

The man nodded—as if to say it certainly did. There were four of them now, not counting Wheels. All bearded, all in need of a haircut, each with the exact same build: not the lean, athletic frames of most PJs and Rangers, but bodies like professional weightlifters—all neck and chest and shoulders. *Bulk for the sake of bulk,* Wheels might have said, but Wheels wasn't going to say it to their faces, and Russell figured if they wanted to carry that extra weight, it was their business.

Wheels climbed the corral panel and handed the blanket to Russell. It was hunter green with dark crimson stripes—thirty inches by thirty inches, made from acrylic. Russell had been taught never to use synthetic fibers on his horses, only leather and wool. He didn't know how the filly would respond, but he supposed it would only really matter if she was used to something else, and this horse wasn't used to much of anything, far as he could tell. He approached her with the lead in one hand and the blanket in the other. He let her sniff him again and then let her sniff the blanket. She recoiled slightly when her whiskers touched the fabric, but then she gave it another sniff and seemed not to mind.

"Blanket," he told the horse. "Not going to hurt you."

He brought it up and touched her neck with it. He ran it down her shoulder and rubbed it across her flank.

"See," he said. "Blanket."

The horse craned her neck and stared at him. One ear rotated and then stood erect, like a watchdog's.

"You're okay," he said. "Don't be so damn spooky."

He continued rubbing the blanket across the horse's flank and then over her croup, loin, and back, all the way up to her withers. She shivered at each of the small circular motions and then she shivered less and then she just stood there with her ears flicking slightly. Russell placed his hand on her hip and then crossed behind her and went around to her right side, where he started all over again. When he was finished he asked Wheels to bring him the saddle.

One of the Green Berets turned to another and said, "He's doing that to introduce it to the horse."

"No shit," the other man said.

Wheels grabbed the saddle by the horn and cantle, climbed the corral once more, and handed the saddle across to Russell. The blanket rested now over the filly's back, and Russell stepped beside his horse, swung the saddle up, and planted it atop the blanket. The horse just stood. Russell had half expected her not to accept the saddle, or not to accept it the first time, but the filly didn't seem troubled by the weight, maybe thirty-five, forty pounds. He let the cinch just hang for several minutes, unbuckled. He spoke to the filly and petted her down, left side and right, and when he was done, he stepped over and reached under the horse, took up the cinch, and ran it through the buckle. Then he stood back and eyed the horse.

"You doing okay?" he asked her.

The filly stood. Her right ear swatted once, twice. She gave her tail a brief swish.

"If you're going to do something crazy," said Russell, "I'd as soon you did it now."

But the horse didn't do anything, and after standing another minute, Russell bent down, tightened the cinch, waited for the horse to exhale, and then he buckled the cinch and stood.

"What now?" he heard one of the Green Berets ask.

Russell turned and stared at the row of men standing along

the corral with boots propped against the bottom rung. It was turning into some kind of impromptu clinic, but Russell couldn't worry about any of that. He'd learned a long time ago not to try to impress people, particularly where horses were concerned. It was enough to worry about impressing the horse. Or impressing your intentions on the horse. That you wouldn't mistreat them. That'd you'd be firm and fair. Training aside, you were dealing with half-ton animals, and they were going to be who they were going to be. Russell gripped the saddle horn with one hand, put his left boot in the stirrup, lifted himself alongside the filly, and let her feel his weight. He reached down with his right hand and petted her neck.

"What do you think?" he asked her. "You feel like going around a few times?"

The horse was steady beneath him. Her ears relaxed and her tail hung straight down. He leaned across her back, straightening his body and backing his left boot partially out of the stirrup in case he'd need to slide off. He waited several moments and then he swung his right leg over, found the far-side stirrup, and lowered himself into the saddle. The filly pawed the dirt and gave a slight shake of her head. Then she settled again. Russell took up the reins, squeezed his thighs, and put the horse forward a few steps. Then a few more. He reached a hand down and petted her neck.

"That feeling all right to you?" he asked her.

The horse snorted a jet of vapor into the cool mountain air. Russell chucked her up to a slow walk, and they went round the corral, Russell talking the entire time, stopping the horse, starting her, turning to retrace her path. In five minutes he had her trotting, and in five more he'd pushed her up to a canter, circled twice, and then dropped back to a trot, bouncing with the two-beat gait. Wheels watched him give the slightest tug on the reins, the slightest pressure with his boots. He seemed to will her every movement. He seemed to control her with his thighs. He sat perfectly straight, with his eyes forward and his chin up, moving the filly so her hooves printed half-moons in the corral's soft dirt. Then he began to slow the horse. He slowed her and walked her to the center of the pen, turned her twice, three times, and then brought her to a halt. The men on either side of Wheels grinned, and one of them chuckled and shook his head.

Wheels leaned over and spat.

"You can put that horse's feet anywhere you want, can't you?"

"They're my feet," Russell said.

Russell started on the next horse two days later, an Akhal-Teke, one of the oldest surviving breeds, only thirty-five hundred of them in the world. The stallion was golden from the tip of its nose to the last hair on its tail—seventeen hands, its conformation flawless. A stunning horse, perfect and powerful, but a horse half wild and restless in its blood and about an inch away from being a predator. Which meant he'd been made that way: no horse got there on his own. Russell decided to work him very slowly, a little each day. He went on to the Arabian—gentle as you had the right to expect an animal to be—and then he started another of the paints, leading him about the round corral and then going to work with the long line and the flag.

By the afternoon of his fourth day, he was back to working the Akhal-Teke. The corral was lined along one side with his audience of Green Berets, five of them, and all of Wynne's team currently in camp, with the exception of Billings. Wheels stood to one side, like the sorcerer's apprentice, arms crossed, nodding sagely when Russell did something that seemed to bring the horse along. You didn't whip the horse. You did nothing to hurt him. You brought only discipline, and discipline done right was an art form in itself. You had to be an artist. You made the wrong thing feel like work for the horse and the right thing feel like relief. Wrong thing difficult, right thing easy. Wrong thing pressure, right thing release.

The stallion would trot in the afternoon light with the sun glowing along his caramel coat, a metallic look to it, a burnished metal gloss. Bronze-stockinged rear feet and bronze-stockinged front. A white strip down his nose. Gold spangles across his back, darker golden coins on his flanks. He circled the corral blowing, shaking his head, Russell talking to him, the soldiers watching from behind the rail.

"You got a damn bronc on your hands," said Wheels.

Russell leaned over and spat. He held out a hand for Wheels to pass him his flag, and the horse backed nervously several feet. He stood eyeing Russell. Then he sprang suddenly forward and gnashed at him with his teeth.

Russell saw it unfold as if in slow motion—the horse lunging forward and his neck stretching out, head stretching, the muscles striated beneath the golden coat and his mouth hinged open, the perfectly white teeth parted like the jaws on a trap and then closing with a dull, wet snap as Russell ducked and slid to his right, slipping the way a boxer might dodge his opponent's jab.

"Christ Jesus!" Wheels shouted, and the others were calling out, murmuring. The stallion turned and came about to face Russell, but Russell had already backed against the corral, thrown one leg over, and straddled it. He studied the horse several moments where he stood in the sunlight with his tail swishing.

Russell pointed to the stallion. He looked over at Wheels and Pike and the other Green Berets alongside the corral. "Nobody rides this horse but me."

"Don't think you have to worry about that," Pike said, and the men all laughed.

All but Russell. He was staring at the horse. He told Wheels to bring him the Kimblewick bit from the stable.

"Did I say *bronc*?" Wheels asked. "I meant *alligator.*"

"Bring me the Kimble," Russell said.

Wheels shrugged, took his boot off the lower bar of the corral panel, and went toward the stable. Russell was eyeing the stallion and rubbing the palm of one hand back and forth along his jaw.

"That thing could've bitten your face off," one of the men told him.

Russell nodded.

"What are you going to do?" another asked.

Russell shook his head. A horse would lick its lips when it was learning, but this horse didn't lick its lips at all. He glanced over and saw Wheels coming from the stable with the Kimblewick in hand. It was a kind of curb bit, though most didn't consider it a curb, or not a traditional curb. If you had a slotted Kimble, you could apply leverage to the horse's mouth, get him to pay attention. That all depended on whether or not you could get it into the horse's mouth. Even then, it would only help when the horse was saddled and the rider was seated upon it.

Wheels walked around and handed him the bit, and Russell sat holding it by the D-rings and working the joint. He'd have to attach it to the reins and the halter, remove the halter already on the stallion, work the new halter over the horse's head, and get him to accept the Kimble. It wouldn't keep him from biting, and it certainly wouldn't keep him from kicking. He imagined the horse on it back legs, reared to full height, hoofs pawing the air. He pushed that image away.

By early evening, he'd managed to get the old halter off, the new halter on, the Kimblewick in place. They'd saddled the stallion, and it stood now on the far side of the corral, head down, left ear twitching. The muscles along the horse's shoulder would flex and release, flex and release. Russell walked to the edge of the corral and leaned his flag stick against the panel, paying out the long line as he went, never taking his eyes from the horse. Wheels watched him as he approached the stallion and brushed a hand under the horse's chin, down his throat, stepping to the horse's left side, rubbing the horse's neck, telling him it was okay. The horse didn't look okay. He looked like something about to explode. Russell didn't seem to notice. He stood there talking to the stallion. Then he placed his left boot in the stirrup, grabbed the horn in his left hand, the cantle in his right, and lifted himself alongside the stallion, leaning slightly over him, standing in the stirrup one-footed. The horse began instantly to sidle and then to turn, Russell still talking calmly.

Wheels watched. Horse and man looked to be involved in an intricate dance—Russell perched along the animal's left side, clucking softly with his tongue, the stallion tossing its head and turning, tossing its head and turning, rotating in wider and wider circles, dust rising from its hooves in the late-evening light. Then, just as quickly as the horse had started moving, it stopped. Stopped and stood motionless, the dust passing eastward through the corral, fleeing the sunset in a red drift of smoke. Russell waited several moments for the animal to settle. The air had a sharp edge to it. A bird called. He nodded several times, threw his right leg over, found the stirrup on that side, and lowered himself into the saddle. He leaned forward and took up the reins and then reached down to pat the horse's neck.

"Good boy," he said.

He'd just gotten out the words when the stallion bucked. It came without warning, front and rear legs coming suddenly together, and then the rear legs shooting out behind, kicking, turning somehow, Russell trying to lean forward and straighten himself along the horse's neck, lower his center of gravity, the stallion spinning faster, resembling for the briefest of moments a figure skater, corkscrewing, man and horse beginning to blur. And then winding out of this eddy, slowing, the two of them separate again, distinct, Russell still astride the animal, teeth clenched, reining the stallion and pulling him to the left, the horse taking wider steps now, head down, the soldiers along the rail watching as men will watch a fight—wide-eyed, astonished—something of reverence in the air, a ritual activated in the blood, and all the while Russell looking as if he was about to be thrown and yet directing the stallion's movements with a squeeze of the thighs, a tug of the reins.

When he straightened the animal and put him forward, the horse was moving at a canter, loping the corral counterclockwise with Russell bouncing in the saddle and snapping back on the reins, jiggling them. The stallion shook his massive head and blew but began to go slower, dropped to a trot, and then down to a walk. Russell was telling him "good," he was a "good horse," but the stallion's eyes were crazed with fear, and Wheels watched Russell make another pass around the corral and then make another. He circled a third time and then reined more sharply, and the stallion walked to the center of the corral and stopped. The temperature had dropped, and steam rose from the animal's coat like something that might catch fire. He swished his tail and snorted vapor into the evening air. Then he just stood.

There were several moments of silence. You could hear the bellows of the horse's lungs as he drew a breath and released it, drew a breath and released it, drew a breath and released it—imitation of a locomotive idling. Someone cleared his throat. Then the men began to applaud.

Russell looked up at the clapping figures. Several shook their heads, and one placed a thumb and pinky in the corners of his mouth and gave a shrill whistle. The stallion lifted its head. Russell glanced along the row and saw Wheels nodding his approval. Beside him was the woman from the surgical team they'd first encountered on the helicopter flying in. She was standing there with her arms crossed and a strange look on her face. Russell climbed down from the horse, walked him to the other side of the corral, and passed the reins to the Afghan groom who'd been standing there. The man touched his forehead with the tips of his fingers and bowed his head slightly, and Russell returned the gesture.

When he made it over to where the woman was standing, the men had dispersed and Wheels was moving down toward the mess tent with two of the Green Berets, striding between the massive soldiers, gesticulating wildly. Russell walked up and blotted the sweat from beneath his eyes with the back of his shirtsleeve. He asked how she was doing.

She looked over at the Afghan groom, leading the stallion toward the stable. She looked back at Russell.

"Horses," she said, as though she'd stepped into a dream.

Russell nodded.

"This is why you're here?"

"Yes, ma'am."

She stood there, her eyes very green in the failing light. She wore makeup. Not much. Some eyeliner and mascara and whatever it was women put on their cheeks. Her features were very delicate, very fine, and there seemed to be some struggle in them, her eyebrows knotted, a look of enormous concentration on her face. Then the muscles relaxed and she extended her hand.

"I'm Sara," she told him.

"Elijah," he said, taking her hand. It was small and smooth, a little cold.

She said, "I didn't even know we used horses."

Russell couldn't decide if this was a question. He asked how he could help her.

She crossed her arms to her chest and seemed to shiver slightly.

"I was supposed to bring antibiotics down to Sergeant Bixby," she told him, "but they told me he's out."

Russell nodded. He said he was surprised she was still in camp.

"They keep saying they're going to send us back to Kabul, but you know that tune."

"Hurry up and wait."

"Hurry up and wait," she said.

He studied her a moment. A shapely figure, porcelain-pale. A little fragile looking. Like a doll.

The hell with it, he decided.

"Are you hungry?" he asked her. "Would you like something to eat?"

She seemed to give the question serious consideration. She said she'd take coffee if they had it.

"We have it," said Russell, and they started down the path, dusk falling all around them and their breath fogging in the cold.

Sara and Russell sat at one of the picnic tables inside the large canvas tent, while the Green Berets conversed in a steady hum around them, sounds of meat sizzling in the background. There was a cook in camp whose sole duty was to prepare meals for these men, but the team's junior weapons sergeant—a lean and beardless Latino named Rosa—manned the grill at suppertime, cooking steaks, sausage, burgers. He made the best burgers Russell had ever eaten. Tonight he'd prepared teriyaki chicken, and he moved around the room spooning the contents of a cast-iron skillet onto paper plates, standing over the men in his University of Arizona ball cap and a camouflage apron with LIVE BY CHANCE, LOVE BY CHOICE, KILL BY PROFESSION emblazoned on the front. He was a sniper by trade but in another life could easily have been a chef. He came over to Russell and Sara's table, filled their plates, and then stood like a waiter about to inquire if they needed anything else. Two mornings ago, Russell had watched the man group ten rounds in the tennis ball–sized circle of a paper target at 620 meters, lying in the dirt with his eye to the scope, pacing the shots about a second apart.

"Bon appétit," he said.

They sat a moment. Sara asked where he'd learned to do all of that with a horse.

"My granddad."

She smiled and shook her head. It was the first time he'd seen her smile, and his throat went suddenly tight. She stabbed at the chicken on her plate, brought a bite to her mouth, and blew.

"You do that every day?" she asked.

"Not *every* day," he said. "I been doing it the last few days because they need horses and most of these hadn't even been rode."

She nodded and placed the chicken in her mouth. She chewed several times and lifted her hand to cover it.

"What's that called?" she asked. Her nails weren't painted, but they looked glossy and neat.

"Which?" he said.

"What you're doing with them. What you were doing with that blond."

Russell swallowed the bite of food in his mouth and sipped his coffee. He almost put his elbows on the table and then he caught himself and braced his forearms against its edge.

"It's horse breaking," he said. "Or *some* would call it horse breaking. Horse starting. What you might see in a clinic."

"What's a clinic?"

"You know," he said, "a horse clinic. Like a seminar."

"A class?"

"Yeah. More like a short class."

"I guess I imagine a doctor's office," said Sara.

"I didn't think of that."

They sat staring at each other a few moments.

"This chicken is pretty good," she told him.

"It is good. He makes good chicken. Makes good everything."

"He's the cook?"

"No," said Russell. "He just sort of does that. He's one of them."

Sara glanced over to where Rosa stood behind the grill, her eyes reappraising the man.

She said, "Special Forces?"

"Yeah."

"*He* is?"

"Yes, ma'am."

She looked back at her plate, and both eyebrows went quickly up and down.

"Like Rambo."

"Like Rambo," Russell said.

Early morning, and a bird chirping out in the Afghan dawn—a sound like *chur-weet, chur-weet*—but it wasn't the bird that woke Russell. When he rolled over and opened his eyes, he saw a man seated on a folding chair beside his cot. Russell started, raising up on an elbow and backing against the wall, blood pulsing through his carotids and his heart tightening like a fist. The man had blond hair, a blond moustache and beard. He wore the same unmarked khakis as the other operators, but he was missing the ring finger of his right hand. It was the first thing Russell noticed—no stump or stub. The finger was just gone. He'd almost reached for his pistol, but the missing finger had stopped him. He couldn't have said exactly why.

Russell lay there. All remnants of sleep had fled his body.

The captain smiled.

"Come with me," he said.

Russell had fallen asleep in his pants and a T-shirt the night before. He sat up on the edge of the cot, located his boots, pulled them on, and laced them tight. The captain had already crossed to the doorway; when winter came they'd need to get an actual door. Russell grabbed his jacket and, sliding his arms into the sleeves, trailed Wynne outside into the morning chill, his pulse starting to slacken, the translucent specks swirling before his eyes moving slower now. Vanishing.

The captain went toward the stables. He was the same height as Russell, six-one, athletic and very lean, not bulky like his men. He looked to be in his early thirties, but he had to be older, Russell thought. He would have guessed forty, but it occurred to him this wasn't the kind of man you guessed about. Not correctly, at least.

The captain stopped at the corral and stood with his arms crossed to his chest, watching the horses: two paints and the Akhal-Teke stallion. The paints were bunched against each other at one end of the pen, pressed together, trying to get as far from the stallion as possible.

Russell came up and joined Wynne, and they stood for several minutes without speaking. The air stung Russell's cheeks, and he could feel it inside his ears.

"You've been busy," the captain said, his voice melodious and deep.

"Yessir," Russell said.

"How long did it take?"

"I've barely got them started," Russell said. He lifted a hand and pointed to the Akhal-Teke. "Him, I can't even say that about."

Wynne turned to look at Russell and then turned back to regard the horse.

"He's different," Wynne said.

Russell almost said that depended what you meant by *different*, but managed to say, "What's he for?"

Wynne didn't respond. He stood several moments watching the stallion.

Then he said, "We come into these mountains on helicopter." He lifted a finger and gestured at the surrounding hills. "What's the problem?"

"Problem?" said Russell.

"The problem," Wynne said.

Russell thought about it. "They're loud," he said, shrugging.

"What else?"

"Slow."

Wynne looked at him, indicating he expected Russell to continue, but Russell's mind went suddenly blank and he dropped his gaze to the ground. He took a moment and cleared his throat.

"They hover," he finally said. "They don't fly high enough to get out of rocket range."

The captain nodded. He said, "Issue we face in places like this is mobility. Choppers worked in Vietnam. Why shouldn't they work here?" He paused to look at Russell. "Correct?"

"Yessir," said Russell.

"No, sir," said Wynne. "Incorrect." He told Russell this was not Vietnam. Seemed too obvious to even say, but it wasn't obvious to command. They were always fighting the last war.

Then he said Russell was right about one thing: helicopters had to hover to take off and they had to hover to land. They were vulnerable that way. The Taliban was always waiting, and if they managed to knock one helicopter out of the sky, the cavalry came in, and then the cavalry became the targets.

Russell nodded. "Like Robert's Ridge."

"Robert's Ridge," the captain said.

He gestured toward the horses with his chin. He said these animals would confuse the enemy. He said their enemies wouldn't hear them coming. Wouldn't expect it. He told Russell when 5th Special Forces first entered the country in October of 2001, they rendezvoused with the Northern Alliance's General Dostum and pursued the Taliban from Mazar-i-Sharif all the way to the Pakistani border. They'd done this on horseback. A lot of people didn't even know. And, mind you, these were Americans riding Afghan ponies, on Afghan saddles. No one seemed to wonder what they might have done on American horses with American saddles and tack.

Russell toed the dirt with his boot and studied the ground. When the captain quit speaking, Russell said, "You aim to take your men out on horseback?"

"I do," the captain said.

"Up in these mountains?"

Wynne nodded.

"Can I ask you what for?"

The captain ignored this question. He pointed at the Akhal-Teke. He asked how the stallion was coming along.

Russell shook his head. "Captain, to be honest with you, he's just a damn psychopath."

"Psychopath?"

"Yessir."

The captain smiled. His eyes were very blue. They would be difficult to look at for long.

"How long will it take to break him?"

Russell couldn't answer something like that. "Hell," he said, "he ain't even been cut."

The captain's brow furrowed. Then it relaxed.

"Neutered," he said, nodding.

"Unless you're planning on studding him out, I'd do that the sooner the better."

"I don't plan to breed him, Corporal. And I don't want him *cut.*"

Russell cleared his throat. He told the captain that the way he was now, it would be all a rider could do to even stay atop him.

"Show me," the captain said.

"Show you what?"

"Ride the horse."

"Right now?"

The captain said it was waiting.

Russell glanced over. He saw that it was. The Afghan groom would have taken the saddle and blanket off yesterday evening and curried the stallion before putting him in the stall, so that would mean the groom had risen and saddled the horse and led him back out. Russell didn't want to speculate as to why. He brushed the knuckles of one hand back and forth across his chin.

"Sir," he said, "let me go get this little mare I've been working with. She's coming along pretty good. If you want to see what kind of progress we're making, I'd as soon show you with her."

The captain stared at him a moment.

"Go get her," he said.

Russell nodded and told the man he'd be right back. He turned and went off toward the stables, entering through the tack room at the side of the building, then turning down the hallway that led him past the stalls. Third door down, he opened the latch and swung the door back on its massive hinge. Fella looked up at him out of the half-light of the ten-by-twelve enclosure. Smell of hay and horseflesh. The scent of sweet feed and pine. Underneath everything, that rich odor of manure like the oldest and most luxuriant soil. Russell took a halter from the nail on the wall and began to buckle it around the mare's head. She snorted and raised her left forefoot.

"Don't you make me look bad," he told her.

Fella exhaled a long hot breath against his chest. Then she lowered her foot.

He ran a hand beneath her jaw and patted her neck.

When he led her out of the stable toward the round corral, the captain was seated on the split-rail fence. Russell nodded to him, opened the gate, walked his horse through, and then turned to pin the gate shut behind him. He put a boot in the stirrup and hoisted himself into the saddle. The horse was a little tight, but her back was round, head down, and he took her about the corral at a trot, feeling her beginning to soften beneath him. He spoke to her as they made a revolution, as they made another. Then he gave the slightest pull on the reins, turned the horse, and walked her to the center of the corral, bringing her about to face the captain, who had climbed from his perch and come over to lean against one of the corral panels.

"Do it again," he said.

"Do what again?" Russell asked.

The captain raised a hand and, pointing his index finger at the ground, drew a counterclockwise circle.

Russell nodded. He chucked up, turned the horse, and began to make another circuit, this time pushing Fella up to a canter, his ears stinging in the cold, the filly snorting twin jets of vapor out into the morning air. She was going to make a good horse. She was starting to respond to the touch of his heels. He wouldn't have to do much more with the reins, and he thought he could get her to where he'd barely need them at all.

When he stopped her again and glanced over toward the captain, he saw that the man had turned and started for the main pen. Russell sat the horse, watching him go. Then something in his stomach dropped, and before a thought had time to germinate, he'd slid from the saddle, led Fella over to the corral's edge, and dallied the reins across one of the panels. He stepped up and over and followed Wynne, the man now climbing the split-rail fence, then dropping down into the pen where the stallion stood waiting.

"Hey!" Russell called. "Captain!"

Wynne didn't respond. He went toward the animal, approaching the way you might approach a pet. Russell's first thought was that the stallion would lunge at the captain as it had lunged at Russell the day before—more luck than reflexes that had prevented Russell from being knocked senseless—but the stallion didn't lunge and Wynne didn't slow his pace. Didn't reach a hand out to let the horse smell him. Didn't so much as touch the horse until his left boot was in the stirrup and he was heaving himself onto the animal's back—that golden expanse of shining coat and flawless muscle—heaving himself up and throwing a leg over and then seizing the reins. He sat the horse naturally, but it didn't matter how naturally you sat: the stallion could break your neck in half a second. The safest place around a beast like this was on it, but Russell knew the captain wouldn't be seated on it for long. His first thought was that all of this was about to be over and he and Wheels would shortly find themselves back on a helicopter to Bagram. He was surprised to find the thought disappointed him.

The captain took hold of the reins, gave them a snap, and the stallion came forward, going from statuesque immobility to motion in a blink. Russell made the edge of the pen, stepped up, and seized hold of the top rail. He thought perhaps he could vault the fence, step over and grab hold of the bridle before the captain was thrown, but the stallion was already moving at a canter, a quick three-beat gait too fast for a pen this size, the other two horses pressed underneath the overhang at the south end of the stable, clouds of dust rising from the stallion's hooves and the captain sitting perfectly upright in the saddle, with his blond hair and beard and those luminescent blue eyes like jewels lit from behind.

He made two passes around the corral and then he made a third, dropping the stallion to a trot, then slowing him back to a walk. Russell watched as he reined up in the center of the pen, stopped the horse and sat there amid the dust he'd raised, then slid from the saddle and made his way over to the fence. He hadn't even broken a sweat.

Russell studied the captain a moment. He asked him how long he'd been riding.

Wynne didn't answer. He turned to consider the stallion and then looked up at the paling sky. His face was impassive and calm.

"I was just wondering how you learned to do that," said Russell.

"Do what?" Wynne said.

"What you just did," Russell told him, pointing toward the Akhal-Teke. "How'd you learn to handle that thing?"

The captain turned to look at him.

"Watching you," he said.

In the days to come Russell would train the men of ODA-372 to ride, teaching them the correct way to hobble their mounts, load their saddlebags, to lean back and squeeze their thighs when they descended a slope. There were now ten Green Berets in camp, and it took time to distinguish one from another, to learn their names or learn the names they went by, the names they'd give a soldier such as himself, a Ranger, sure, but still just an 11-Bravo, still only infantry.

He'd met Billings up on the hill, the lieutenant who'd escorted them into camp—a man surly by nature, calculative, distant. Russell decided almost immediately he'd keep clear of Billings, but that took little effort given that Billings seemed determined to ignore him completely.

Pike was a different story, the sergeant who served as the

team's senior engineer. It was this man who'd given Russell the T-shirt that day at the corral, then stood watching as he cut it into shreds. A little shorter than the others. A good deal more cheerful. He'd survived an IED in Kandahar Province, though his hearing had not. He was completely deaf in his right ear, and whenever you spoke to him, he'd tilt his head to one side and offer you the left. He was from Aspen, Colorado, and seemed at home in these mountains, or seemed like he would have been perfectly at home if allowed to carry a snowboard or a pair of skis. Russell spoke to him at breakfast and dinner, and he was easy to teach, very coachable. The horses responded to his even-tempered manner. When he petted the animals, he'd grin.

The weapons sergeants—Boyle and Rosa—were also friendly to the Rangers: they'd both served in the Regiment before joining SF. The two men were polar opposites, nearly inseparable. Staff Sergeant Boyle—everyone called him "Ox"—was a huge hulk of a man: six-four with red hair and a bushy red beard. He was the soft-spoken son of Iowa farmers: four hundred years ago he would have walked these highlands in a kilt. He'd been an All-American wrestler before dropping out of junior college to join the army, and spent his free time in the detachment's makeshift gym. Russell had seen him bench press 385 without so much as blushing, his chest like two bowling balls under his shirt, massive arms sunburned red, and veins bulging like blue ropes.

His junior, Sergeant Rosa, was a fourth-generation Mexican American from Yuma, Arizona, his father a member of the Yuma County SWAT team, his grandfather the former Yuma chief of police. Five-eleven, lithe-bodied, and lean: jet black hair and the boyish, beardless face of a sixteen-year-old. He sauntered about camp with a graceful, long-legged gait, seeming almost to glide. A clever young man, quick to laugh and yet possessing that academic air of the world-class snipers Russell had known—a killer by nature and disciplined as a monk.

The two weapons sergeants were accompanied by an Afghan interpreter. Russell rarely saw the three of them apart. The man's name was unpronounceable, so the men called him Ziza or Zero.

He'd fought with the mujahideen when he was just a boy and later trained with American Special Forces when they entered the country in the fall of 2001. He'd been a member of the Afghan National Army Commandos and now was chalked to Wynne's team as a terp. He seemed more than that. He walked like the Green Berets and swore like the Green Berets, his English impeccable, though formal in its cadence. He stood five foot five and had close-cropped black hair, a wispy moustache and goatee, and a compact and muscular frame. He didn't look like the other Afghans. To Russell, he looked Filipino or Thai. He lifted weights with Ox and practiced on the shooting range with Rosa, and he wore a New York Yankees ball cap he only took off for prayer. He carried an enormous knife on his back in a Kydex sheath, more of a short sword than a knife, Japanese in design. Russell never saw Ziza without it.

These men were deferential toward Russell, or deferred, at least, to his expertise with a horse. They listened intently when he spoke. Those like Pike and Rosa didn't have far to go; others like Ox needed all the attention he could muster. The weapons sergeant looked about as at home on horseback as a horse looked in water—struggling constantly not to drown. Russell could tell that, like many men of his size, he was used to muscling his way through the world, and what he couldn't accomplish by physical strength mystified him completely. He was all quiet brawn, lacking the effortless finesse of Sergeant Rosa, and after lunch one day, he'd just dismounted the massive paint Russell had paired him with, when the horse backed without warning and stepped on his foot, tearing through the leather upper of his boot and cutting him to the bone. Russell watched as the man's face went a deep shade of purple, then as he dropped the reins and tried to hoist the mare off him like you might a sofa. The horse merely turned his neck to look back at the sergeant, as though trying to gauge exactly what this man might want, and Russell sprinted up, took her by the bridle, and led the horse forward several steps. When he looked back at Ox, the man was standing there with his hands on his hips, studying the blood welling up from the top of his boot.

"I'll be goddamned," he said in an almost casual whisper. He pursed his lips and bent to probe the wound with an index finger. He glanced over at Russell and shrugged.

Russell was leaning against the split-rail fence of the corral that evening, watching the sky darken and blush, when the team's medical sergeant came out to give him a report. The sun had just dropped below the lizard's back of the western hills, and he studied Bixby, the man Sara had been down to visit a few weeks before, as he made his way along the talus path. There was a weariness not only in the man's stride but in the slump of his shoulders, in the way his hands hung loosely at the ends of his arms like something else he'd been given to carry.

He walked across to Russell, took a deep breath, and nodded.

"Corporal," he said by way of greeting.

"Sergeant," Russell said.

The man was average height, average build. Back home, in civilian clothes, he'd not be mistaken for a member of Special Forces—or a member of anything at all. He'd let his hair grow long and his beard grow out, but his hair was thinning and you could see scalp through the brown fluff, red in the declining light. He had a soft, kind-featured face and the intelligent eyes common to medics. A largish nose. Lips chapped by windburn and sun. He would've looked perfectly at home behind a desk with a passkey clipped to his belt, but he had a gun holster clipped to it now. A MultiTool. A three-magazine pouch that held ninety rounds of 5.56 NATO.

"How's your patient?" Russell asked.

Bixby turned and glanced over his shoulder as though the man might be standing there behind him. He waved a hand vaguely in that direction and turned back.

"He'll be fine," he said.

"I didn't think the horse would back up on him. Looked like he was bleeding pretty good."

"Don't worry," said Bixby. "He seems to enjoy it."

Russell shook his head, and a horse whinnied from somewhere in the stable. He said, "How long you been out here, Sergeant?"

"A while," Bixby said.

Russell asked him what he did back home, and the medic said he designed software for a firm in Seattle.

Russell coughed. He never asked this many questions. He was working his way to the one he really wanted to ask and he couldn't get himself to stop.

"The captain's kind of different," he heard himself saying.

Bixby nodded.

"You known him a long time?"

"Long time."

"Don't know that I've ever met an officer like that."

"You won't," Bixby said.

Russell cleared his throat.

"What's he want with these horses?" he said. "He told me you need them to ride up in the mountains, but that doesn't make a lot of sense."

Bixby stood there a moment. His lips tightened and he looked out toward the corral. "I'm not a planner," he said.

"Roger that. I'm not asking for logistics. It's just like I told the lieutenant—" He paused, fumbling for the name.

"Billings," said the medic.

"Billings," Russell said. "I'd be able to do a lot better job of training these guys if I knew anything about what I was training them to do. I mean, I know they'll be riding. I know they'll be up in these hills. But where they'll be riding and for how long and anything else you can tell me—"

"Corporal," said Bixby, "I'm just here to kiss it and make it better. Anything else, you're going to have to ask the captain."

"I asked the captain," said Russell. "Didn't make any more progress than I'm making now."

"Well," said Bixby, "there you go."

The mission was covert. That much was clear. If the medic wouldn't talk about it and the lieutenant wouldn't talk about it and the captain wouldn't talk about it, they were doing all of this off the books. The army had a term for everything, and the term for this was *deniable operations.* Which basically meant there'd be no medevac for the Green Berets if they took casualties—and no artillery or air support. If they were captured, their government wouldn't claim them. No cavalry would come to get them out. About as close to a suicide mission as you could get. He didn't envy them. Not even a little.

Wynne supervised for several days, coming out in the evenings to stand at the corral. Then Russell woke the next week and discovered that the captain had taken half the team and gone out on recon, back into the hills. Left behind were Pike and Billings and Ox, Sergeant First Class Hallum, and Staff Sergeant Perkins, the ODA's junior engineer. Russell didn't worry about it anymore—which team members were in camp and which were out with Wynne. He concentrated on his work with the horses. Getting them soft and supple. Getting them to accept saddle leather and the touch of human hands.

Sara would come down in the evening and watch quietly as he worked, leaning against the corral with her arms crossed one over the other and her chin atop them. Watching the horses. Watching Russell work the horses. Whenever he led the Akhal-Teke into the pen, she'd lean forward and her eyes would go big and bright. He'd glance over and see her sitting on the edge of the fence, and he knew if he hadn't been there to caution her back, she would've tried to approach the animal and touch it.

Lying on his thin cot in the minutes before he descended into sleep, Russell thought about her and the captain and the way the stallion seemed to draw something out in them. Or drew something out in Sara. With Wynne the process was inverted. Reversed. He seemed to siphon the creature's wildness and rage. He seemed somehow to drain it. And without a doubt it was rage that Russell felt down in the animal's bones—rage and madness. Seated on its back, he could feel that constant chaotic simmer. It could erupt at any moment into outright bedlam. How you could take that out of the horse was beyond Russell entirely. The most he could manage was to channel it. As always, his grandfather's words circled inside him—*Make the wrong thing difficult and the right thing release.*

But Sara was herself pulled along by the stallion's manic electricity, something essential drawn out of her as she watched Russell steer the horse around the pen. He could see it on her face, the attraction of it. Wildness was a quality Russell had been taught to govern. You didn't run toward it and you didn't dare to flee. You tried to take hold of it—firmly, respectfully. You tried to steer it toward order. And what you couldn't govern, you tried to identify before it broke you to pieces. There was a wildness in the world that couldn't be governed at all.

His grandfather taught him that like knew like. And a lesser wildness would always be drawn to a greater. Which meant, thought Russell, turning toward sleep, that Sara moved toward the stallion's wildness and the stallion toward that of Wynne. Like recognizing likeness, lesser flowing into greater. Where Russell fit into all of this, he hadn't yet decided.

Mornings, he would rise before dawn, lace his boots by feel, and navigate out to the corral by flashlight. Hamid, the Afghan groom, would always be waiting. The man didn't speak a word of English, but he and Russell had already established an intricate series of gestures that allowed all the communication they required. He was a short man with sunken cheeks and few teeth left in his mouth, and Russell liked him immensely. He had his prayer beads constantly in hand and never seemed to sleep. He was with the animals when Russell walked out to the stables in the morning, and he was with them when Russell curried Fella and retired to his quarters at night.

They squatted across from each another one afternoon in the cool stable, looking out at the November day, heat shimmer on the bare dirt of the corral, the shoulder of the mountain just beyond. Russell's clothes were drenched with sweat and coated with a fine layer of talc. He'd stripped off his jacket and laid it on a hay bale and opened a pack of beef jerky he'd taken from the camp's mess. He chewed in silence, staring at the dirt between his knees, and then he looked up at the groom and offered him the plastic bag.

Hamid regarded Russell's gift with curiosity. He took it in hand and removed a strip of dried meat. He raised it to his nose and sniffed and then put it in his mouth. Russell realized that the man wouldn't be able to tear the beef with his gums, but it didn't matter, because a grimace stretched across his face and he handed back the bag of jerky and then the strip of meat he'd sampled. He shook his head and presented his wrinkled palms, pressing them forward as though he were pushing something across the ground.

"You don't like it?" Russell asked.

Hamid made the pushing gesture. He shook his head.

Russell smiled. He selected another strip of jerky from the bag and took a bite.

He spent his mornings and evenings at the stables, working the horses, packing and ponying, teaching the Green Berets in camp to saddle and ride, how to keep their horses' heads up, keep the animals soft, the proper way of tailing them up an incline. Of the men on Wynne's team, only four had ever ridden, and only one of these had ridden enough to be considered anything but a novice. Most of the men he'd met in Special Forces were southerners, many from Tennessee and the Carolinas, but several of these soldiers had scarcely been in the woods before joining the army, and large animals such as horses seemed to unsettle them. The first thing Russell had to teach was how to approach a horse, to let it see you, smell you, let your idea become the horse's. He'd fallen back on those words of his grandfather's so often they'd become a kind of mantra.

His grandfather was on his mind as he moved softly around the stable, righting pieces of tack hanging from galvanized nails. Outside, the autumn morning was growing warm. Fella walked in from the corral and rested her head against the rail.

"Hello there," Russell said.

The horse walked along the length of fence. Russell watched her sleek brown form. The gloss of her hide, her brown eyes flashing. He went over and leaned against the rail and crossed his arms atop it.

"Oats?" he said. "You want oats or carrots?"

The horse worked her mouth, the muscles along her jawline quivering. Russell thought she was coming along. He was making a nice horse out of her. Another of his grandfather's sayings: *Making a nice horse.* As though the real horse, the horse you want, is down inside the animal, obscured by hair and bad habits.

His grandfather had a number of these proverbs: *Taking the fear out of the horse. Riding from the hind-end forward, not front-end back.* He used to tell Russell constantly, "If you can't do it slow, how are you going to do it fast?" His grandfather knew horses, and Russell had inherited his knowledge, along with the old man's height and his oil black hair. He believed he'd come into his grandfather's knack for soldiering, though this was never something the man had encouraged.

Russell's early years were all barnyards and livestock arenas. He imagined a career as a trainer, working competition horses. His grandfather had broken just about every type of horse—the broncs and buckers, the just plain crazy. You didn't turn your back on such animals. You were better off not to mess with them at all.

In 2000, when they celebrated his grandfather's eightieth birthday, the old man had shown no signs of slowing down. He didn't seem to need to. Other than arthritis in his wrists and ankles, he was in excellent health and sharp as he'd ever been. He could lift a fifty-pound dumbbell from the ground with one hand and then straight up above his head. Seated beside his grandfather at the VA hall for the party, Russell studied the man's forearms, burned brown and corded with muscle. His eyes bright blue. Animated. He wouldn't have guessed that in another year he'd be dead.

It was hard on Russell in the months after. His grandmother had passed during the winter of '97 after a brief fight with bone cancer, and he was alone now in a ranch house in the middle of 640 acres. His aunt Teresa insisted Russell move into town with them, but Russell wouldn't. The city of Cleveland, Oklahoma, had a population of just over three thousand, but he couldn't get to sleep in town. He needed the baffle of oak trees, thick stands of them blocking out the faint noise from the highway half a mile away. Oil trucks and cattle trucks and the occasional semi. Late at night, the carnival of coyotes as they crossed the south pasture, their barks like the laughter of children. He'd lie in bed listening to the chirp of crickets and the steady moan of bullfrogs. The stables were on the other side of the house, and he could hear, from time to time, the whinny of horses—his grandfather's horse, Sugar. She was a painted mare with white stockings and a splotch of white coming down her nose. Russell couldn't look at her without his chest going tight, so he tried not to look.

He began his senior year of high school, cumbersome as a saddle, came home every afternoon to scatter fresh hay and pour sweet feed into the horses' trough, then drove to his aunt's house for supper. She'd try to get him to take covered dishes. She'd try to get him to spend the night. One Friday evening when he walked in the front door, he saw that she'd already made the living room couch up into a bed—sheets and pillows and a blanket folded over one arm. She told him he was staying over and that they'd stay up late watching movies, and she wouldn't take no for an answer. Then she had him take off his boots, which she promptly confiscated and didn't return until the next morning. They'd been shined with great care, and she brought them in and put them on the carpet next to his feet, then sat down beside him on the sofa, placed a hand to his cheek, and began to weep. She was his mother's sister, and he knew she loved him intensely, and if she could have taken him as her own son, she would've. She and her husband didn't have any children—whether by choice or chance, Russell never knew—and with him, her maternal instincts welled up from some deep reservoir of feeling and need.

Winter came, and with it a dampening of Russell's thoughts, everything inside him muffled, gradually going mute. He felt as though his life were happening underwater. He'd walk about the house, toward the kitchen to heat his aunt's meals in the microwave, down the hallway to his grandfather's room. Now was the time for mourning. Now was his turn to be visited by ghosts.

It wasn't just the loss of his grandfather. It was and it wasn't. The old man's death made him feel the loss of his grandmother, and, strangely, for the first time, his father, as though his grandfather's passing was the gateway to an even greater sorrow. Russell stood there in front of the antique mahogany dresser, opening drawers, closing drawers, going through his grandfather's things. Treasures wrapped in yellowed newspaper. Belt buckles embedded with turquoise. Another adorned with a silver dollar. Cufflinks he was certain the man had never worn, and everywhere the small blocks of cedar that the old man believed kept out bugs.

In a velvet-lined box, Russell found the Bronze Star Medal and its accompanying ribbon, his grandfather's two Purple Hearts, his combat infantryman and Expert Rifleman badges, the latter in sterling silver and tarnished almost black. Lastly, he pulled out the diamond-shaped patch of the man's old battalion, RANGERS in gold lettering against a bright blue field. He took these decorations to the bed and arranged them there on the quilt, an intricate counterpane made by his grandmother and her sewing circle before he was ever born. He lifted the Ranger patch to his nose, but there was no smell other than cedar. No sea salt of Normandy or sweat of combat or the metallic scent of blood. He slipped the belt buckle into his pocket.

That spring, he began selling their livestock, cattle by weight —sixty-three cents a pound—and the horses one by one. Without his grandfather, he couldn't care for them, couldn't really afford to feed them. Other than this ranch and the animals, they had almost nothing in the bank. For years they'd lived off Social Security and his grandfather's pension and what the old man had been able to make at the stockyard and state fairs. Stable fees, stud fees, riding lessons, and roping. Russell sold the last of the beef cattle—his grandfather had bought a herd of Black Angus eighteen months before his death—and had five horses left by the end of April: his horse, his grandfather's, his aunt's, and two ponies they'd traded for and didn't know what to do with. He graduated the first week of May and was offered $500 for both ponies and $750 for the ponies with saddles and tack. He accepted the man's money but didn't help him load, and he didn't wave as the man pulled away with the trailer, the heads of the ponies receding as the buyer rounded the driveway's bend.

The summer of 2002 was hot and very dry. Grass fires on the roadsides and a drought on the prairies that burned everything to dust. Russell spent his time riding the pastures and old cattle trails leading through the stands of blackjack and pine. Birds called to him from the branches. Squirrels ran the length of tree limbs and then sat with tails twitching. Russell spoke to Duncan and told him what was happening—to his prospects, his resolve. He told the horse whatever the case, he'd be all right. He'd be ridden and cared for and curried. The animal's neck dipped slightly with each step, a flip of the ears when flies landed, a shake of the head as they buzzed about.

August 2, the day after his grandfather's birthday and twenty days before his own, Russell went down to the local army recruiter's—a sparsely decorated office in downtown Cleveland that used to be a western apparel shop—signed an Option 40 contract, took the physical that Friday, and the next week was on a bus bound for Fayetteville, North Carolina. His aunt wept and shook her head and told him how proud she was, then asked if there was any way he could back out.

Fort Bragg in August. Still ninety degrees at sundown. Rain in the early afternoon, and then the sun back out by evening and a steam rising in thin wisps from the pavement and grass. Russell in the sandpit drilling combatives, hand to hand with Wheels. Their drill instructor said that watching the man sprint was like seeing a cartoon animal with legs pinwheeling, going nowhere fast. Therefore, "Wheels." Russell had liked him instantly, his thick drawl and good-natured grin. He was the son of a highway patrolman and said he'd be better qualified for his father's profession if he had a few combat tours in the Middle East.

"Once you been shot at with automatic weapons," said Wheels, "ain't nothing going to faze you. How's anybody going to compete with that?"

Russell nodded. The man had a point of some kind.

They completed Basic Combat Training October 11 and then were shipped out for Advanced Individual Training, both to Infantry School, both to Fort Benning. Another six weeks of southern humidity, the leaves just beginning to turn and the slightest chill to the air when they rolled out of their bunks at 0430 for PT, standing in formation in front of their platoon barracks wearing gray T-shirts and black shorts and tennis shoes. The sergeant ran them through a circuit of pushups and sit-ups and jumping jacks and burpees, then fell in alongside them as they began their four-mile run, calling out the lines of a running cadence and then pausing for the recruits to parrot his words in response.

Men complained about the robotic nature of these activities, but for the first time since enlisting, Russell knew he'd made the correct decision. Running the stretch of blacktop with his shirt soaked and his lungs burning, heart huge inside his chest, the cadence in his ears like the very first song.

Russell completed Airborne School February 2003 and went to the four-week Ranger Indoctrination Program, the sole purpose of which was to weed out as many of its recruits as possible. The first days at Cole Range in the Georgia woodlands caused up to 40 percent of the trainees in Russell's class to voluntarily withdraw. You get cold enough, tired enough, hungry enough, wet enough—none of this seems like a good idea. It seems like the torture it actually is. All you have to do is tell one of the cadre members that you want to Victor-Whiskey and you're given a hot meal and a shower. Then they put you on a truck the next morning and send you back to your parent unit to spend the rest of your days in shame.

Russell wasn't about to do that. He'd come too far to withdraw, and he realized that this level of suffering cleared his thoughts and emptied him of emotion. After thirty-six hours without sleep and one twenty-one-hundred-calorie MRE, he entered a strangely euphoric state where there was only cold mud and the ruck straps cutting into his shoulders, the falling rain, the weight of his weapon. Something inside him seemed to switch on—he hadn't known it was there—and as he watched his fellow students fall away, the thing burned brighter. By the time he entered Ranger School, he felt as though he'd shed his skin to find some stronger, stranger hide beneath.

Ranger School was hell in three phases, sixty days and a wake-up's worth of being starved and wet and frozen. Navigating obstacles. Solo night navigations through dense pine forests with a small map, a ninety-pound ruck, and a dim flashlight you could only use when you stopped to take a reading. Cadre members catch you using it while walking, they immediately remove you from the course. Cadre members catch you using an actual road or path, they remove you. Cadre members out there in the bush with night-vision and thermal-imaging monoculars, no hiding.

He and Wheels didn't get a full night's sleep until they started Mountain Phase in the hills of Dahlonega, Georgia. Still hungry, still exhausted. Learning knots and belays and fundamentals of climbing. The two recruits shared a pup tent, and one night between four-hour patrols, Russell had just closed his eyes to slip below consciousness when he heard Wheels's voice at his feet.

He didn't bother to open his eyes or raise up on his elbows. "What was that?" he asked.

"Why'd you do this?" Wheels asked.

"Do what?"

"This course," said Wheels. "The army. Why didn't you stay on your ranch?"

Russell lay there several moments and then he did open his eyes. Dim light through the thin fabric of the tent. The soft patter of drizzle. He could see his breath fogging from the cold.

He said it had felt like his only move.

"What," said Wheels, "—because of your granddad?"

"Yeah," Russell told him. He listened to the rain against the canvas a few feet from his head.

Then he said, "Wait. What do you mean?"

"He passed away, you said. You enlisted right after."

"Right," Russell said.

"What were you thinking, I meant?"

Russell mumbled. Something incoherent. He was hoping his friend would just let it lie.

A few quiet minutes passed.

Then Wheels said, "Was it because he'd been a Ranger?"

Russell cleared his throat. He'd never thought about it quite that way. He didn't exactly know.

Wheels said, "Your dad was a Ranger, too, right? Vietnam?"

"Vietnam," Russell said. "He'd started off in the LRRPs. Then they folded those recon units into the Regiment. Not sure: 'seventy-two, 'seventy-three. I think that's how it was."

"Your granddad," said Wheels. "—this was your dad's dad?"

"No," said Russell, "my mother's."

"Still," said Wheels. "It's tradition. It's family."

Russell lay thinking about that. It was family. It was family for certain. Except now his family was all but gone: his grandparents, his father. His mother was a prescription-pill addict, and Russell hadn't seen her since his father was killed more than sixteen years before. He thought that if he made it through Ranger School he'd earn a new family. One that could never leave.

"I guess," said Wheels, "considering your history, doesn't sound like you had a lot of choice."

Russell told him no.

He didn't guess that he did.

It turned colder in the mountains and the skies clouded, and early one morning as he was trotting Fella along one of the dirt trails that wound into the hills behind camp, he felt something brush against his cheek and then moisture, glanced up, and saw it had begun to snow—small flakes hardly distinguishable in this light, gliding mutely in the windless dawn. Russell reined to a stop and sat the horse, watching the white flecks descend like ash and melt instantly against the earth. He'd not seen snow in nearly seven years, or not up close he hadn't, and he'd forgotten how it quieted everything and closed you in. He put his horse forward, and the animal took several pensive steps. He gave the horse her head, and she blew and carried him up the trail.

By afternoon patches of white had begun to accumulate, and by evening there was a thin blanket all across the ground. It brought the soldiers out of their huts, and they stood there, staring up at the sky. They performed stand-to in the hushed blue light, and just before dark there was a whistling sound from the ridgeline and then the dry, flat pop of a rocket detonating, a brief moment's silence, and then an echo through the valley, a long series of ghost explosions back along the hills. Russell looked over at Wheels, and both of them took off up the trail at a sprint. Billings had taken two of the other men out to rendezvous with the captain—or that was the plan as Russell understood it—and there was no one to stop the two Rangers and no one to caution them back. The snow along the hillside was ankle deep in places, and their breath fogged before them in the dusk.

The sky had all but cleared when they reached the hilltop fortress, and another rocket struck and blew a cloud of white against the stars. Russell leaned over and palmed his knees, struggling to get his breath, and he glanced beside him and Wheels was doing the same. They watched the soldiers scurry about the firebase, and they watched a third rocket scream in and disappear into a snow-covered embankment. They started for the medical tent, but before they reached it, they heard a woman's voice calling their names. Russell turned and saw a hand beckoning them to the mouth of a bunker about fifteen meters away. They went along a series of sandstone steps, ducked under a plywood lintel, and climbed down into the earth. Sara was crouched there along with several soldiers and the other woman on her surgical team, the woman's face lit from below by the green glow stick she held.

Another rocket struck, this one closer, and Russell felt the ground shudder beneath his boots and something sprinkled onto the back of his neck. When he glanced over, Wheels was squatting against the wall of the bunker with both palms to his ears, his chin tucked and his elbows pressed together in front of his face.

Russell and Sara stared down at him. He looked like a child hiding in a closet.

Wheels looked up at them.

"We came to save you," he said.

The rockets started to fall again at daybreak. Russell awoke just before dawn in the bunker where he'd first been quartered, took his pants from the head of the cot, slipped them on, and fastened the belt, a few extra inches of slack in it—the work and stress and diet. He slid his sidearm into his thigh holster and took up his carbine. Then the familiar shriek of a mortar came from outside the bunker, followed by a low concussion that shook the cinder-block walls and sprinkled grains of sand from the ceiling. Instinct sent Russell to the floor, and he rose wiping at his eyes and checking himself for wounds.

It had taken a while, but the hostiles had finally found positions from which they could range in their mortars, their rockets, and Russell emerged from his bunker into a bedlam of scrambling soldiers and smoke. He followed three men down an earthen trench toward the command bunker, which he saw, once he came onto the packed ground at the center of camp, lay in a smoldering rubble of sandbags and concrete and aluminum sheeting. A young soldier sat in the snow with his rifle across his lap like a child's toy, head shaved, eyes wet, saying, "You got no idea. You got no idea." There were men already searching the debris for survivors, and Russell fell in and began to heft bits of broken rock toward a pile that was forming several yards from where the bunker had stood. They'd just uncovered the first body when a man in his observation post called "*Incoming!*" and they dove behind what cover they could find and waited for oblivion.

He spent the rest of the day digging through rubble or taking shelter in the nearest bunker while the rockets pounded. The men called for air support, and in half an hour two Apache gunships appeared over a spur to the north, strafed the valley below, emptied their munitions, and returned to base. All was quiet for several hours. They unearthed three dead soldiers from beneath the ruins of the command bunker and conveyed their bodies to the medical tent. Late afternoon, the rockets returned.

He sat with Sara in the bunker that evening. The rockets would strike and the ground would tremble and bits of earth dislodged and fell.

"How long you think they'll keep this up?" Sara asked.

"I don't know," Russell told her. "I reckon until someone goes out there and stops them."

"Who'd do that?"

Russell had been staring through a crack in the plywood. He turned and regarded her for a second.

She shook her head. "Why'd I even ask?"

Russell smiled. Even with a grime-streaked face and a sweatshirt she'd likely been wearing for seventy-two hours, she was still very pretty.

"Can't they call in choppers or something?"

"They already called in the choppers or something. They're dug in like ticks. As soon as they hear our air, they slip off the back side of that ridge, wait until we've murdered half a dozen monkeys, then come out when the coast is clear and get right back to it."

Sara was sitting on the ground with her legs pulled to her chest and her arms wrapped around her shins. She rested her chin on her knees.

"Frustrating," she said.

"Yes, ma'am," Russell said.

A few minutes passed. A mortar struck and there was a burst of machine-gun fire from one of the emplacements. Sara looked at him.

"You were in Iraq before this?"

"Yeah," said Russell. "Mosul."

"Did the insurgents do this there?"

"Not really," Russell told her. "I was chopped to a task force. They had a platoon of us Rangers and a couple Special Forces teams. There was a company from the 101st, and we maybe had about a dozen or so commandos on loan from the Brits."

"What did they have you doing?"

"Doing how?"

"Your job," said Sara. "Were you training horses?"

"No," Russell told her. "I was part of a QRF. Me and another—"

"What's a QRF?"

"Quick Reaction Force. If a coalition element in our area got in trouble, we'd hop on board a Black Hawk and go play cavalry."

"Did you like it?"

Russell considered the question. He hadn't thought of liking it or not. He told her you were always waiting for something to happen. You were never the happening itself.

They were shelled the next morning and every morning after for the following week. Russell would wake in the half-light and find Sara curled on one of the bunks, a tuft of dark hair poking out from beneath the sleeping bag, her small, slender form under the olive fabric, rising and falling. After several nights of playing cards with the Rangers, Sara sought refuge here with them.

When he awoke on the fourth day of the shelling, the first thing he heard was the noise of a distant helicopter, and the second thing was the low rumbling of Wheels's voice. He smelled cigarette smoke and coffee.

Wheels said, "That's the real reason we're here."

"In this outpost?" Sara asked.

"In Afghanistan," Wheels said. "People say 'natural resources,' but they don't know what they're really saying. It's natural resources, all right. It's gold."

Russell lay there. *Gold,* he thought. A few months ago it had been lithium. He flexed his calf beneath the blanket, considering whether he should tell Wheels to knock it the hell off, but then decided to hear him out.

"So Alexander . . . ," Wheels said.

"Right," said Sara.

"When he conquers Bactria—"

"Where's Bactria?"

"North," said Wheels. "It's up in the north. Anyway, he comes in, conquers Bactria, marries one of the princesses or whatever they called them, and then all the gold and gems he'd been winning in his battles, he stows them in the treasury there and then ups and dies."

"I thought he died in Babylon."

"He did die in Babylon," Wheels told her. "Just let me finish."

"Sorry," Sara said.

"So all this gold and treasure gets buried for a couple thousand years, and then they start digging it up in the seventies—"

"Nineteen-seventies?"

“Let me finish,” Wheels said. “Start digging all this treasure up, this Russian archeologist or whatever, and then Russia invades in ’seventy-nine, and the gold goes into the vault in Kabul. You could go see it there in Kabul, but they won’t let you, of course. Anyway, there’s that gold—the Kabul gold—but there’s all this other gold from these graves that the Taliban dug up, how come them to be able to afford their weapons in the first place.”

“I thought they did it with drug money,” said Sara. “Opium.”

“They did do it with drug money,” said Wheels. “Drug money and Bin Laden money and gold from the tombs they pillaged. And don’t think for a second we don’t want in on *that* action, cause since when have you ever known Americans not to be interested in gold?”

There were a few moments of silence. Russell wanted to look over, but he managed to keep himself from it.

“That wasn’t a reticular question,” said Wheels.

“Sorry,” said Sara. “I wasn’t sure you were finished.”

“I’m finished,” Wheels said, and he had just said it when the thin whistle of a rocket screamed over camp and then a sharp crack from the valley on the other side of the range.

Russell raised up on the cot and rubbed his eyes. He looked over at Wheels and Sara where they sat at the card table, Sara with one leg pulled to her chest and her arms around the shin, chin upon her knee.

“Morning,” Wheels said.

Russell and Sara met for lunch in the mess tent when the all clear had sounded, and they met again for supper that evening. They talked about the outpost and where they were from, and they talked about how they’d ended up in the mountains of a country they’d not even known had existed before the Towers fell.

Sara was at the end of her second tour. She’d done her first a few years prior, serving as medic aboard a C-130 and working the overflight from Riyadh to Ramstein Air Base in Germany. The post didn’t suit her. Or she didn’t think so at the time. She got out after her rotation was up, went back to Nevada, and started nursing school. She used the pay she'd saved up during her deployment to put a down payment on a two-bedroom house, and she set about starting an average middle-class life, working as a med tech in the laboratory of a small hospital and taking classes in the evenings.

It was all she'd dreamed of during her deployment, and in six months depression had closed around her throat. The words in her textbooks swam, and doctors prescribed sleeping pills and anxiety medication, bottles of alprazolam, which she chose one night to empty into her mouth and choke down with half a bottle of Chardonnay.

They were seated on a wall of sandbags beside the compound's entrance, sharing a can of soda. She stared off toward the mountains.

"Xanax won't kill you," she said.

Russell coughed into a fist.

"Maybe that was too much," she said.

"No," he told her, "I just . . ." He made an ambiguous gesture and trailed off into silence.

"Did you go to therapy?" he said after a few moments.

"No therapy," she said. "I mean, they *put* me in therapy. Or the nuthouse, actually. Two weeks."

Russell shook his head.

"It's where I belonged at the time," she said, shrugging. "I got lucky it didn't end up affecting my reenlistment. My aunt works in the county clerk's office, and she was able to keep a couple things under wraps. Otherwise, I'd never have gotten back in."

"You're the first medic I ever met who was happy about getting another deployment."

"Well," said Sara, "they don't have the same advantages as me."

"Such as what?"

"Being crazy."

"You ain't any crazier than me," Russell said.

"No?"

"I don't think so."

"Swallowing a bottle of Xanax?"

"People do stuff like that," said Russell.

"They do," she agreed.

"Well," he said, "you don't seem crazy to me."

"I don't?"

"You're helping a lot of people."

"You haven't considered they might go together?"

Russell looked at her. "You think you have to be crazy to want to help people?"

"No," she told him. "But you probably have to be a little crazy to do it in a war zone."

Russell shrugged. "Someone needs to."

"I agree," she said. "Someone does. It just so happens those someones tend to be nuts."

They talked longer and decided to walk back to the surgical tent so Sara could fetch her jacket, when a commotion came from outside the walls. They looked down from their perch into a swarm of bodies, men shoving each other and shouting and a blur of robes and *pakol* caps and the intermingled legs of Americans in fatigues. Russell watched a few moments and then looked at Sara.

"I think they got somebody," she said.

So they did. There were a dozen Afghan militiamen who worked out of the firebase as translators and guides, and they had in their possession a very thin man dressed in a soiled linen shirt that went just past his knees, sandals, a suede leather vest. He had a burlap sack secured over his head and tied with a length of rope, and his hands were bound with what to Russell looked like wire. The Afghans were leading him toward the center of camp on a paracord leash that had been wrapped around the man's waist. Every so often one of them would reach out and slap the base of his skull. They brought him to a pile of dirty snow and pushed him to his knees. One of the men stepped up and pulled the sack from his head, and the prisoner knelt very still, studying the ground.

Russell watched. The Afghans seemed to be arguing some point of custom or law. Russell saw that they were divided in their opinions, and he wished he spoke Dari or Pashto, whichever was being used. The American soldiers kept their distance, seeming reluctant to intervene or uncertain of exactly how.

There was a private standing beside the gate. He couldn't have been more than nineteen and looked even younger than that. Russell called to him and asked what was going on.

"It's one of the enemy spotters," said the young private, "for the mortars that've been hitting us."

Russell nodded. The Afghans continued arguing. They gestured at the kneeling man and they gestured at the sky—either at their ultimate destination or perhaps the cobalt expanse through which the mortars had fallen. Then an elder among the men stepped forward and lifted a hand and all went instantly quiet, and he regarded them with an almost clerical calm. He spoke very softly, and his listeners' brows furrowed with concentration, and some began nodding. He touched their prisoner gently on the shoulder. He pointed at the earth on which they stood. Then he raised an enormous knife in his fist. Russell didn't see anyone pass it to him, and he didn't see the man draw it from anywhere about his person. His hand had been empty and then it wasn't. The blade was a machete of strange manufacture, its edge curving obscenely outward, and the elder took one step forward and, with a single, practiced stroke, severed the prisoner's head cleanly from his body. Russell felt something buzz across his skin, and he watched in amazement as the man's skull went tumbling among the rocks. The headless torso pitched sideways and began to geyser blood onto the snow, and the elder, his robes freckled with the spray, passed his blade to a subordinate and stepped clear. One of the Afghans gave a shrill cry, and the cry was echoed by the others. The Americans had begun to stagger backward, and one young soldier turned and fled down the path toward his bunker.

But the ritual had yet to conclude. Two Afghan men came forward, each taking an arm of their prisoner, bringing his torso once more to a kneeling position, the blood all but subsided and turned now to seep. A third Afghan—a leader of the local militia whom Russell had heard several Americans refer to as Bari—came up with a five-gallon jerry can and began, without hurry, to pour the contents into the corpse's neck. Then he flung the can aside and began to rummage in the pockets of his robe. He produced a small box of matches, struck one and then another against the side of the box, and tossed it toward the corpse. Tongues of fire erupted and flames licked the bloody shirt of the headless man, reaching, at last, the cavity between his shoulders. The two men still holding the torso released their grip, and a ball of bright blue flame went up in the dusk and the torso fell forward, bent as if in prayer.

It didn't stay bent for long. Gasoline had filled the dead man's stomach, and gasoline had soaked his clothes, and as the fire consumed the corpse, it began to writhe. The Afghans once again released a piercing call as the torso wrenched upright and began to cavort in spasms, standing and falling, performing a macabre and frightful dance.

"Sweet Jesus," said Russell and turned to look at Sara, but Sara was no longer seated beside him. He glanced at the wall of HESCOs, then over at the gates. He looked back toward the spectacle in the center of camp, and that was when he saw her. She'd managed to slip from the wall of sandbags and was threading her way among the soldiers, through the swarm of militiamen, now approaching the ring of elders, this small figure in surgical scrubs—girlish, petite—moving closer and closer to the dancing corpse.

Russell jumped down and went after her, moving past the astonished Americans, past the murmuring Afghans. She was within ten yards of the burning body when Russell caught up with her. He seized her by the wrist and began to lead her away. She came without struggle, limp as any doll. They went down the sandbag-lined path in the cold evening air until they came to the medical tent and stood for several breathless moments.

Sara looked up at him. Her pupils were large as dimes and her expression that of someone coaxed from a trance. Euphoric. Enthralled. Her breath fogged in the blue twilight.

He stood there with her hand in his until the color came back into her face and her eyes shifted and she seemed to be returning.

"That—" he told her, when he managed to speak, "*that* was crazy."

The next morning a storm rolled in from the west, and it began once more to snow, the white world descending, muffled and mute. The air was very quiet, very cold. Russell rubbed his hands together, cupped and blew into them, then reached down in a cargo pocket for his gloves.

All that day an unease gnawed his stomach. It wasn't just the mortars and rockets, the thought of his death screaming in from above. The hollow beneath his sternum began to ache. His temples pulsed. Snow and the all clear only seemed to make it worse.

At dusk he glanced out from the tent where he and a few other soldiers had gone to seek warmth and saw three figures walking across camp, two large, one small—Ox and Pike and Wheels—watch caps pulled down to their ears and their jacket collars turned up against the cold. Wheels wore a checkered shemagh—black and brown—no telling where he'd gotten his hands on it. Russell walked out onto the packed white path with the snow crunching under his boots. He lifted an arm to wave, but the three men had already seen him and started his way.

As they approached, Russell saw that Ox had a chaw protruding from the left side of his jaw and then that Wheels had lined his lower lip with the stuff. He kept leaning over every few steps to spit. He came up, slapped Russell's shoulder, and pointed to his mouth.

"Sergeant loaned me a dip," he told him.

"Good for you," Russell said.

The four of them stood several moments.

"We need to go out and stop this," Pike said.

Russell agreed. He said the problem was how.

Then he said, "*We?*" pointing a finger at himself, then at Ox and Wheels and Sergeant Pike.

"You be up for that?" said Pike.

"How would we do it?" Russell asked.

"Sergeant was thinking an ambush," Ox said. His lips parted

and he spat expertly between his teeth, a thin stream arcing to the ground, not a drop clinging to his beard or the front of his jacket.

"We're going to try to ambush them?" Russell asked. "We'd have to know where they were. We'd have to know where they're *going* to be."

"I know where they are," Pike said.

Russell stood thinking about it. He thought the odds of Pike knowing the precise—or future—location of an enemy mortar team was slim to none.

Pike said, "How long before one of these rounds goes long and ends up hitting *our* camp."

"Or the horses," said Ox.

"Or the horses," Pike said.

For some reason, Russell had yet to consider that as a possibility, as though the mountain and this hilltop fortress would prevent any wayward shell from killing everything in the corral.

"When would we go?"

"I think the sooner the better. Don't you?"

"Just the four of us?" said Russell.

"Just us four," Pike said.

Russell looked at Wheels, his friend standing there with pupils quivering. He opened his mouth as if to tell Russell his opinion of this plan, but he spat instead. Or tried to spit. He kept his teeth together like Ox, attempting to eject the tobacco juice between them, but unlike Ox, his technique was off and spit dribbled from his lips and down onto his beard. He leaned forward, palmed a knee with one hand and swiped the back of his sleeve across his chin.

He looked up at Russell. His Adam's apple jerked.

"I think I maybe swallowed some," he said.

They left Dodge just after midnight. Pike had procured tactical vests for Wheels and Russell, kneepads and helmets and pouches for their ammo. Their rifles were back down in camp, but Ox handed them a pair of Colt carbines with the sixteen-inch barrel, ACOGs mounted on the sight rails, night-vision optics on the quad rails just in front. Precision buttstocks. Suppressors screwed into the threaded muzzle breaks. The weapons still had their unmarked factory finish—you could run your thumb across the receiver and feel that powder-textured coating—and when Russell asked the sergeant where they'd come from, Ox simply told him to try to return it in one piece.

They were the better part of an hour working their way onto the valley floor, and when they reached the basin, the air was cold on Russell's face and the moon lit the bare oak limbs and cast spidery shadows against the snow and the bare patches of scree. The mortar team they hunted had been launching from about four kilometers out, and Pike thought the enemy position lay in a little draw that came down the throat of the mountains on the valley's opposite side. The sergeant's thinking was to try to get there before dawn and lay up for an ambush. That was provided, of course, the mortar crew wasn't already waiting.

"You think he's right?" Wheels had asked Russell just before they set off.

"Do I think *who*'s right?" said Russell. "About what?"

"The sergeant. You think he knows where these Talibs are posted up?"

Russell told him he had no idea.

"I don't see how he could know," said Wheels. "Unless he's been out there. And if he hasn't been out there, he can't know anything."

"Then I don't suppose we have to worry about getting shot," Russell said.

Wheels stared at him.

"The fuck crawled up your ass?"

"I'm fine," Russell said.

Wheels studied him a long moment. Then he said, "You can't afford to be thinking about any of that."

"Thinking about what?" Russell said.

"She's a pretty girl," said Wheels, "but this ain't the time."

Russell didn't say anything.

"I haven't brought it up because you know how you can get."

Russell said, "No. Tell me how I get."

Wheels exhaled very slowly and shook his head. "Russ, I'm not trying to get on your case. I'm just saying."

"We haven't even done anything," Russell said.

"Not yet," said Wheels. "But I've seen the way she looks at you. I've seen you looking at her. Save it for stateside. Right now it'll get you cross-threaded."

Russell looked at him. His platinum hair grown out into a short rooster's comb. His pupils quivering back and forth.

"Since when did you become the voice of reason?"

"Since always," Wheels said.

They deployed along a gorge that twisted across the valley floor. It had been a stream at one time but was bone-dry now and lined with egg-shaped stones, perfectly polished, glowing in the moonlight. Russell kept glancing down to monitor his footing. Easy, in such circumstances, to roll an ankle, pick up a mechanical injury, and then the entire mission would be a wash. He stopped at one point and pulled back the sleeve of his jacket to check his watch. First light was two hours away. He readjusted his rifle sling and continued walking.

The gorge began to angle northward, and they climbed its southern lip and shifted course to the east. They hadn't spoken a word since leaving camp and they didn't speak now, walking soundlessly and fifteen meters apart, scanning the country through their rifles' sights. Russell kept his eyes sweeping back and forth, dividing the terrain into sectors. A Vietnam veteran who'd done his tours with Long Range Reconnaissance had once told him that anything worth looking at was worth pointing your gun at. *Good advice,* Russell thought.

They reached the first slopes of the eastward range and defiled along an uneven goat trail heading south. They went several hundred meters, and then Pike brought them to a halt, raising his left fist in the air and then lowering himself onto a knee. The three men behind him knelt in unison. Anyone watching would have thought they'd rehearsed. Pike looked up a draw to his right and then pointed his index finger toward the stars and rotated it several times. They rose and moved into the gorge.

The walls of the culvert were slick with ice, and through the night scope the world burned with a sea-green light. Russell lowered the rifle and glanced at the moon, put his outstretched hand between it and the horizon. They had an hour's dark left, and here was where they'd lose it. He trailed Ox, taking great care to step in the man's tracks, like a child following his father.

After a ninety-minute climb—slow, treacherous—they reached the clearing Pike was searching for, fanned out and shouldered their rifles. There was no one about, but the snow had been marked by footprints, and in the middle of the clearing lay the perfect impression of a mortar's baseplate—this frozen, concave square, blue in the dawning air. The four of them stood looking at it. Wheels took a knee beside the indentation, reaching out a hand to trace its borders. He looked up at Sergeant Pike, then over at Russell.

"I will be damned," he said.

Russell lay in the snow beneath the live oaks on the eastern edge of the clearing, blinking every few moments to brush the sleep from his eyes. He watched his breath dissolve in the air like smoke, and every few minutes he'd turn and stare back toward the melancholy hills where Firebase Dodge sat on its impregnable perch, waiting for the sun to crest the ridgeline. The dark forms of birds jerked against the sky. Dozens of them, swarming like insects. Russell watched how they seemed to spasm in flight and shift direction, a constant and crazed flapping. He blinked again, massaged his eyes with his forefinger and thumb, and he realized these were not birds. They were bats. Dipping down beneath the tree limbs, feeding on the wing. It was a mean omen, and he concluded one of two things would happen in the next hour: they'd either see no sign of the mortar team they sought or they'd all of them die in this place.

He was mistaken in both assumptions. As light was spreading among the leaves and limbs, he heard a sudden exchange of low voices and then watched in disbelief as four men came down the trail toward the clearing. Four Talibs. He blinked and counted again. There were five. They were dressed in oversize black shirts and thin black trousers, turbans that were a lighter shade of black, gray almost, and three of them lugged an ancient Soviet-era mortar that would have weighed well over a hundred pounds. There was no practical way of transporting this weapon if the wheel base was lost, and it was apparent to Russell that this was precisely the case.

The three men set the mortar crunching into the snow and began attaching its bipod. One of them—tall and lean, shod in cheap plastic sandals—unslung a canvas bag from his shoulder and started removing rounds, placing each six-pound shell within reach of the launcher, nose-down in the carpet of white. The others kept up a whispered exchange in Pashto or Dari, and the shape of the words caused a tremor of panic to run the length of Russell's body and settle like a boot in his back. He watched as the men finished assembling the mortar and began to dial in coordinates, one of them peering through a set of binoculars toward the hills where the American firebase was awakening in the early dawn. Russell drew a bead on the torso of the nearest combatant, aligning the red dot of his gunsight with the center of his enemy's chest, aiming center mass. He thumbed the selector, pressing it very slowly to SEMI, following the switch with the pad of his thumb and catching it before it clicked. He curled his finger inside the trigger guard and felt the cold metal against his callus. Then he just lay there, focusing on his breath.

One of the men had set a spotting scope on its tripod at the far end of the clearing and was staring at something to the north. He'd just turned back toward his comrades when a vulval slit perforated his Adam's apple and he went down very hard in the snow, legs crossed under him, a strange movement that almost looked vaudevillian. He gripped his throat with both hands as though he were choking. Blood welled between his fingers. Several of the Talibs had turned to watch. They seemed not to understand what was happening, and two of them went sprawling face-first and another's head burst like a melon and he staggered three steps before collapsing.

The suppressed rounds buzzed through the clearing like wasps. The remaining man didn't even raise his rifle. He took off sprinting toward the trees where Russell was concealed. Russell pressed the trigger twice very fast—two shots spaced on top of each other. He saw the man's face very clearly—eyes stretched wide, brows slightly raised, beads of sweat visible on his forehead. When the bullets struck him, he spun to one side and fell forward, his momentum carrying him until he collided with a tree. Russell came up on his knees and, keeping his rifle trained on the man, got his feet under him and moved up. The man lay on his stomach, both arms around the tree trunk as though he were embracing it. Russell stood a few moments and then lowered his rifle to the low-ready position and toed the man with his boot. The man just lay there. Russell glanced at the other bodies in the clearing. Pike and Wheels and Ox were entering from the south side, sidestepping the terrain with rifles to their shoulders, staring out over their scopes. Russell raised a hand and motioned to them, and Pike motioned back.

The two of them met on the level expanse of snow. The sun had crested the eastern mountains, and Russell turned his back to the light, squinting.

"You smoke him?" Pike asked.

"Yeah," said Russell.

Pike swiped a gloved hand through his beard and glanced toward the man Russell had killed. Then he looked at Russell and gave him a tight-lipped nod.

Russell massaged the skin just above his left eyebrow. He turned and looked at the spotting scope on its tripod.

"What were they looking at?" he said.

Pike seemed not to hear him. He walked over to one of the corpses and began to search the body for intel. Russell watched him a moment and then he stepped across to the scope. It was a brand-new Bushnell 60x65, the kind the marines were using north of Baghdad, and Russell knew it had been taken from American personnel. He bent to look through the eyepiece.

The haze of mist and vapor rising from the rocks. Shadows. Tones of white muted brown. He stood and slung the rifle over his shoulder and leaned to look again. He drew a breath and began adjusting the focus. What came into view didn't make sense, and he blinked several times to correct the picture, but there it was: a man in a clearing much like the one in which Russell stood, staring at him through an identical scope. This man, however, was dressed in black—turban, shirt, and trousers—and to his left were several more men, likewise dressed, hovering above a mortar tube. The man was staring through his scope at Russell and gesturing to the men beside him. They were repositioning the tube, and the spotter seemed to be motioning them to hurry. Russell's breath caught in his chest and he turned to look at Pike. He'd just opened his mouth when he heard the barely perceptible hiss of the mortar round.

He fell to the snow with both hands cupped to his ears and his elbows pressed together. His knees had risen to his chest, and he lay there as the air went hot and pieces of earth rained around him. His head was buzzing and he couldn't hear anything but the blood rushing inside his skull, and before he opened his eyes he began to check his limbs to see if they were there. Smell of gun smoke. The sharp smell of shredded pine. He rose onto his hands and knees. The sun that shone through the dust and smoke was an orange morning sun, and he saw Wheels and Ox lying very close to one another, almost touching. He called to them but he couldn't hear the sound of his own voice, and when he looked to his left, he saw Pike.

The sergeant lay on his back beside the overturned mortar, eyes blinking and a bright arterial mist spraying from the cut on his jugular, a thin serum leaking from his ears. He'd lifted a hand toward the sky and seemed to be grasping for something which only he saw. He closed the hand into a fist and turned it slightly, the motion of someone unlocking a door. Russell crawled to the sergeant and pressed his palm against the man's neck. He reached into a pocket and pulled out his bandana, then folded it over the wound to make a compress. Pike's eyelids were fluttering, and Russell shouted for the men to bring their trauma packs, but his words were sucked away into a great humming void.

He pulled the sergeant to the edge of the clearing and was joined by Ox and Wheels. Together they began to drag Pike deeper into the trees, leaving behind them a trough of snow and frozen earth and the bright dribble of blood. Another mortar detonated up the slope about a hundred meters and then another even farther. Russell stopped and applied pressure to the sergeant's neck. He looked up at the faces of the two men across from him.

Ox leaned toward him and began mouthing words, but Russell stopped him, gestured to his ears, and shook his head. The large man studied him a moment, then reached and touched his hand to a torn place on the outer thigh of Russell's fatigues. Russell glanced down to examine his leg where shrapnel had torn through the fabric. He couldn't feel his injury through the adrenaline, but the wound didn't seem deep. He took hold of the drag handles on Sergeant Pike's body armor and motioned for Wheels and Ox to take his feet. They picked the man up and started down the hillside, finding their way among the pine trees and oaks, the sun bright on their faces and the sergeant's pupils widening.

They fought their way onto the valley floor. They bore Pike on a foldable litter they carried, but there was no hurry in this regard now, for the sergeant was dead. They'd shot through most of their ammunition, and Russell's back felt strange and his rifle had malfunctioned. He'd fired through twenty-eight rounds, and when the bolt slammed back and he slapped in a fresh magazine, he couldn't get the weapon to go into battery: the bolt release lever was locked in place and wouldn't budge. He tried to pull the magazine out, but it was locked in place as well. They laid the sergeant's body on the ground and tried to form some kind of a perimeter. Russell scoped the terrain farther out onto the valley floor, looking for cover. The rattle of an AK came from the higher hills. Russell went prone in the dirt, laid his rifle in front of him, and pressed the bolt release hard as he could. The paddle was frozen solid.

There was a wadi about fifty meters out, but he didn't know if they could get to it. He looked over to Wheels and Wheels looked back. The man glanced toward the hills from which they were taking fire. Then he glanced back to Russell. His eyes were calm, the pupils motionless. Russell had seen this before during firefights: the surge of adrenaline seemed to act as a sedative. He slung his rifle, got to his knees, and motioned toward the dead sergeant. Then he moved over and took up the litter's front handles. A rifle shot passed overhead—the sharp crack of it several feet from his ear—and he hunkered into himself. Ox and Wheels came up behind and grabbed hold of the litter, and they set off at an ambling shuffle with bullets caroming off to either side.

They made it to the wadi and down the embankment to the hardpan bed. Russell tried to determine if it was the same trench they'd traveled along the night before, but he wasn't sure. Ox went to cover their backtrack, and Wheels knelt above the corpse of the sergeant as though he'd resuscitate him. Russell could see plumes of smoke rising from the mountains to the east. Mortars were falling once again on the firebase. He fetched another bandana from his pocket and spread it on his lap, sat and began disassembling his rifle, pressing the takedown pins and pulling them out the other side of the receiver with his thumbnails. He laid the upper across his thighs, took his knife and began prying at the magazine, trying to work it free of the well. When this didn't work, he fit the upper and lower receivers together and pressed the pins back into place. Sweat was running into his eyes. He smacked the magazine with the heel of his palm and then he took the rifle by the stock and forward grip and slammed the magazine against the ground. He sat there a moment. The pain in his back was a dull red knot. He glanced at the frozen ground on either side of his legs, dug a fist-sized piece of sandstone from the snow, and, laying the rifle across his thighs, struck the bolt-release paddle. The sandstone cracked in half, but the paddle gave way and the bolt snapped forward and chambered a round. He pointed the rifle at the sky and fired. Then he fired twice more. He pressed the magazine release and the clip fell into his lap. He examined it to see whether there was anything he could see that might have caused it to stick, but nothing looked damaged. He snapped the magazine into place, fired two more rounds, then moved to the lip of the gulch and stared out through his scope toward the mountains, the mortars, the bright winter sun.

• • •

They expected to be all day bearing back the sergeant's body, but at noon a Black Hawk appeared over the ridge to the north, and fifteen minutes later they'd loaded Pike onto the craft. A medic knelt over him, searching for his pulse. Then the helicopter lifted into the sky, snow blowing up on either side of it in great fountains of white.

There were two air force PJs on the helo—one large, one small. Russell sat on the rumbling seat with the terrain blurring past the Plexiglas window—very clear, someone must have cleaned it with Lemon Pledge—and then the smaller PJ reached to touch the torn place on Russell's fatigues. This man's nametape read DIAZ, and he pulled back the fabric to study the wound, then produced a pair of scissors and sheared away the pants leg to Russell's thigh. He was pressing gauze against the quarter-sized gash when he looked up and his brow furrowed. He put a hand to Russell's vest, and Russell looked down to see that blood had soaked the brown fabric. Something had gotten through the ballistic panel on the left side, but Russell had just watched five men die, one of whom he'd killed, and his entire body had a numb, floating feeling. The PJ set about removing Russell's body armor, removing his undershirt and jacket. Russell closed his eyes.

When they landed at the firebase, there was a small crowd awaiting them, members of the surgical team standing to one side. A row of wounded soldiers lay along the sandbag wall, Sara and the other nurses attending them. The chopper put down, and two medical techs came up with a litter. It took Russell a moment to realize they were coming for him. Sara was watching. She nodded to Russell and massaged the skin just below her throat. Russell looked at her and waved. His hearing had partly returned and he told the med techs he could walk on his own, but they didn't seem to care what he could do, and finally one of the surgeons approached.

"Soldier," he said, "they do it for a living."

Russell stared at the man. Then he turned to seat himself on the thin canvas stretcher. He felt the doctor swipe something cold across the skin below his shoulder, and when he looked to see what it was, the man sank a needle into his deltoid and pushed the plunger.

Then he was in the medical tent. He could tell that his back hurt, but he couldn't feel it beneath the drugs. *Could tell it hurt but couldn't feel.* He'd have something he wanted to say and then he'd try to form the words and they'd evaporate from the tip of his tongue. Something seemed to have caught up with him. He kept closing and opening his eyes. The scene unfolded before him like bodies caught in a strobe: the doctors across the room, the doctors up close. There were men on tables screaming. Men wheeled past on gurneys.

Then a surgeon was speaking to him. Time seemed to have passed. They'd removed shrapnel from his torso and thigh, debrided the wounds but for some reason hadn't stitched him. He both seemed to recall the procedure but couldn't remember a thing about it.

"You have a mild concussion," the surgeon was saying. "Mild TBI. On the scale we use, about a thirteen."

"What did you give me?" asked Russell.

"Fentanyl," said the surgeon. His tone suggested they'd already been over this. Maybe several times.

Russell closed his eyes. Opened and closed them. He kept sucking his bottom lip inside his mouth to wet it. The man said something else about concussions. It seemed to be a question.

"I've had three concussions," said Russell. "I had two in one semester playing high school ball. I had another not too long ago." He made a plosive noise with his lips and lifted one hand to mime a detonation.

"There are different kinds," the surgeon told him. "Are you having trouble hearing?"

"Not now," Russell said.

The doctor nodded. He had gray hair in a buzz cut and wire-rimmed glasses. He pulled a penlight from his jacket.

"Follow my finger," he said.

He held his index finger six inches from Russell's nose, and shining his light into Russell's eyes, moved the finger up, down, and then from left to right, like a priest administering rites. He seemed satisfied. He nodded again and patted Russell's shoulder.

"You've strained the muscles in your lumbar spine, but I don't believe it's in the vertebrae or discs. Can't know without an MRI, but I'd be very surprised. You're not having any numbness and you're not having referred pain. Doesn't mean it won't hurt, but it seems to be muscular. You might need a CT at some point. We'll get those wounds stitched up."

"What did you give me?" Russell asked.

"Fentanyl," said the surgeon, smiling.

Russell closed his eyes. When he opened them again, he was sure only a few seconds had passed, but the light in the room had slanted into evening and Sara stood beside him wearing surgical scrubs. There was a stainless-steel tray beside his bed, and Sara laid something on it, some kind of instrument, and began repositioning the lamps so they focused along his rib cage and leg. She set about cleaning the wounds, opening two packs of Betadine swabs, working along the cuts in a circular motion. She used all six of the swabs and then gave him a shot of penicillin, explaining everything to him as she went. She gave him a tetanus booster and then she took another syringe from the tray, held it up to her eyes, and pressed the plunger. Fluid sprayed from the needle's tip.

"All ready?" she asked.

Russell nodded. He didn't know quite what he was agreeing to and he was still too high to care. He could feel his lips again, but the lamps glowed with a warm narcotic light, and he watched her put the needle into the skin beside the inch-long wound on his thigh—red in the lamplight and gaping from debridement, like a bright toothless mouth. Sara injected about a third of the fluid into one side of the gash and then she retracted the needle, put it in the skin on the other side, and injected the rest.

She reached over and sat the syringe on the tray and looked at him.

"We'll give you a few minutes to numb up," she said.

"What was it?"

"Just your local," she told him. "Lidocaine."

Russell nodded. He lay for a moment.

"They blew up Sergeant Pike," he said.

"I know," Sara whispered.

"He had blood coming from his ears."

She cleared her throat. Said she needed him to relax.

He looked away and blinked the wet from his eyes. He said there wasn't anything he could do.

When he turned and looked back at her, she was staring at him. She reached and laid a hand on his cheek.

"We'll get you good and numb," she said.

Sara started with the wound on his thigh, removing the suture from its pack, taking it in the jaws of the needle driver. Russell drew his chin to his chest and watched Sara with a detached, academic interest. He'd learned to administer stitches from a Ranger medic at FOB Marez, cross-training in case he ever had to do it in the field, but that opportunity had never arisen. Sara pushed the needle through the flap of skin on one side of the wound, then the flap on the other. She glanced at his face as she drew the thread taut.

"How we doing?" she asked.

Russell couldn't feel a thing through the local, just a kind of pressure. He told her he was doing fine.

She nodded, made another stitch, tied off and snipped it, then started on the next. She worked quickly, effortlessly: through, through, and pull. Through, through, and pull. Under, through the loop, tighten up, snip. She was very good it at. She told him she used to practice on quilt squares.

When she was finished, she dressed the site with antibiotic salve, then reached to angle her light toward the wound on his side. She glanced over at the tray, said she'd need to get more lidocaine, took off her gloves, and exited the curtained enclosure.

Russell lay there. The fentanyl had started to fade. The sensation had returned to his face, and he could no longer feel his heartbeat in his skull. He closed his eyes and inhaled a deep breath. There was Sergeant Pike, standing in the clearing with the morning sun coppering his face. Head tilted to one side, his good ear inclined toward the sky, listening. Then he was lying in the snow like a discarded doll. One moment standing, the next moment prone. Russell opened his eyes and exhaled. He lifted a hand and massaged his temples with his thumb and middle finger. As if he could rub it all away.

When Sara came back, she bent to study the wound below his rib cage, and she studied the one she'd just sutured on his thigh. There was a worried expression on her face. She shook her head.

"That was the last of the lidocaine," she told him.

Russell lay there. He asked her what she meant.

"They used it all," she said. "Not supposed to be able to do that, but they did. We don't have any other locals, so I can't give you anything for pain. Not with a concussion, I can't. I was surprised they gave it to you in the first place. I don't think they realized yet you'd been concussed." She stopped and stared at him a moment. "Are you understanding me?"

Russell nodded. He was understanding parts.

"I've got to suture this other one," she said. "I can't just leave it open."

Russell nodded. He could see the wound on his thigh without straining, but he couldn't manage to twist his neck far enough to get a glimpse of the one on his side.

"It's going to hurt," she told him. "It's going to hurt you really bad."

Russell said that was all right, but that didn't seem to be what Sara wanted to hear. Her face seemed to tighten. She pulled on another pair of latex gloves, opened another suture pack, and took up the needle driver. She asked once again if he was ready.

"Ready," Russell said.

There was pressure and then pain, so sharp it nearly took his breath. Then the pain vanished for a moment, as if the fentanyl was chewing it. Then the opposite started to happen: the pain was eating the fentanyl and the fentanyl was consumed. Suddenly, he felt very sober, very alert. The pain was warm, then hot, and then his side was on fire. He clenched his teeth, clenched shut his eyes. The pain moved up his torso and reached his chest. Then it crept toward his throat and took up residence in his jaw. He'd heard that courage was holding on for one more second, but he thought if there were many more seconds of this, he'd crack his teeth. He had the feeling she was stitching herself to him, stitching the two of them together. He was going to ask for something to bite down on, but the pain wouldn't allow him to work his mouth, and then it moved to his sinus cavity and finally behind his eyes. They burned red-hot. He opened them.

Sara's face was a mask of concentration. She said to stay with her. She said it'd only take another minute. She seemed to have said this several times. It had taken several minutes. It would take several minutes more.

Something strange happened. He felt his entire body begin to lift, lift and then hover above the bed. It wasn't the drugs and it wasn't the concussion. He didn't think that's what it was, but he wasn't exactly thinking. The pain seemed to lift him, buoy him up. It was in his side, his chest, and his chin, then behind his eyes, and now it had brought him out of himself, out and away from his body. It might have been the drugs. Might have been the concussion. Didn't really matter what it was or wasn't: he was definitely rising. At first, centimeters. Then actual inches. He'd left his body back behind him. He was floating free. Sara was driving the needle, drawing the thread, tying off, and snipping. She paused and looked at him. There wasn't anything to say. He was floating and his eyes were inches away from hers. If they'd been any closer, her eyes would have blurred, both eyes merging into a single olive orb. His junior year of high school, he and his girlfriend would drive back from the ball game in his pickup, his hair still wet from the showers, muscles aching. He'd turn onto the gravel drive that went snaking up through the black oaks toward the ranch house, but they'd pull off onto the lease road, turn off the headlights, and navigate by the moon. Twin ruts in the milkweed and thistle, grass brushing the undercarriage. They'd park down beside the oil tanks overlooking a field of alfalfa, roll down the windows. In spring they rolled them down, stripped each other in seconds, that teenage impatience with buttons and snaps—can't get the clothes off too fast. He'd remove the bulb from the cab's dome light, open the passenger door so they could stretch out their legs. And after they'd made love there on the bench seat, he'd lie with her beneath him, nose to nose. He couldn't recall them saying much. She'd stroke her nails very gently along his back, and he'd hold her face between his palms, watching her eyes. And then it would happen. His vision would tire, or they'd be near enough, and her eyes would creep closer and closer until it was one blue eye staring up at him. It was the closest he could get to the feeling that this wasn't just a high school romance that would end as soon as Elaine left for college on her tennis scholarship—which it was; and she would. But to have that brief narrowing—it was enough to make him forget.

Russell closed his eyes and the pain reached up and took him. He could feel himself begin to fall. Wasn't more than a few inches, but there was definitely the plunge of it, coming back inside himself, everything in reverse. Elaine on the seat beside him, the door shutting, his pickup backing down the lease road, backing down the gravel drive. They were on the highway. They were in the parking lot behind the stadium. He was standing under the stream of the locker-room shower with the water hot on his neck.

He lay there several moments, trying to get his breath.

When he opened his eyes, Sara was standing at his bedside, sorting through her tray. She reached over and picked up the tube of antibiotic ointment and squeezed a dollop onto her finger. Then she saw him staring at her. She told him how good he'd been for her, how brave. Her eyes were moist and her face looked very soft. It seemed to glow in the light of her lamp. She smeared the salve across the row of sutures she'd just made, the swipe of her finger like an electric lash below his ribs. Then she removed her gloves and placed them inside the tray.

"How we doing?" she asked.

Russell didn't answer. He lifted his hand from the mattress and she took it between her palms and held it.

They stayed like that for several minutes. He could feel the residue of talcum powder on her skin. He thought she was beautiful.

He thought she'd hurt him very badly. He thought of how the universe had conspired to place both of them right here. He cleared his throat to tell her what he was thinking, but she stopped him.

"Hey now," she said. "Shhhhhh."

He woke past midnight in the dark of the tent, the only light coming from the electrocardiograph propped on its stand beside his bed. The doctor had explained as he'd hooked up the device that he was just being cautious. The concussion Russell had sustained was minor, but he wanted to hook him up to the EKG in the event of a seizure. Russell wasn't certain this would help. Would it record the seizure or notify the medical team he was having one? It certainly couldn't prevent it. The green line on the monitor beside him dipped and rose, strobing the room with a pulse of emerald light.

He'd been awake a few seconds when he realized someone was in the room with him. He hadn't seen or heard anything. He could just tell. He craned his neck to the right—the muscles very tight in his shoulders and his upper trapezius—and saw a thin form standing just inside the room. Rising from the pillows, he reached to pull the IV catheter free of his arm, but the form stepped closer and the light from the EKG flickered across Sara's face.

She placed a hand to his chest and pushed him gently back against the pillows. He'd been sleeping in an elevated position to accommodate the wires and tubes, and the woman reached to the back of the heart monitor and switched it off. The machine gave a just-audible whine. He could no longer see her but imagined he could, a darker form against the black. She smelled of shampoo. Something with the scent of berries. He could hear her breathing. Neither of them said a word. They'd never been alone like this, and he was afraid that the smallest thing might break the spell.

He felt her weight on the mattress and then her thighs on either side of his hips. All that was between the two of them were his boxers and a sheet. He didn't know what she was wearing, but he could feel her struggling out of it, and then her lips were on

"Carson," the medic said.

Again Wynne ignored him. As though he weren't in the room. Russell had the strangest sensation. Might've been the concussion, but the thought occurred to him that Bixby was a hallucination and only Wynne was real.

"You'll be coming with us," the captain said. "Grimes can replace Breeburn."

Russell turned to look at him. Blond hair and close-cropped beard, blue eyes like sapphires inside his skull.

"On the mission?" said Russell.

"On the mission," Wynne said.

Bixby cleared his throat. "Captain," he said, and his voice shifted in tone. "Corporal Russell might have to be medevaced. We'll need to get him back to Bagram for a CT."

Wynne looked at Russell a few more moments and then he looked at Bixby. The captain's glance confirmed the reality of the medic, and Russell felt somehow relieved.

Then he realized he'd had it wrong.

It wasn't that the captain was real and Bixby wasn't.

It was the captain's decision to look at you.

That's what made you real.

He saw Sara a final time a few days later. They stood next to the helipad in the morning light, watching members of the surgical team load their packs and personal equipment onto a Chinook as their replacements disembarked, a new group of medics and surgeons, blinking in the Afghan dawn.

The sky in the east blushed a pale shade of rose, and the jagged mountains stretched away into the Hindu Kush. Birds twittered from the gargantuan pines. He looked at Sara in her winter jacket and gloves, a watch cap pulled over her hair, her nose and cheeks flushed from the cold. The green of her irises were shot through with shards of amber. Her nose was small and straight. She'd plucked her eyebrows into slender half-moons, applied mascara very lightly. He wanted to tell her to be careful, but the words caught in his throat.

"How much longer will you be here?" she asked.

"Spring," he told her. "Early spring."

"Where will they send you after that?"

He told her he really couldn't say.

"'Can't say' as in 'don't know,' or 'can't say' as in you just can't?"

"Both," Russell said.

She looked down a moment, biting the corner of her lower lip. Then she looked back up and nodded.

"Would you say good-bye to Wheels for me?"

"'Course," Russell said.

"Try and take it slow," Sara told him. "Take your anti-inflammatory. I know you're going to stop the pain meds before you should, but if you start having numbness in your feet or legs, tell Sergeant Bixby. Numbness or tingling, either one. I think it's just the muscles, though. Will they fly you to Bagram for the CT?"

"I suppose that kind of depends," said Russell. He didn't say on what.

"Well," said Sara, "they need to. That and an MRI. They really should just—" Then she seemed to catch herself. She inhaled a deep breath, then exhaled it long and slow. "Okay," she told herself. She forced a smile.

Then she reached and touched him very lightly on the arm. The index finger of her gloved right hand. The slightest, muffled touch. It lasted maybe a second, and then her hand returned to her side, but in that moment something had passed between them—a signal, a current—and Russell knew like he knew his own heartbeat that he was in trouble. He realized that by now he'd prepared himself to die a number of times, but he hadn't—not in any way that mattered—prepared himself to live.

THEY RODE OUT of camp in the blue light before dawn, thirteen riders, four mules, six riderless horses bringing up the rear in the remuda. It was the first week of March, and there was still snow in the shadows of the trees and in the stony draws on the northern slopes, but by noon the air was warm enough for shirtsleeves. The horses stepped briskly, vapor rising from their nostrils like steam from a grate. Wynne rode at the head of the column, Russell at the rear, the other soldiers in single file following their captain into the hills on a narrow trail that snaked up through the pine trees and cedar.

That first day they rode without speaking or even pausing to consider their maps. They'd reconned up this very trail in training with Russell, but they kept noise discipline regardless, the only sound the muted clop of horseshoes against the packed earth, or the fall of a dislodged stone as it skittered among the loose scree and talus. They'd sent two Afghans ahead of them as scouts, and these men were to steal half-day journeys and report back in the evenings. The air grew thinner and the trees fell away, and they traveled a high pass along the hillside where the tops of these mountains rose up around them and birds circled in the cobalt sky and the sun was a bright companion in that perfect blue expanse.

They made camp on the other side of this peak in a sheltered bowl of rock and waited for the return of their scouts. Russell saw to the horses and helped the men hobble their mounts, checked hooves and horseshoes, and then he stayed behind with Fella while the others dug their Ranger graves and Wheels built a fire. Russell curried his horse and then stood speaking to her in soft tones with a hand to her neck until he felt the muscles loosen beneath his palm. He ran his fingers down her back and told her she was a good horse and then turned and made for the fire.

Wheels and Russell had been briefed by Lieutenant Billings the day before they rode out, the two of them struggling to keep up with the flood of data, the flow of the narrative spilling from the assistant commander's chapped and petulant lips. Russell never thought he had the capacity for hatred, but he'd begun to hate this man: a political maneuverer bitter about his role as second-in-command. He couldn't imagine how Wynne tolerated him or why he kept him on. Even after they'd helped ambush the enemy mortar team, Billings seemed reluctant to brief these Rangers, outsiders both of them, not to mention corporals.

He told them that a SEAL Team had gone missing the previous summer: six operators dropped off in the northeastern part of this province with orders to patrol into the mountains on foot. They'd made radio contact with headquarters the day after their insertion and they'd made contact a few days later. Then all contact stopped. They seemed to drop off the grid. The drones couldn't locate their heat signatures and IR beacons, satellites couldn't detect their GPS. As if they'd walked into another dimension and vanished entirely.

Other teams were sent to look for them—search and rescue—but such efforts were dicey given their location along the border. Special Operations had kept up the search for several weeks, considered bringing the Pakistani military into the hunt, then decided they'd better keep the matter in-house. Command began to give up hope, families were notified, and the men from the team were formally listed MIA.

Then one of the SEALs walked in to a marine outpost, staggered in out of the mountains and was medevaced to Bagram. The

CIA went to work on him but got nowhere. Then they'd called in Captain Wynne.

Which, Billings said, was where the situation became more complicated still. The SEAL was half-crazed from his ordeal, and seventy-two hours of what was basically an interrogation had not made him any saner. Wynne knew the terrain better than any officer in the coalition, and Special Operations wanted his opinion of the man's story. CIA didn't want to believe him even when his credentials checked out, so they took blood and DNA samples. They couldn't believe anyone could just walk out of the willowwacks, Navy SEAL or not.

It was Wynne who'd got him talking. They'd choppered him over the evening of August eleventh, and the captain sat at this man's bedside the better part of a week. The SEAL told him how his team had gone in through the valley, proceeded up through the mountains following their maps and GPS. How they got into day two of the mission, dug in that morning to wait the day out, and when they got on the move around nightfall, everything had gone to hell.

Their maps were wrong. The terrain was wrong. They lost GPS signal for several hours, and when it came back up, north didn't look like north anymore, and they were off course. Their coms operator wanted to scrap the mission, try to backtrack to the insertion point, but the team leader wasn't having it, and he marched them all night through the mountains, and by morning, they were lost.

That evening they got in contact with an enemy element, took casualties, and humping their wounded to a fallback position, were overrun by Taliban and taken into the hills. The wounded died on the way up, so the enemy stripped their gear, burned the bodies, scattered their ashes on the mountainside. The other four SEALs were brought into camp blindfolded, then taken back into one of the compound's caves and locked inside a cell. No food. They were watered from plastic bowls like dogs. One of the men came down with dysentery and died a week later. The other three were led out one by one and tortured. A few more days of this and two of them woke one morning and found their buddy dead. He'd soaked one of his socks in the water bowl and suffocated himself. So then there were only two.

It was at this point in the man's story where Wynne and the CIA officers had a difference of opinion. This SEAL in the hospital bed, who claimed to have escaped an enemy stronghold and walked out of the mountains in his boots and boxers with no food or compass, was in bad shape, and several of his American interrogators didn't believe there was a Taliban camp at all. They thought the team had gotten in contact, taken causalities, then died off trying to get to a fallback position, this SEAL being the last man, his mind broken by his trials.

Others believed he had been taken prisoner, that his buddies had been tortured, that he'd escaped. What they didn't buy was his claim that there were other POWs at this camp, six or eight of them—he could never decide the exact number—that the Talibs had collected. They didn't believe the enemy would want to keep prisoners more than a few weeks, and they didn't believe they'd keep prisoners they hadn't used in propaganda films and then relieved of their heads. Their conclusion, though, was the same as the first set of analysts: that this SEAL had gone native and ought to be remanded to psych.

Wynne disagreed with both camps. He believed this solider was telling the truth. The man, half-psychotic—had the twitch in his thumbs; he'd break down at the drop of a hat—but there wasn't any lie in his eyes and he never contradicted himself. The group responsible for his debriefing split about 90–10: 90 percent of them thinking the SEAL was a Section 8, the other 10 that he was providing actionable intelligence. Wynne, another Special Forces captain, and the JSOC colonel they answered to were the outliers.

They fought it out for two days. The other SF captain who agreed with Wynne wanted to go right then, insert another team by helicopter and perform the raid. He managed to convince a few of the analysts, but most of those in the room wanted to ignore the SEAL entirely. Didn't think he was credible. Didn't think there was any chance of there being actual American POWs. By day two, they were arguing drones and Delta Force, coming in the back door through Pakistan, and there were a couple of spooks from Langley who wanted to send in a team of their own. They were shouted down, and somebody got pushed, and a young major got in a shoving match with one of the analysts and Wynne stepped in to break them up.

This is when the colonel spoke from the back of the room. He'd been with 5th Special Forces Group at K2 when they moved into Northern Afghanistan in October of 2001, and he proceeded to remind them that SF had negotiated this terrain on horseback. He said a reprise of this method would provide a number of advantages to any kind of rescue operation. Stealth. Speed. Reliable transport. Renewable fuel source. He said if it was his op, there's no question he'd use horses. And he wouldn't use these shaggy Afghan ponies. He'd have real horses choppered in, American horses, and he'd bring in someone to train them.

Which was where Russell came in, said Billings. Wynne had seen the footage of the incident with the horse and then he'd seen the stories about Russell's grandfather. It took the captain less than thirty-six hours to get him transferred.

"So it's a rescue?" Russell asked.

"It's a recon," Billings told him. "We don't know what we're going to find, but we can't afford to just ignore it."

Russell sat a moment, trying to think all of this through. He had questions, but before he could ask them, Wheels said, "It's an ass-covering mission. It's us covering our asses in case all this turns out to be true. So we can look good to the press. So we can actually look like we tried."

The lieutenant had stared at Wheels for several moments.

Then he'd turned and exited the room.

Over the next several days, their way would take them through arroyos of sandstone polished smooth by winds and weather, overhangs of granite. The soldiers, staring up from their horses at these vaults, saw, etched in the rock, ancient pictographs, runic engravings, who could say from what millennium: sun and moon and stick-figure representations of hunters and the beasts they pursued. They slowed their mounts to study the carvings, then emerged into bright daylight, the trail winding down into a forest of twisted juniper and pine.

On the fourth day, pausing to take their midday meal, a shadow fell across Russell's lap where he sat on the ground cross-legged, and he turned to see the captain, blocking out the sun. The man beckoned him with a brief twitch of his index and middle fingers, and Russell rose and followed him to the other side of the trail about fifty feet from where the soldiers sat eating. Wynne passed a hand across his face.

"We need to check on our scouts," he said.

Russell regarded him a moment, and Wynne added, "I'm thinking Zero and Corporal Grimes."

"I can go," said Russell, but the captain shook his head.

"Yourself excluded," said Wynne, "those are the two best riders?"

Russell thought, excluding himself, the captain was their best rider, but he said, "Yessir. Ziza and Wheels."

Wynne considered this for a long moment, his blue eyes fixed on something at the horizon's edge.

Then he nodded. He turned and began to call orders to his men.

Russell helped Wheels drop gear, sort through his saddlebags, strip his load-out light as he could get it: three MREs, twelve pints of water, ten thirty-round magazines for his rifle. The two Rangers stood there in the noon heat with the air buzzing on the bare rock slopes and their nerves tight as a snare. Russell boosted his friend into the saddle, held the reins while Wheels got himself situated, and then handed them up.

"I don't reckon I got to tell you to be careful," he said.

Wheels looked down at him. His eyes quivered back and forth.

"You see any bad guys," said Russell, "do not engage."

"Don't need to tell me about engaging," Wheels said, gesturing toward Ziza. "Tell him about engaging."

"Just try not to get shot," said Russell.

"Will do, doggy daddy."

"And don't let Ziza get you in a tight. You can hurt a horse at this altitude. You can hurt a horse in this heat."

Wheels nodded. He squared his ball cap, crimping the bill with both hands and then smoothing his palms across his thighs.

Ziza was already in the saddle. He rode up beside the two of them and looked at Wheels. Then he chucked up his horse, pushed it to a slow trot, and started down the bed of cracked clay they'd be using for a trail. Russell tapped his fist lightly against Wheels's shin and the man glanced down at him.

"See you this evening," he said, and pushed his horse forward to follow the commando. Russell watched the riders maneuver along the creek bed and disappear around a ridge.

He barely had time to worry. The two men had been gone just a few hours when they were spotted riding back down the creek bed toward camp, the two Afghan scouts trailing behind, startled expressions on the men's weathered faces and their horses stepping wearily in the heat shimmer and mirage. Ziza rode his big bay up through camp and into the half circle where the men stood watching. He nodded to his captain and motioned back down the creek with a tilt of his head.

"We have hostiles," he said.

"How far out?" Wynne asked.

"Five klicks," said Ziza. "Maybe less."

The scouts had entered camp by this point and sat their horses nervously. Russell studied them. If they still thought volunteering for this post to get out of the Afghan National Army was a good decision, they didn't anymore.

Ox stepped toward Ziza's horse and brushed his knuckles across its cheek. "Is it an ambush waiting down there for us or what the fuck?"

"It's not an ambush," Ziza said. "They're walking around with AKs, but they don't even have ammo belts. Some aren't carrying weapons at all."

Wynne waved up the scouts and Ziza addressed them in Dari.

The leaner of the two paused a few feet from the captain and stood with his eyes slightly out of focus and the pupils tilted upward, as though attempting to read the words he was searching for off the inside of his skull. Finally the scout said in English, "He is having much fear, this man."

"Of what?" Wynne asked.

"He is having fear of this place we see. Ziza and your man see it also. There is much wrong in this place."

Bixby was standing beside Wynne listening intently. "Can we go around?" he asked.

The scout squinted for a moment, thinking. Then he shook his head.

"We must to go backwards."

"Backwards," Wynne said.

"Yes. These are too many. We don't have enough man to make the battle. We must to go backwards."

The captain told him they weren't going backward. He ordered the team to mount up.

In these mountains when it rained it rained without warning, and soon the stretch of sky above them had clouded and a light drizzle fell. The men donned their ponchos and followed the captain along a wadi where a shallow stream had begun to flow. Another hundred or so meters and Wynne walked his horse up the bank beside the brook, turned in his saddle, and motioned for the riders to do likewise.

Wheels looked over at Russell. He pointed to the stream that had appeared to their left.

"Flash flood."

"Apparently," Russell said.

For the next several hours, they rode in a steady pour beside what had become a river, the brown water rushing and carrying lengths of driftwood past, brambles, the body of a small goat. Russell thought he saw a clear plastic bottle, but he couldn't be certain, and it stayed in sight for only a few seconds before the water took it away. Wynne led them on, and the rain began to slacken and then suddenly it stopped. Lightning strobed the hilltops to the north, and the sky grew paler and they could see strips of blue in the canopy above. Another hour and the sun broke through the evening sky, and soon the entire front had moved off to the east and the earth all around them steamed as though it had been removed from an oven. Wynne brought the column to a halt, dismounted, and waved up Ziza. When the man reached him from the rear of the line, Wynne asked him how close they were.

Ziza glanced around at the terrain, vapor rising from the rocks and tree trunks.

"I'd say about another thousand meters," he said. "We found the scouts behind that spur. We could set up overwatch on the ridge."

Wynne looked to the rise of land where the commando pointed. He nodded and then directed Rosa to get his rifle.

"You're with the sergeant," Wynne told Morgan. "You're spotter."

"Roger that," Morgan said.

"I'm taking Ox, Perkins, and Russell. We get into trouble, Mother, Hallum, and Zero are the cavalry."

"Who's Mother?" asked Wheels.

"I'm Mother," Bixby said.

Wheels studied the ground a moment. Then he looked back over at Bixby.

"Then who's Father?" he asked.

Russell shook his head. He rose and walked over to Fella, made sure of the picket line to which she was tethered, a simple picket line—a hemp rope strung wither-high between two trees. Each of the horses had been secured to lines such as these about the sparse grove, short lengths of hay twine tied in breakaway knots to lead lines and bridles. Russell checked the line and checked the lead and then he spoke to the horse and rubbed a hand along her neck. If they were killed out here, these animals would likely be found and taken by the very men whose compound they were about to assault. Russell thought about that. He told his horse that everything was going to be all right.

They formed up behind a low berm in the early dusk—Wynne

and Russell, Perkins and Ox—kneeling and checking magazines, grenades, tightening their harnesses and belts. A light haze lay over the valley and up along the pine-covered slopes where tree trunks stretched horizontally and foliage seemed to grow from rock. Russell glanced over and saw a heron standing in a shallow pool about twenty yards distant, little more than a puddle, fed from some invisible source. The bird turned its head on a long gray neck to study them with a detached, avian interest. Then it looked away.

When Rosa was in position on the ridge overlooking the enemy compound, Wynne nodded to the three of them, and they followed him along the spur of the mountain. The evening had turned cool and cloudless, and the four soldiers went silhouetted against the fading sky—shades of rose and crimson and a dark band on the horizon where night was forming in the east. They stepped soundlessly through a sparse grove of scrub oak and cedar—the rich smell hitting Russell with the force of an actual blow and bringing back the small dresser that had stood in his grandmother's sewing room—and then along the bed of what was once a stream. They went down thirty meters, and Wynne raised a fist and they halted and took a knee. The captain proned out on his stomach and crawled to the lip of the creek. Russell watched him maneuver his rifle up and stare for several minutes through its scope, then slowly push himself backward, dragging along the silt. He rose to a crouch and came over and squatted beside them.

"Compound's just to the left," Wynne whispered. "Adobe walls, steel doors on the entrance."

"They're going to be reinforced," said Perkins.

The captain nodded. He reached a hand back, got his radio from his belt, and pressed the talk button.

"Underchild Actual to Underchild Five," he said.

There were a few moments of silence and then Rosa's muffled voice came through the walkie-talkie:

"Go ahead, Underchild."

Wynne glanced at Russell and then looked up at the sky.

"How is your line of sight? Over."

"Line of sight's good," said Rosa. "Looking into the compound. We got a Tango just inside the walls and we got another on the northeast corner."

"You have eyes on the gates?"

"Affirmative."

"Steel?" Wynne asked.

"Say again."

"I say again: verify—are the gates steel?"

"Wait one," said Rosa. The radio crackled and went silent. When the voice came back it said, "I verify. Looks like steel to me."

Wynne glanced over to Sergeant Perkins. "We're going to have to blow them," he said.

Perkins nodded.

Wynne lifted the radio to his lips. "How many Talibs are you counting? Over."

"They're not Talibs."

"Say again."

"I say again: they're not Talibs. They're white."

Wynne's brow furrowed. He looked over at Ox and then he looked at Perkins and then he studied the ground between his knees.

"Chechens," he said. He repeated the word into the radio.

"Affirmative," Rosa said.

Russell had heard about Chechen militants who'd come down to fight the infidel alongside their Taliban brothers, but until now it was just a story. They were supposed to be harder than the locals. They were supposed to be better trained.

Wynne said, "Do you have a shot?"

"I have two," Rosa said.

"Say again."

"I say again: two Tangos, two shots."

"Execute to follow," Wynne said. He lowered the radio and tapped it lightly against the packed earth. He looked up and asked his men if they were ready.

Russell nodded along with the others, but it was a bald-faced lie and he couldn't imagine when it wouldn't be.

The captain rose from his squat and brought the radio to his lips. "We're moving up. When we blow the gate, bust 'em."

"Wilco," said Rosa. "Five out."

"Could've wished us luck," said Perkins.

"Luck's ass," said Ox.

If the gate had been reinforced, it hadn't been reinforced properly, and when Sergeant Perkins blew it, the sheet-iron plates caved and went flying inward. Wynne's fireteam had stacked against the wall to the left of the entrance, and before the smoke had cleared, the four of them were inside and moving toward the main structure—torsos hunched over their rifles, hips locked, walking from the knees. The sentry Rosa had reported on the north side of the building was lying in the dirt with a bullethole in his right temple and the left half of his skull missing. Both the man's eyes were open and his tongue lolled on his bottom lip. Wynne waved the others toward the building's front door. Russell glanced at the last of the daylight in the west, and as he did, another sentry came around the corner. This man held a rifle at his waist, and he seemed merely curious about the noise he'd heard, not concerned enough to have his weapon shouldered. Wynne shot him in the chest and the sentry sat down very hard. Wynne shot him again and the man pitched backward and lay twitching.

There was a low adobe structure in the center of the compound, and they took positions at either side of the door, two on the left, two on the right. Russell was behind Ox and he could see the muscles along the right side of the massive man's jaw flexing and relaxing, flexing and relaxing. His face was very red. Russell looked across and saw Wynne turn to Perkins and slap his knee, and the demolitions sergeant nodded, removed a small brick of C-4 and a blasting cap from one of the pouches on his belt, stepped around Wynne, and squatted in front of the door. This door was made of the same sheet iron as the one they'd blown entering the compound, but it opened out instead of in. He'd have to blow the hinges. Perkins was standing to mold explosives around the top hinge when the captain said, "Try the handle."

legends in Cyrillic. A upended baby crib stood in one corner. A PlayStation without controllers or wires lay there on a beige carpet sample. No television. No power outlets that Russell could see. There was another door at the far end of the room, and the four of them formed up to either side of it, taking knees, catching their breath. Russell thought he heard voices from beyond the doorway. Then he was sure he heard them. He looked at Ox on the other side of the doorway and saw that the muscles along the man's jaw were still bulging. He studied him a few more seconds from over Wynne's left shoulder, and he'd just looked back to the doorway when a figure in a tracksuit burst into the room, sprinting. It was a blond man, blond hair and beard, and he was already past them and in the room's center before he realized he wasn't alone. He'd just started to turn when Ox and Perkins opened fire.

Russell watched the man in the center of the room turn and pitch to the ground. Perkins stepped farther away from the door, turkey-peeking around Ox to see if another enemy would be following the one they'd just shot. Wynne glanced at the dead man and then back to the doorway. He lifted a hand and motioned Ox and Perkins through. Russell's ears continued to ring. Wynne waved him to the other side of the doorway, and he rose from his crouch, moved opposite the captain, scanned his sector, and then followed Perkins and Ox.

They went along a hallway, and then the hallway turned back to the south and they went down another short stretch, their boots making muted slaps against the floor.

The passage terminated in small room where a laptop sat closed upon a card table. Maps on the walls. A corkboard with thumbtacks pinning torn scraps of paper. A narrow window into which the last sunlight came. There was a thin man in olive-colored fatigues seated on the floor, leaning against the far wall with both hands crossed over his stomach, fingers interlaced, and his shirt blooming with dark arterial blood. His Kalashnikov lay beside him, but he made no attempt to take it up. He sat watching the Americans without interest, his eyes starting to glaze. The room smelled of feces and iron.

Wynne walked over to the man and kicked his rifle, which went skidding across the concrete. The captain studied this soldier for several moments and then he knelt there in front of him. Ox and Perkins had already turned back to the doorway they'd come through, Ox open-mouthed, massaging the left side of his jaw. Russell watched him a moment and then he turned to watch Wynne and the dying Chechen. He thought the captain would get back on the radio and inform Rosa and the others that they'd cleared the building, but instead he seized the man's hands and pulled them away from his stomach.

"Where is it?" he asked.

The man just stared. He was struggling for his breath. His blond beard was long and matted with blood.

"We can make it quick," Wynne told him. "I know you understand."

The man closed his eyes and drew a breath. Russell could see his chest expand. He reached down to his med kit, which he kept in his right cargo pocket. The kit had trauma shears, decompression needles, and a nasal airway. A half roll of QuikClot and a tourniquet. A fentanyl lozenge. He'd just pulled the kit out of his pocket when the Chechen blew a long breath into the captain's face.

"The fuck you," he said.

Wynne let go of the man's wrists, reached and grabbed the collars of his olive jacket, and ripped it open, buttons tumbling between the Chechen's legs, scattering across the floor. The man wore no shirt beneath the jacket, and the bullet hole was about two inches above his navel and pumping blood in time with his pulse.

Wynne studied the man's face a moment and he studied the man's stomach. He undid the Velcro strap on his right glove, pulled it off, and dropped it beside him. Then he drove his naked index finger into the wound.

The Chechen's eyelids snapped open and his eyes bulged from their sockets. Sweat broke out on his forehead. He began panting.

"The fuck you," he told the captain, spitting the words. "The fuck you."

Wynne smiled. He pressed his finger deeper, twisting it.

The Chechen wheezed and then began to cough, and his face was a mask of torment. Russell stepped toward his captain. He raised a hand to place it on Wynne's shoulder. Then he lowered it.

"Tell me where and I'll make it stop," Wynne said, his voice surprisingly calm. "Don't pretend you don't know, because we both know you know. We both know that, don't we?"

The man was still coughing, his eyes clenched against the pain. He looked across the room and gestured with his chin. Wynne watched. He turned and glanced over his shoulder to where a poster was taped to the wall. The poster showed a man in an A-shirt and tight blue jeans holding a bottle of malt liquor, a caption in Cyrillic beneath.

"Perkins," he said.

Russell watched the sergeant step over to the poster, remove his knife from his belt, slide it under the strips of tape, and pry it from the wall. Beneath the poster, a crude hole had been knocked in the wall, and Perkins reached inside and removed a small velvet sack with a bright yellow drawstring, bright yellow writing stitched along the crimson fabric. Russell couldn't make out what it said. Before he had a chance, Perkins turned and tossed the bag to Wynne. The sack struck the captain's palms with the sound of marbles clacking.

Wynne undid the drawstring and reached his naked hand down inside. Then he pulled a dark blue stone from the sack. It was knuckle-sized and polished so that it shone, shot through with striations of gray and white. The captain held it toward the narrow window, and there was an odd moment where Russell watched the light hit the blue of the stone, the blue of Wynne's eyes.

Then the captain dropped the stone into the sack, pulled the drawstring closed, and tied it.

"That all?" he asked the Chechen.

The man stared up at him. Then he closed his eyes.

Wynne slapped him twice very quickly, very hard. "This can get a lot worse," he said.

The man began panting.

"Are there more?"

The man seemed to wilt. You could see something in him break, like a plate shattering. He began to shake his head.

"No," he said.

"Convince me," said the captain.

"No more," the man told him. His breath was coming to him in rasps.

Wynne studied him for several more moments. Russell had readied a pair of flexicuffs and he was stepping forward to hand them to the captain when the captain stood, swiped his finger along his pants leg, and pulled back on his glove. He slid the sack into a cargo pocket.

Then he pulled his pistol from its holster, pressed the muzzle to the Chechen's forehead, and fired.

They made camp that night in a narrow draw and watched wolves thread their way along the slopes, down toward the compound to pick at the bodies. The gunfighters took turns with a night-vision monocular, staring at the furtive forms and their reflective eyes as they trotted with tails tucked between their legs, seven of them, eight. Wheels passed the device to Russell and he passed it right back. He didn't want to see, and when he awakened in the dead of night to the alien yipping, he lay there in his sleeping bag gripping the earth beneath the layers of Gore-Tex, feeling as though he'd fallen through the world into an alternate plane: predatory, carnivorous, a universe of tooth and bone.

The ground underneath him felt like rock. He shifted his body and tried not to think. During the raid, Ox had bit down so tightly he'd splintered a molar. After they'd exfiltrated from the compound, Ox walked back to Bixby and collapsed. The medic had examined his mouth with a penlight, and then they'd loaded the sergeant on a Skedco, dosed him with fentanyl, and dragged him up into the hills. He lay several feet from Russell now, twitching in his opiate dreams.

They performed stand-to in the dark before daybreak, the Rangers seated back-to-back with rifles propped on their thighs.

Russell could feel Wheels's muscles knot and tense. He glanced over at Ox, the sergeant holding the bridge of his nose pinched between thumb and forefinger, lying there with his mouth stretched wide. He would tire, allow it to close, but as soon as his teeth met, his mouth would snap open like the jaws on a trap.

Russell turned his head and whispered back to Wheels. He told him that the captain knew.

"Knew what?"

"About the compound. He knew what we were walking into."

"Didn't seem to me he knew shit."

"I don't think he knew they were Chechen," said Russell. "I don't think he knew that. But he definitely knew the place was there. He took something out of there. That's what the whole thing was about. He wanted to go in and get it."

Wheels asked him what it was.

"It was a bag of stones."

"Stones?"

"Blue stones," Russell said.

"Like jewel stones?"

"They were in this cubby in back of a poster on the wall. One of those bags like liquor comes in. Stone I saw was about the size of a quarter. Blue."

Wheels sat for a moment.

"Sapphires?" he said.

"I don't think so," said Russell. "It wasn't clear, but I don't know what sapphires look like before they've been polished."

"Cut."

"Whatever," Russell said. "There was a whole sack full. Or I assume so. I only saw the one."

They sat for a moment.

"Lapis," said Wheels.

"How's that?"

"Lapis," Wheels said. "They mine it here."

"Is it worth anything?"

"It's worth something," Wheels said. "Why you think they were hiding it?"

A few seconds passed. The morning blew a cold breeze across their faces. Russell could see his breath in the air.

"He executed one of the hostiles. Just straight-up greased him."

"Shit's bad all over," Wheels said.

They followed the trail north, mounting up at dawn and riding until the sun set behind the western hills. They ascended low mountains by rocky switchbacks and descended to forests on their far side: scrub oak and holly, trees of gargantuan size, the soldiers dwarfed by the perfectly straight trunks from whose high branches monkeys screamed, sending down acorns and bits of bark. Their horses stepped nervously. Russell would lean down and straighten himself along Fella's neck, speaking in a soft voice, telling the animal she had nothing to worry about. That she was a good horse. She was a sweet little mare.

The next day Ox fainted under the noon sun and pitched sideways in his saddle. He would have dropped to the ground but for Ziza, who, riding behind the sergeant, pushed forward and managed to pin Ox between their horses and get an arm around his waist. He called for help, and several of the men dismounted, and together they lifted Ox and carried him to a level space beside the trail. The sergeant's eyelids fluttered. He came to for a few moments, gave a low, guttural moan, and then his eyes rolled back in his head and he went unconscious. Bixby, who'd been riding toward the column's rear, walked up and knelt over the man. Russell watched the medic take off his jacket, roll it up, place it under Ox's head, and then, very gingerly, part the man's lips and open his mouth. He retrieved a small penlight from his cargo pocket and spent several minutes inspecting the man's teeth. Wynne was standing there in the circle that had formed around Ox, and the medic looked up at him.

"That tooth's got to come out," Bixby said.

Wynne nodded. He hitched his pants and squatted beside the sergeant, reached over, and placed a hand on his sternum. Russell could see the man's chest rising and falling under the captain's palm, rising and falling. Wynne motioned for Bixby to hand him

Wynne considered the question. Then he shook his head and ran his fingers through his beard.

"Let's just get it over with," he said.

Bixby wrapped the sergeant's wrists with gauze, then took a length of paracord, made a honda knot at one end, slipped the loop over Ox's right wrist, and drew the slack through until the loop was tight. He walked over to an oak sapling several feet away, passed the paracord around it, tightened until the sergeant's right arm came off the ground and extended out from the shoulder, then secured the rope to the tree with a highwayman's hitch. He did the same with Ox's left arm, tethering it to a low limb that jutted from the pine, and motioned for Wynne to bind the man's ankles. Wynne took the spool of paracord and built his lasso, slipped it over the man's boots, and trailed the rope back between Ox's feet. He drew it taut and stood for a moment.

"What are we tying this to?" he asked.

The medic's brow furrowed. He glanced to either side of him.

"Stake it," Russell said.

Bixby and Wynne looked over to where he squatted beside the trunk of a low cedar.

"Sharpen one of these branches, drive it into the ground, tie off from that," Russell explained.

Wynne stared at him a moment and then turned to consider Bixby. The medic nodded.

Russell cut a limb from one of the pines, stripped it of needles, then began to whittle it with his knife. It took about five minutes, and when he was finished, he pounded the stake into the ground with an entrenching tool about a yard away from Ox's feet. He'd cut a nock in the stake for the paracord, and Wynne stretched out the sergeant's legs, looped the cord around the stake, and tied it off. The three of them stood over the man. Bixby looked at Russell.

"Come hold him," he said.

Russell stepped over Ox, turned, and sat in the dirt, cradling the sergeant's head in his lap, interlacing his fingers and making a cup of his hands into which he fit Ox's chin. He flexed his forearms, tightened them along the man's temples, and pulled. When he thought he had him good and tight, he glanced at the medic and nodded. He could feel Ox's pulse against his wrists.

Wynne had squatted above the sergeant's legs and grabbed him by the hips. Bixby knelt beside him. He had his needle-nose pliers in one hand and a few antiseptic swabs in the other. He swiped the pliers' stainless-steel jaws, one and then the next, threw a leg across his patient, and sat upon his chest. He paused a moment and looked at Russell, and then the two of them just stared. Russell was the first to look away. He seized a tighter grip on the sergeant's chin, his forearms beginning to burn. He hoped that the man would remain unconscious.

Bixby had to have been hoping the same. He braced his free hand against the man's collarbone and, squinting, lowered the pliers to Ox's mouth, inserting them between his lips, working around the bit. He squinted and craned his neck to one side, mumbling something. Russell thought he might be able to perform the procedure quickly, and then they could untie the sergeant. He felt the steady beat of the man's pulse. He felt the pliers click against the broken molar, and as soon as they did, Ox's eyes sprang open and he began to scream.

Or tried to scream. With his tongue pinned beneath the Mullen, the noise was just a gurgle. Ox tried to pull against his restraints, but there was no slack. At times like these, you learned to duck into yourself. That's how Russell thought of it—head dipping between his shoulders. Hunching into himself. Ducking. He'd been doing it so long, he couldn't remember when it started. He thought, inexplicably, of Sara. Their time at Dodge had been the opposite of ducking, and he knew in a strange kind of flash that he loved her. He tightened his grip on Ox's chin and pulled.

Bixby withdrew the pliers and settled a hand against the sergeant's neck. He told Ox it was all right. He told him he'd fainted. He said he'd just given him fentanyl and that the procedure would take a minute at most.

"The tooth's got to come out," he said. "We can't let it get infected."

Ox's eyes rolled up in his head, and when Bixby reinserted the pliers, the sergeant's body began to shudder as though wired to a circuit. There was a muted, underwater click, and the medic removed a bone-white fragment from Ox's mouth and dropped it beside him in the dirt. He swiped the back of a hand across his forehead and bit his lip.

"Just a couple more," he told Ox. "You're doing good."

It didn't look to Russell like Ox was doing good. It looked like sheer agony. He glanced up and saw a falcon in the blue vault above them, riding the thermals. When he looked back down, Bixby had inserted the pliers once more into Ox's mouth and then tightened his grip. Russell heard a dull, wet snap.

"Shit," said Bixby.

"Just fucking finish," Wynne said.

"Going as fast as I can."

"Mother," said the captain, "I swear to fucking God."

Russell closed his eyes. He saw himself following Ox into the compound. Haze of gun smoke with the noise of American boots against the packed dirt floor. The rustle of gear and hiss of fabric, thigh against thigh, brushing—*swick, swick, swick.* The sneeze of their suppressed rifles. The burning in his throat and the copper taste on his tongue and the pain that always came with shooting a weapon indoors: the overpressure caused your eyes to ache for weeks. Firing and moving and fighting gravity with every step and his heart going like mad, and he tightened his grip on the sergeant's chin and opened his eyes and found himself looking at the captain, sprawled now against Ox's legs, his hands pressing against the sergeant's hips, the two of them, Wynne and Russell, with maybe fifteen inches between them, face-to-face, staring at one another, and why was he shocked to see the captain weeping?

When Russell woke in the night, Sergeant Bixby was seated there beside him, legs crossed and palms upon his knees, moonlight silvering his face. Russell lay a moment wondering whether he ought to pretend sleep, but then the sergeant spoke:

"You don't like what the captain did."

He thought, at first, that Bixby was referring to Ox. He reached and unzipped the sleeping bag, rolled onto his side, and sat. The night was cold and clear, and thin wisps of cloud trailed across the moon like ink inside a water glass, bleeding out, dispersing.

They'd made camp earlier that night three hundred yards from the trail they'd followed, tying their horses to picket lines and bedding down in a thick grove of pine. Russell and Wheels had moved a little apart from the others, up to where they could see stars through the canopy of limbs.

"He wasn't always like this," Bixby said.

Russell glanced up at the moon and then back to the sergeant's face, half in shadow, half in light.

"Do you know what he did before?" said Bixby.

"Before the war?" asked Russell.

Bixby nodded.

"Wheels told me he was a hedge-fund manager," Russell said. He didn't go on to tell the sergeant that he'd researched it and found that it was true.

Bixby regarded him a moment.

"I see what you're thinking," he said. "He was some kind of shark who stole old people's savings. It wasn't like that. He wasn't greedy. You won't meet a more principled man."

Russell glanced over to where the others were sleeping, dark forms crumpled across the pine-needle floor. A mist moved through the tree limbs.

"I watched him execute an unarmed prisoner," said Russell. "I never seen anything like that. Not from an American, I haven't. Not from an officer."

Bixby turned and looked out into the night.

"He walked away from it all," he said. "Manhattan. The money. He would've been a millionaire. For all I know, he was a millionaire. After the Towers came down, he could've cashed in his portfolio and cruised down to some tropic isle. Could've stayed on at the firm and *bought* a tropic isle. What's he do instead?"

"Joins the army."

"He quits a six-hundred-thousand-dollar-a-year job and takes one that pays forty-four thousand and where any given moment the odds are decent you'll be shot or shelled or blownthefuckup."

The sergeant's voice had started to rise, but he caught himself. He swiped the palm of one hand across his cheek, cracked his knuckles. "I'm trying to explain," he said. "I can see that he likes you. That's not true of very many men. I'm not sure it's always true of me. I know he does things that don't seem right. Things that *aren't* right—no question about it. But it bothers me you might have a bad opinion of him."

"I don't know that's how I'd put it," said Russell. "'Bad opinion.'"

"However you'd put it," Bixby said. "I need you to understand. Because you're going to see things you might not get at first, things that are going to be pretty hard to square. He's not some egomaniac. Plenty of those in this line of work, but that's not who the captain is."

"Who is he?" Russell asked.

Bixby sat there.

Then he said, "Last year we were working these villages north of J-Bad. Little line of adobe settlements. We'd go in and distribute vitamin packs and solar-powered radios tuned to the pro-American station run by our Bravo team. I'd do inoculations on the kids the farmers brought in, do what I could for the villagers. Their nutrition was pretty poor, and you had to treat them symptomatically. Pepto-Bismol and aspirin.

"There was this one village along the river that allowed us to work out of it. Kind of use it as a central hub. They'd let us spend the night, get our Humvees behind their walls. They put out word to the locals that Americans were providing medical assistance, MREs, paying bounty for artillery shells, explosives, anything you could use as an IED. The village elder was younger than you'd normally see, maybe forty, forty-five. He had a little boy about five years old that took a liking to the captain. Massoud. His father had named him after the G-chief that the Talibs assassinated in the fall of 'oh-one. He didn't have any use for the Taliban, and he had brothers who'd fought and died with the Northern Alliance.

You could tell Wynne admired him, and the captain would teach his boy the English words for all the stuff he was wearing: his vest, fatigues, helmet, and patches. Got a New York Yankees cap sent over, gave it to Massoud. Boy never seemed to take it off. This was still the hearts-and-minds campaign, before everything went completely to hell."

Bixby paused and ran a hand through his beard.

"But go to hell they did, and for two months straight they had us in Kunar doing raids. By they time we got back to working the villages, there was something nervous in the air. We'd been in a bad gunfight in Fallujah, back in 'oh-four; helo took fire and we almost lost the captain—"

"Wheels told me," Russell said.

Bixby looked at him. He asked how Wheels knew.

"He said he'd heard it from a medic when we were stationed at the Rifles Base in Ramadi."

"You were in Ramadi?"

Russell nodded.

Bixby was quiet for a few moments. He said, "Captain nearly died. They actually *pronounced* him dead. I think that's when all of this started. Maybe he went away and came back, and when you come back from something like that you don't come back all the way. I don't know. I was just glad we hadn't lost him. Saying he's the best officer I've ever served under doesn't do him justice. Best *man* I've served with. Period."

"I think I might've gotten you off track," Russell said.

"No," said Bixby, "I got myself off track. So we were reestablishing contact with the locals, or trying to at least, but no one wanted to be seen talking to us. Farmers whose names we knew would go inside their houses whenever we passed. When we finally got down to the village by the river, we knew something bad had happened. Captain had us park the Humvees off beside this stand of mulberry trees, left Rosa and Perkins in the gun turrets to pull security, then we got out with our rifles and went in expecting an ambush.

"We smelled it before we ever saw it. Stopped us like we'd hit an actual wall, and we just stood there, blinking. Piles of excrement on the ground, trash all over. The huts fallen in on themselves. Smell was so bad I got an instant migraine. When we got back to the outpost, I had to throw away my uniform. Brand new Crye Precision and I just pitched it. Ended up taking the stock and rail panels off my rifle and tossing those too. Threw away my go-to-hell bag. Threw out the case for my med kit. Changed out the bladder on my Camel and tossed the Oakleys I was wearing. Ox ended up cutting off his beard and shaving his head down to the scalp. . . ."

Bixby trailed off into silence and sat there a moment. He said, "No one left but the kids, Corporal. An entire village of children. And I don't mean eleven, twelve-year-olds. I'm talking little kids: four, five, six—about the same age as Massoud. All girls, by the way. Just standing there in the doorways, staring at us. Only sound we could hear was the flies and our footsteps. We went down the little thoroughfare like sleepwalkers.

"Outside of one of the larger huts there was an old Afghan woman seated on a stool against the mud wall. Ziza walked up and started talking to her. Wynne said, 'Ask her what happened,' and Ziza would question her in Pashto. Kept referring to her, when he'd translate, as 'grandmother,' and from what he could gather, the Taliban had come into the village several weeks before. They'd executed the men, took the boys prisoner, beat the women bloody. Wynne was kneeling there beside the woman with a hand on her shoulder, listening to Ziza, shaking his head. Then he looked up and saw Massoud. He'd heard our voices and come from inside the hut to stand in the doorway."

Bixby sat very quietly for several moments. It was after all, a story Russell was listening to, but he could feel the panic rising in his chest. Like climbing that first steep hill on a roller coaster, that moment before you level out and the world drops away and you are betrayed to the fall.

"His eyes had been burned out and his ears cut off. They'd pulled all his teeth. When he opened his mouth, his gums were purple as a chow dog's. I knelt there between the captain and

Ox. Ox was so furious he was shaking. Captain was calling Massoud "son": 'Who did this to you, son? Tell us who did this?' They seemed to have forgotten what language he spoke. I put my hands on the boy's shoulders—he couldn't have weighed thirty pounds. His bones felt like the bones of a bird. The Talibs had taken him to their cave and tortured him for several days. Then they brought him back to the village as a kind of living message to anyone who aided the infidel."

"Why?" Russell asked.

"Why what?"

"Why would they do that? Why would you do something like that to a kid?"

"That's who they are," said Bixby. "That's who we're fighting. In this culture, women are nothing. But sons? The son of an elder?"

"His eyes," said Russell. "So he can't identify his kidnappers. At least it makes some kind of sick sense. But his teeth? What the hell for? What possible reason could you have for removing a kid's teeth?"

Bixby stared at him for a long moment. When the answer to his question dawned on Russell, a spasm of nausea and then of rage ran through him.

"You've got to be shitting me," he said.

Bixby's voice, when it came, was very quiet, very calm.

"You have to understand. Rape, torture: these are our enemy's weapons. Like a rifle or grenade—"

"Not the same," said Russell. "Not the same thing at all."

"I agree with you, Corporal: it's *not* the same. But these are their weapons."

"Bastards," Russell said, and though the night was cold, he felt too warm inside his clothes.

Bixby nodded and then they just sat. Russell thought that if they'd do these things to a child, what the hell kind of hope did a POW have?

"So we called in an infantry platoon to evacuate the village. They loaded everyone into trucks and took them away."

"Away where?"

"I don't know."

"What about the boy?"

"Don't know that either," said Bixby. "The captain called around to different bases, looking for him. For all I know, he still is.

"We started hunting them the next day. I watched the captain over the coming weeks. I'd never seen him more . . . I don't know what the word is. He'd been different after Iraq. Maybe dying does that. Or almost dying. Maybe it changes something in the brain. Chemically. But I saw it now, the difference. In some ways he was better, sharper. He barely slept. He'd sit there in the TOC going through hours of drone feed until he was able to track the guys who'd decimated the village to a cave in the mountains to the east."

"He did that from drone video?"

"He did it from drone video," Bixby said. "Not only that, he got hold of footage showing the bad guys coming down to the village the day they assaulted. Not the attack itself, but the infil."

Russell shook his head.

"So," said Bixby, "the mountain range they were operating off was right on the Pakistani border. Pretty ideal, because they could come out and wreak absolute havoc, and then when we tried to run them down with Apaches or airstrikes, they could slip over the ridge and be in another country's airspace and our gunships would have to return to base.

"Frustrating and very effective. But once we'd confirmed these were our guys and got the green light from command, we decided to go in on ATVs, little four-wheelers—"

"You had those?"

"They flew them out to us from Kandahar. You ever ridden one?"

"Not in the army," said Russell. "We had them growing up on the ranch. Granddad and I used them when we built fence."

"I liked them a lot."

"They're great," Russell said.

"Carson didn't think so. I don't have to tell you why."

"The noise."

Bixby nodded. He pointed toward where the horses were tethered out in the dark. He said, "What I'm telling you is really the genesis for what we're doing now. I don't know that I've even thought about it that way. But it's true. Carson got fed up giving away 'tactical advantage.' 'Breaking noise discipline.' His words, obviously. But I'll give it to him: that's precisely what happened. We went in at night, of course, with the headlights disconnected and parked two klicks out from our target, and still they were waiting for us. Almost got ourselves in an ambush. Ox took frag in the shoulder. Our warrant officer—man named Joel—was shot through the leg and ended up with a shattered pelvis. Almost bled out on the medevac bird. He's back in Bragg working as cadre in the Q Course. Which is how we ended up with Billings. He—"

"How'd you get the green light?"

"For the raid?"

Russell nodded. "Why didn't they send in the Rangers? Why didn't they send Delta or the SEALs?"

"Why do you think?" Bixby said.

Russell thought about it. The captain had obviously convinced one of the shot-callers in higher that his team should get to conduct a direct action assault, even though that wasn't what Green Berets were supposed to be doing, necessarily, and their involvement with the kidnapped boy and his village ought to have disqualified them. He sat with it a moment.

"Just how high up the food chain do the captain's supporters go?" Russell asked.

"Pretty high," Bixby said.

"Can you not tell me?" said Russell.

"I can tell you."

"Will you?"

"Of course not," Bixby said. He leaned over and took another sip from his hydration tube, wiped his mouth and beard. "Thing is, you have friends in high places, you're going to have enemies in high places, too."

Russell looked at the ground. He thought about that and then he thought about the disfigured boy.

"Least tell me you got them," he said.

"We got them," said Bixby.

"All of them?"

"All," Bixby said. Then he said that when they'd assaulted the stronghold, they discovered what a cancer this particular cell had been.

"They had cardboard boxes—old boxes for Samsung VCRs—filled with jewelry, gold and silver. Boxes of wedding rings. *Boxes.* Think about that, Corporal. They'd been robbing the locals since the Talibs had taken over in 'ninety-six. Then we found the fillings."

"What do you mean, 'fillings?'"

"I mean fillings," said Bixby. "Gold fillings. For teeth. There were entire ammo boxes of teeth."

Russell took his face in one hand and massaged his temples with the thumb and middle finger. "I don't see how you didn't go absolutely berserk."

Bixby turned and looked away.

"I'm not sure that we didn't," he said, his voice lower and just at the edge of hearing. "You should've seen the captain. We did a body count, confirmed our kills, collected weapons and intel, and then started stacking up the boxes of plunder. What—nine, ten years worth? Carson stood there in the middle of all that. Cave was lit by torchlight, and the gold sparkled like a dragon's treasure. He started to preach. Never heard anything like it. Wish I'd written it down. He told us to look. Said this was what the enemy used to buy their rifles. Their rifles and mortars and roadside bombs. Provisions. He pointed to one of the boxes of fillings.

"'You see that? Every one of those is a dead American.' We all just stood there, and he went quiet a couple of minutes and let it sink in. Then we set explosive charges on the weapons cache, wired it to blow, sent half the team out to get the ATVs, bring them up to load the ammo and VCR boxes, called in the medevac chopper for Joel, and started stacking bodies. And then he said—I'll never forget it—he said, 'Eye for an eye?' He looked at us and shook his head. 'Eye for an eye won't cut it. *Two* eyes for an eye. You take my eye, I take both of yours. That's our math now. That is how we win.'"

Afternoon of the next day, the captain waved him up from the rear of the column and then sat the gold stallion as Russell walked Fella past the other riders. They seemed to watch with great interest, Wheels and Rosa and Sergeant Bixby. Ox sat gripping his saddle horn in both hands, eyes glazed from the fentanyl, and one side of his mouth stuffed with gauze. When Russell reached the captain, Wynne turned in the saddle and looked back over his shoulder, staring for several moments. Then he looked at Russell, the Akhal-Teke perfectly motionless beneath him.

"We're being followed," he said.

"Are you sure?" asked Russell.

"Pretty sure," the captain said.

"Talibs?"

Wynne's mouth tightened and his brow furrowed. He asked how the horses were going to hold up around a lot of shooting.

Russell glanced down and patted Fella's neck. He'd done what he could to gunbreak the animals, but nothing got used to the noise of automatic weapons.

He glanced back up at Wynne.

"My honest opinion?"

"Your honest opinion," said the captain.

"I think they'll go completely apeshit."

"That's what I was afraid of," Wynne said.

"We could split the team—half of us ride ahead leading the other half of the horses. Get a mile or so up the trail."

The captain seemed to be considering it. Then he said, "I don't want to get in contact with only half our shooters, and I don't want to send you guys into an ambush of your own."

"What do you want to do?"

"Scouts will be back in an hour. Let's hear from them."

The scouts were late that evening. The team had made camp in a dry wash ringed by oak and holly. Ziza was posted near the trail on sentry, and when the captain's radio crackled to life, it was the commando's voice that came over the speaker.

"Scouts are coming," it said.

"Copy that," said Wynne, and then told the man to bring them on down to camp. He sent Sergeant Hallum to relieve his post, and the team waited in the gathering dusk. Fifteen minutes later they heard the crunching of dry leaves and then saw the two Afghan scouts following Ziza's short, athletic form through the trees. Wynne was seated cross-legged on the ground and he waved the three of them over, Ziza walking up and squatting beside his captain, the two scouts stopping several feet away, like children awaiting punishment. Russell listened as Ziza spoke to them in their native tongue, questioning them, it sounded like, and then the commando lifted a palm and turned to Wynne.

"They say there is a tower. Three, four kilometers down the trail."

The captain looked at him a moment. He said, "*Tower?*"

"That is what they say."

"What kind of tower?"

Ziza turned back to the scouts and barked at them in Pashto, the scouts responding in soft voices, deferential, and then the taller of the two knelt and began making a crude sketch in the dirt with the middle finger of his left hand. The team watched. Bixby came over and turned on his flashlight to get a better view. When the man was finished with the drawing, he spoke once more to Ziza and then fell silent.

The captain gestured at the sketch with his chin, illuminated in the circle of Bixby's flashlight. "What's that?"

Ziza lifted a hand and held it several feet off the ground. "They say this is a very tall building. The word they know to say is *tower.*" He shrugged an apology.

"How tall?" Wynne asked.

"One hundred meters," Ziza said.

Ox was seated beside the captain—hadn't spoken all evening,

hadn't done anything but stare at the ground and sway. At this figure, his head jerked toward Ziza and his eyes came alive.

"Bullshit," he said.

"Ask again," Wynne told the commando.

Ziza turned and spoke to the scout, his tone harsher, and when the scout answered, Ziza turned back to address the captain.

"They say one hundred meters."

"Bullshit," Ox said.

Wynne glanced at the weapons sergeant. He looked as though he was about to tell him to secure it, when Rosa spoke up. He'd been squatting over a pot of cold chili, stirring it with one of the cleaning rods for his rifle.

"If they have that kind of crow's nest, it's going to make for a hairy approach."

The men began to murmur their agreement. Wynne nodded. He motioned Ziza toward the scouts.

The commando began to interrogate them and then he cleared his throat and stared down between his boots for several moments. Russell noticed the gray hairs that had grown in his moustache and beard—how long since any of them had had a shave?

"They are saying this tower is deserted," Ziza told them.

"Deserted," said Rosa, the way you might repeat the word *aliens* if someone told you they'd just landed in your backyard.

Wheels leaned over to Russell and whispered, "How can they know that?"

Russell shook his head. He motioned for his friend to listen.

"Did they go inside?"

Ziza told him they hadn't.

"How long did they observe?"

Ziza asked the scout and the scout answered. The man looked terribly ashamed.

"Several hours," said Ziza.

"And there was no movement?"

"None," Ziza said.

Billings was seated several yards away, massaging his legs, sulking as he always did in the evenings. Now he lifted his head and spoke.

"Captain," he said, "I don't like this."

"Fuck's there to like?" Wheels muttered.

The men fell to arguing. Dark closed in around them, and the stars winked on between the spidery shapes of the trees. There was no agreement as to the accuracy of the scouts' claims and none as to how the team should proceed.

When Russell woke the next morning the captain sat sipping coffee he'd brewed over a can of Sterno. Russell walked over with the sleeping bag draped across his shoulders like a shawl. He seated himself beside Wynne on a downed tree trunk that Ox had dragged into camp the previous evening, and the captain took the pot from where it sat smoking on its metal grate, poured a cup three-quarters of the way full, and handed it across. Russell thanked him. He inhaled the rising steam, then tested the coffee with his tongue. He blew into the cup for several seconds and then took a sip—rich and very strong.

They sat there in the half-light, birds calling from the darkness beyond the trees. Then he felt the captain looking at him.

"I was in the Regiment," said Wynne.

"Didn't know that," Russell said. "I knew you'd been through Ranger School. I saw you were tabbed."

"It was only for two weeks," Wynne told him, shrugging. "I'd dropped my SF packet about a month before and I was still unpacking boxes there at Benning when I got the call to head to Fayetteville."

Russell nodded.

Then the captain said, "Your grandparents raised you."

Russell couldn't tell if this was a question or a statement, but he told Wynne that yes, they had.

Wynne sipped his coffee. He asked what his father did.

"He was in the army," said Russell. "Did three tours in Vietnam with the Lurps. Or his first tour was with them. After that, they all got folded into Ranger units."

"What about now?"

"What do you mean?"

"What's he do now? Your father."

"Nothing," Russell said. "We lost him when I was real small."

The captain was silent a moment.

Then he said, "Over there?"

"No, sir. Over here. He was killed in Tulsa."

"Murdered?"

Russell said no, not murdered. He told the captain how his father's pickup had stalled on the tracks of the Frisco Railroad, how he'd stayed in the cab trying to get it started until he was hit by a train.

"I was only eighteen months old," said Russell. "I don't even remember him."

"What about your mother?"

"I remember her just fine."

"How'd she deal with all of it?"

"Percodan," said Russell. "Percocet. Vicodin and Valium. Anything else she could get her hands on."

"Did she ever come out of it?"

"Couldn't say. Last time I saw her was the day after my seventh birthday. I don't know where she is. I don't even know if she's still alive."

"Your grandparents were your father's parents?"

"My mother's," Russell said.

They sat there, the sky paling against the ink black limbs.

"Children of adversity," Wynne said.

"How's that?"

"Friend of mine. Operator named Eric, one of the first guys ever selected for CAG. He—"

"Delta Force?"

"Right," said Wynne, "Delta. He told me that right after they'd stood up the unit, the head shrinkers were interested in figuring out what made the elite elite. If there were any common denominators. The men who made it through selection were from all walks of life. Every ethnicity, every kind of background. Short, tall, rural, urban. On first glance, they didn't seem to have much of anything in common.

"So they ran their tests. Psych evaluations. Questionnaires. And what they found was that, to a man, these operators came from broken homes. Had abusive fathers, mothers who were addicts. A lot of them were orphans. They'd been beaten and molested, in and out of foster care. The phrase they came up with was *children of adversity.* Guys with deep psychological scars but whose trauma hadn't wrecked them. Because usually it does. They end up in prison. End up on drugs. Drunks and derelicts. Institutionalized. But the small percentage who don't—these men were somehow stronger. Stronger and stranger. Children of adversity."

Russell raised the coffee to his lips but he didn't drink. He bent over and sat the mug on the ground.

He said, "Be real honest with you: I can't say my life's been all that bad."

Wynne studied him.

"I mean," said Russell, "there's plenty of folks that have had it worse. My grandparents were real good people. They treated me like I was their son. They might as well have been my parents."

Wynne nodded. "Except they weren't."

"No," said Russell. "Not technically speaking."

They sat there. Across camp, one of the men cleared his throat and spat. There was the sound of sleeping bags being unzipped.

"I guess," Russell said, "I feel like, all things considered, I've had it pretty good. I wouldn't want my life to be any other way than what it's been." He looked at the captain. "That make sense?"

"Makes sense," Wynne told him.

The captain rose and pitched the dregs of his coffee out onto the carpet of dead pine needles. Then he turned back to Russell.

"And yet," he said, "here you sit."

Dawn had just broken when they struck a trail that veered north and passed along a narrow gorge where crows squawked to one another from the crags high above them and the noise of the horses' hooves echoed off the sandstone walls. They emerged into a wooded vale, and up ahead they could see the scouts waiting in a grove of pine, gargantuan trees climbing toward the sky like ancient totems. Wynne led them down a dry creek bed and then along a slender path that snaked its way through the evergreens. When they reached the scouts, Ziza rode up to speak with the men for several minutes and then came back to report to the captain. Wheels and Russell were sitting their horses to one side, and Russell touched his heels and put Fella forward, approaching Wynne's stallion from the rear.

"Not worried about any of that," the captain was saying. "If we all go up there together, they take out the whole team in the funnel."

"I don't think there is a 'they,'" said Ziza.

"There's always a 'they,'" Wynne said.

The captain reined his horse about to face the others and waved them close.

"Structure's on the far side of these trees," he said, "four hundred, five hundred meters. Our scouts' 'tower.' We're going to need to clear it room by room. If there's intel, we need to collect it. Can't just pretend it doesn't exist."

"What kind of intel?" Bixby asked.

"I don't know what kind, Mother. This isn't even on our maps."

"Or the drone feeds," Billings added.

The captain glanced over at the lieutenant.

"Or the feeds," he conceded.

"How do you want to do it?" Rosa asked.

Wynne nodded. "Going to send in a fireteam to recon the building. After they clear it, we'll leave the scouts with the horses, get a couple of you to pull security, and I'll take in the rest. Any volunteers?"

"For the fireteam?" asked Bixby.

"The fireteam," Wynne said.

"I'll go," said Ox, speaking around the gauze.

"Negative," said the captain.

"I'll be fine," said Ox.

"You're fine now," said Wynne. "I plan on keeping you that way."

Rosa lifted his hand and Wynne nodded, and then Ziza lifted his.

Wynne said, "You get in there, Zero, get yourself shot, who's going to talk to the scouts?"

"What about me?" said Rosa. "What if I get shot?"

"Then we'll miss your cooking," said Wynne. "Who else?"

"I'll go," said Wheels, and Russell snapped his friend a look.

"You ever cleared a room?"

Wheels nodded.

"Two more," Wynne said.

Russell lifted his hand, but Hallum and Perkins were quicker. Wynne told the four of them—Rosa, Wheels, Hallum, and Perkins—to stay in radio contact. They dismounted and handed over their lead lines and then stalked single file up through the trees and disappeared over the rise. The rest set about tying the horses. Russell sat on the ground next to Wynne, watching Ziza ready magazines, check gear, tighten the straps on his rig.

Ten minutes passed. Then ten more. Russell stared at his watch, picturing Wheels lying on the bare dirt floor of a compound, slowly bleeding out. He shook the thought from his head, but another quickly took its place—Sara in some godforsaken outpost, crouched in a tent as rockets screamed overhead. The captain's radio squawked.

"We're in," said a voice that sounded like Sergeant Rosa's.

"Copy that," Wynne said. "What kind of structure is it?"

There was a moment's pause. Then Wheels's voice came over the radio: "Big one, captain."

Wynne looked over at Russell, but Russell only shook his head.

"Is it a tower?" Wynne asked.

"Not a tower," said the first voice. "Nine or ten stories, though. It'll take a while to clear."

"Do you require assistance? Over."

"Negative," the voice said. "Looks like we have it to ourselves."

They sat and waited. It took the fireteam the better part of an hour to clear the building bottom to top, and when they'd done so, the junior weapons sergeant came back over the radio and told them they could walk on up.

The captain keyed the talk button.

"We're all clear?"

"Roger that," said Rosa.

"You're positive?"

"Say again."

"I say again: you're positive the building is clear? Over."

"Building's deserted," said Rosa. "Nothing but rat turds and sand."

Wynne sat a moment, staring at the ground. His eyes seemed to flash on and off, a trick of the light, Russell thought. Then he rose, slid the radio into its pouch on his chest rig, took up his rifle, and started moving.

They moved up through the pine trees and sycamores, Wynne walking point with Ziza at his heels, Russell behind the Afghan Commando, Billings bringing up the rear. The trees fell away and they emerged into a clearing. Two hundred meters out stood the building that the scouts had reported the previous night. The four of them took a knee at the edge of the tree line and knelt there staring up.

"Jesus God," Billings said.

It wasn't a tower, but for this country it was impressively tall: 140, 150 feet, rectangular in shape, gray in color, glassless windows climbing into the sky. It looked to be built of concrete and cinder block, though Russell had no idea how those materials found their way out here.

Wynne pulled out his radio and held it to his mouth.

"Front door," he said.

"Copy that," said Rosa.

"What's your twenty?"

"You see the roof?"

"Affirmative."

Russell glanced up. What he'd thought was a vent or chimney

atop the building appeared to sprout an arm. The arm waved back and forth and then promptly disappeared.

"Got you," Wynne said. "How we looking?"

"Good shape," Rosa told him. "I can see two klicks, every direction."

"Where's the butcher and the baker?"

"I got Hallum on a third-floor window facing west and Perkins up on the sixth. Ranger's on the ground-floor lobby."

"Where's this lobby?"

"He'll be set up on the stairs when you come in. Just to your left."

"Copy that," said Wynne. "Tell him not to get trigger-happy. We're moving up."

Wheels's voice came over the radio, some joke about being trigger-sad.

Wynne sat there a moment and then he cleared his throat.

"Corporal," he said.

"Yessir."

"You frag one of us, I'll have Ox skin you and make himself a pair of boots."

"Roger that," Wheels said.

Wynne put the radio away, rose, and moved toward the building, the three of them following. Russell looked over and saw that a worn gravel road breached the tree line in the distance and wound across the open stretch of field, approaching the building's front. Nothing about this place sorted with him. Nothing made sense. That old Ranger maxim imprinted on his brainpan: "Just Don't Look Right."

They reached the entrance and stepped inside onto the bare concrete floor, sand grinding beneath their boot soles and the clop of their footsteps echoing off the walls. There was a stairwell on the north side of the room, and Wheels sat on the first step with his rifle at the low ready. When the captain glanced at him, he moved his right hand off fire-control and waved.

Wynne took several steps farther inside, and Russell moved off to the right. Unpainted cinder-block walls, a dusting of talc across the floor, and the bootprints of what must have been Rosa's fireteam, tracks leading toward the stairs. He turned back toward the entrance and saw the enormous cast-iron doors opening out into the gravel lot they'd just crossed. He hadn't even seen them coming in, that adrenal funneling-down: forest for the trees, trees for the branches, branches for the bark. Wynne had noticed the doors as well, and now he stepped over and pulled the left one creaking backward on its hinges. A large steel handle was welded to the inside, and an identical one welded to the outside. He dragged the door completely closed, then went to the one on the right and pulled it shut as well, a half-inch seam of daylight shining between them. He stood there with his back to them in the dim chamber, the only light filtering in from the stairwell. He looked over at Wheels.

"Anyone carrying cordage?"

Russell had several long strands of paracord in his left cargo pocket, but before he could offer it, Ziza stepped up and handed the captain an enormous coil. Wynne pointed to the set of iron handles on the inside of the doors and passed the paracord back to Ziza.

"Secure that," he said.

"What are you worried about?" Billings asked.

"Burglars," said Wynne. He removed his radio and asked Perkins if he was carrying a Claymore mine.

"I've got two," Perkins said.

"Good," Wynne told him. "Come down and set one just inside these doors and relieve Corporal Grimes."

"I think we'll be fine," said Billings, but the captain told him he wasn't going to risk it.

"I'm not seeing the risk," he told Wynne. He gestured at the concrete walls surrounding them. "This is the most secure I've felt in weeks."

"Maybe you could stay," Ziza said.

Russell glanced at the two men, just shadows standing about ten feet apart. Billings towered over the Afghan, but if it came to fisticuffs, Russell's money would be on Ziza.

sell saw it was a necklace, joined together by links of gold. The necklace caught the light, and there was a muted metallic click as it dangled from Ziza's hand.

"You got to be fist-fucking me," Wheels said.

Ziza passed the necklace to Wynne. Then he reached back into the box.

When he pulled his hand out, there were several rings in his palm. He set these to the side and, using both hands, began combing through the sand. He came up with half a dozen more rings, gold and silver, then a small platinum choker set with what looked like emeralds. He handed all of this to the captain, who stowed the items in the cargo pockets of his pants.

Ziza watched him a moment.

"We need to leave this place," he said.

Wynne nodded. He pulled out his radio and asked Perkins if he'd set the Claymore.

"Roger that," said Perkins.

Wynne keyed the talk button and asked Rosa if he read him.

"Five by five," Rosa said.

"How're we looking?"

"No change," said Rosa.

"Get ready to move," Wynne told him. "We're about to get in contact."

"Say again."

"You heard me," Wynne said.

He turned and walked toward the stairwell, calling for Bixby on the radio, telling him to ready their mounts.

"What's going on?" asked Bixby.

"Just get them ready," the captain said.

The five of them had just started toward the first floor when Rosa's voice came back over Wynne's radio, echoing in the stairwell.

"You're a goddamned psychic," it said.

"How many?" Wynne asked.

"Eight," said Rosa.

"Eight," Wynne said.

"Correction," said Rosa, and then his next word was garbled.

Wynne told him to repeat the transmission.

"Eyes on foot-mobiles, six hundred meters."

"Speak slower," the captain said.

"From figures," said Rosa, "One Zero Tangos."

"Ten?" Wynne asked.

Rosa said, "I spell—Tango, Echo, November—ten enemy foot-mobiles, proceeding north-northwest."

The captain asked if he had a shot.

"Affirmative."

"Execute to follow," Wynne said.

They reached the first floor, where Billings and Hallum were backed against the far wall and had their rifles pointed at the double doors. Wynne walked over and knelt beside them, motioning Russell and the others to do the same. Then he lifted the radio to his lips.

"Send it," he said.

Russell heard the dry flat pop of the rifle shot. Then another a few seconds later.

Wynne's radio crackled: "Two Tangos down."

"Continue engaging," the captain said.

"Wilco," said Rosa, and the sound of the next shot came partly through the radio speaker, Russell wondering why Rosa hadn't suppressed his rifle. Everything went quiet for several heartbeats, and then the rifle fired twice in quick succession.

"Two more," said Rosa.

"Keep it up," Wynne said.

The captain turned his head left and right, glancing at the men on either side of him.

He said, "When Rosa clears us to move, Perkins packs his Claymore, cuts those cords, and pushes open the left-side door. He'll post up just behind it. I want Russell and Zero on the right side. You two are the first two out. Perkins provides cover, Hallum falls into the stack behind Zero and gives covering fire from the right. If they need it. Wheels and the lieutenant are next. Zero and Russell move to cover, shoot and scoot, wait for Billings and Wheels. Then

Perkins. Rosa and myself are last. We'll leapfrog back to the horses. Everyone roger?"

The men nodded.

"Ox and Mother will have the horses ready. We hit the tree line, mount up, and haul ass. Don't stop until dark, don't—"

"We're aborting?" Billings said.

"Negative, lieutenant. Just falling back."

"Unless we get ourselves murdered," said Billings.

"Atta boy," said Hallum. "Keep thinking positive."

Billings shook his head. He told Wynne maybe this was a sign.

"Sign of what?" Hallum asked.

"That we're about to get our asses kicked," Billings said.

Russell drew a deep breath and waited for Rosa's voice to come back over the radio to tell them they could move, but when the sergeant's voice came, it told them they had an enemy element approaching from the south, hadn't noticed them until now.

"How many?" Wynne asked.

"Wait one," said Rosa, and his rifle popped twice.

"I count twenty-plus," he said.

"We're fucked," Billings concluded, turning toward the captain.

Wynne seemed not to hear.

"How close?" he asked Rosa.

"About to knock on your front door," said the man.

"Can you engage?"

"No shot," said Rosa. "Going to have to—"

The sergeant interrupted himself with his own rifle, firing, Russell assumed, at targets farther out.

"Get ready," Wynne told them. "Work your way from near to far."

"You fucked us," said Billings.

"Keep your groupings tight," Wynne said.

"Right in the ass," said Billings.

"Lieutenant," said Wynne, "you don't shut your mouth and get your gun in the fight, I'll have Zero hogtie you and we'll carry you out of here like a casket."

Russell thought that Billings would have a comeback for this, but he raised his rifle like he was told.

The captain's radio crackled and Rosa's rifle rang out, and then the doors began to rattle and Russell could see bodies moving back and forth on the other side of the gap.

"Roger up," Wynne said. "After Perkins detonates and they start through the funnel, we open fire. Wait for my order."

But the doors stayed right where they were, and soon the rattling stopped and the shadows outside disappeared.

Wheels said, "This is good, right?"

Rosa's rifle snapped above them. It snapped twice more and went silent.

"We got squirters," he said.

"Which direction?" said Wynne.

"Looks like they're moving—" and his voice over the radio grew unintelligible for several seconds.

"Say again."

"I say again: enemy is breaking contact and moving south."

Wynne knelt there. Sweat beaded his forehead and dropped to the floor, perfect wet medallions forming in the talc. His blue eyes had begun to smolder. It wasn't Russell's imagination and it wasn't a trick of the light.

"They're withdrawing," said Billings.

"Bullshit," Hallum said.

"We need to get out of here," Perkins said.

The captain keyed the radio and asked Rosa if they were clear to move.

"I don't have a three-sixty," Rosa said.

"Do you see Tangos? Over."

"Negative."

"Are we clear to move?"

"I do not know," Rosa said.

"Could be posted up outside," Russell whispered. "Either side of the door. Could be trying to draw us out."

Wynne glanced at him. His lips tightened and he nodded. He motioned for Perkins to move up, told him to disarm and pack the Claymore, cut the paracord lashings off the handles, and kick one of the doors back on its hinges. They knelt and watched as the demolition sergeant moved his rifle to one side and let it hang from its sling. He walked toward the center of the room, approaching the mine as though it'd been planted by the Talibs. He squatted over it and disconnected the wires from the fuse wells, rolled them around the clacker, and tucked the wires and clacker into one of his pouches. Then he took up the actual mine—small, crescent-shaped, FRONT TOWARD ENEMY embossed across its convex side—folded up the pairs of scissor legs on the bottom of the device, and slid it back in his bandolier. He paused a moment, then rose and approached the door, taking his rifle grip in his right hand and pulling his belt knife with his left. Russell realized, watching him, he'd forgotten to breathe. He could feel his pulse against his jacket collars, and he suppressed the urge to call out and tell the sergeant to get down, and then Perkins was passing the blade of his knife through the paracord, sliding the knife back in its Kydex sheath, reaching for the door. He gripped the steel handle and pushed it. Or he tried to push. The door traveled about an inch and stopped. Perkins pulled back and pushed again, pulled back and pushed, a metallic jangling against the outer side. When he turned toward them, his face had gone completely white.

"They chained us in."

"The fuck," said Wheels, rising from his crouch.

"They chained us in," Perkins said.

Russell felt the sweat break out along his spine. His legs had begun to ache from kneeling, but the surge of adrenaline washed the pain right out of him, and he twisted his head to the left and popped his neck. He knew they were about to die.

Wynne rose and crossed the room with the air of a man getting up to check the thermostat—everything about him exuded confidence; everything suggested calm—and Russell felt fear rise into his throat like something that would strangle him. Certainty of death, you accepted. Perhaps dying, perhaps not, put your teeth on edge and set them chattering.

The captain checked the doors, left and right, put his eye to the seam between them, pushed and pulled at the handles. Then he turned to Perkins.

"You have enough C-4 to blow them?"

Perkins said he had enough C-4 to bring the entire building down.

Wynne nodded. He told the sergeant to rig them. He pivoted on a boot heel, pointed to Ziza and Russell, and motioned for them to follow. As they started back up the stairs, Russell could hear Billings ask what the plan was, but the captain ignored him. They went up the first flight, then up the second and third, Wynne taking the steps two at a time, Russell and Ziza struggling to keep up. Rosa's rifle grew louder, and they ascended the remaining flights and emerged gasping onto the building's roof.

Blue sky very close, and the sun above the tree line like the portal to another world. All around them a sea of evergreen and cedar, terraced slopes in the distance, gray mountains and purple mountain shadows, white-capped peaks floating at the horizon's edge. Russell stood with his breath fogging and the sunlight coppering his face, and when he glanced back beside him, he saw that Wynne and Ziza had gone prone on their stomachs. The captain had a handful of his pants leg in his grip, and as Wynne jerked him to the deck, a whip cracked a few inches from his ear, that noise of a bullet breaking the sound barrier just beside you, the thump of the rifle's report following seconds behind. He lay for a moment with his heart hammering the thin shield of his sternum and then he looked at Wynne.

"Two seconds," said Ziza. "Six hundred meters."

The captain's eyes cut toward Russell. "Thought you knew better."

"I thought I did, too," Russell said.

Rosa had set up his firing position behind some loose cinder block at the edge of the building, and they snaked their way over to him. The weapons sergeant kept his eye pressed to the scope, never once turning to look behind him. When the captain came up on his left side, Rosa cleared his throat and glanced down to jot some figure on his data card.

"They're setting up a suicide rig out there," Rosa told them. He spoke as if all of this were happening to someone else and he was observing it on a monitor.

"A what?" said Russell.

Wynne lifted his own rifle and stared out through the optic.

"Eight hundred meters," said Rosa. "On the road out there. Just west of the tree line."

"Got it," Wynne said.

"What's a 'suicide rig'?" Russell asked. "What's going on?"

Ziza was just to his right, and the commando leaned over and began to whisper.

"They have a truck," he said. "They fill it with explosive and drive it into us." He puffed his cheeks and lifted one hand from the deck, miming a blast.

Russell glanced toward Rosa and the captain, who seemed to be studying the device Ziza had just described. The optic on Russell's carbine was a red dot with no magnification, and he'd left his binoculars in his left rear saddlebag.

"Captain," said Russell, "we need to go."

"Working on it," the captain said. He pulled out his radio and apprised Bixby of their situation, then raised Perkins and asked if the doors were ready to blow.

"Affirmative," Perkins said.

"Get the team back on the stairwell. When you detonate, come out shooting. Don't stop till you get back to Mother."

"What about you guys?" Perkins asked.

"Ziza and Russell and Rosa are going with you," said Wynne.

"Then what about you?" Perkins said.

"We got a truck down there on the road with some kind of bomb. They're going to try and ram us and bring the roof down on our heads. I'll stay on overwatch until the rest of you are clear."

"Carson," said Bixby's voice, "I don't—"

"Not up for debate," the captain said.

He told everyone to wait for his order and then motioned for Rosa to move aside and let him have the rifle. Rosa looked at him for several long moments.

"Rather not do that," he said.

Wynne told him to take Ziza and Russell and get moving.

"You need a spotter," Rosa said.

"I'll be my own spotter."

"Let me stay."

Wynne shook his head.

"I don't like this," said Rosa. "I formally object."

"Formally noted," Wynne said. "Get gone."

Rosa's face tightened and he studied his captain. He exhaled very slowly and took his hands off the rifle. He rolled to his right and allowed Wynne to get behind the weapon, waited for him to pass his carbine. Then he just laid there on his back.

Wynne already had his eye to the scope. He thumbed off the safety and then he thumbed it back on and looked at the sergeant.

"Robbie," he said, "it's all right."

"I don't know," said Rosa.

"If I don't make the mission, you know what to do?"

"I know."

"Make sure you Charlie-Mike. Don't let him derail it."

"I won't," Rosa said. He reached and touched the captain on the shoulder and then rolled onto his stomach and began crawling back toward the stairs.

Then they were descending the steps, Russell following the lean sergeant, trying desperately not to trip. Everything inside him seemed to be floating, and then he heard the captain discharge the rifle: one time, two times, a third. They reached the rest of the team bunched back on the stairs near the second floor. Perkins had his radio in one hand and a detonator in the other. Russell and Wheels exchanged a look, nodded to one another in greeting or good-bye, and then the captain's voice came over Perkins's radio.

"Execute," it said.

The men hunkered into themselves and clapped their palms to their ears. Russell closed his eyes very tightly and pressed his forehead to the cold concrete wall. He counted backward from ten.

Nine.

Eight.

Seven.

The explosion pitched him onto his side, and something seemed to rattle loose inside his chest. When he opened his eyes, the air was fogged with a very fine dust, years of it shaken from the walls and ceiling, and the men were coughing. They rose one by one, their clothes powdered a light gray, and Wynne's voice over Perkins's radio was saying, "Now, now, now," the words muffled in the clouded air.

They began moving. They reached the first floor and went through the smoke-filled lobby, paused at the ruined doors for the briefest moment, and then exited the building at a sprint. Those ahead of him were firing their rifles, but Russell couldn't see what they were shooting at. He ran, coughing and trying to clear his throat, bright sunlight in his eyes and bright green grass beneath his boots. He'd lost his sunglasses at some point—no idea when or how. Rosa was just in front of him, and he could see Wheels about fifty yards ahead. The sound from the captain's rifle echoed from behind, and enemy gunfire barked from the trees to their south.

He reached a trench and then a low berm, scrambled up it, then set out for the pine trees at a run. He'd just gotten up the slope and back onto level ground when the toe of his left boot caught something and he tripped. It happened very fast: one second he was all movement with the breeze stinging his ears, and the next he was sprawled on the grass with his rifle underneath him. He heard several closely spaced shots, and then Ziza was kneeling there, helping him to his feet. Russell felt a spasm in his lower back and when he pulled up his rifle, he saw that he'd jammed it muzzle-down into the ground and that the barrel was packed with dirt.

"Are you hit?" asked Ziza.

"I don't think so," said Russell.

"Can you walk?"

Russell told him he could run.

Then they were moving through the trees, dodging limbs, Ziza's hand on his shoulder the entire way. They went down the slope through the pines, and he smelled the horses before he saw them. He sprinted along a stretch of trail and emerged into the clearing, where the other men were untying their mounts from the picket line and heaving themselves onto their backs. Bixby already sat his horse, and he walked it up beside Russell.

"You're going to have to lead us out," he said

"Out where?"

"Captain says take the trail on the other side, then on into the hills."

Russell almost asked him the other side of what, but he knew the answer already. He sat a moment, shaking his head.

"We're riding into an ambush," he told the sergeant.

Bixby nodded. He asked how the horses would behave.

Russell imagined a lot better than him. He reined Fella and turned her and began leading the riders up the goat trail that slipped along the hillside through the pines.

By the time they reached the tree line, the horses had begun to nicker and stamp. Fella went immediately tense beneath him, and he leaned down to pat her neck. He heard the crack of the captain's rifle and thought he could see his scope winking from atop the building in the sun. He couldn't locate the enemy, but there were intermittent bursts from their rifles, and he put Fella forward on tentative hooves. He heard the clap and clack of gear as the others fell in behind him, and then there was the snap of rounds passing overhead. He touched his heels and pushed Fella up to a trot. The building now was about two football fields away, standing to their left like a monolith against the morning sky. The noises of the horses' hooves against the turf rose to a rumble you could feel inside your chest, and the smell of crushed grass filled his nostrils, rich and very fragrant. He heard another series of rifle shots, and when he glanced toward the building he saw that the suicide truck they'd sighted was moving toward it, maybe ten, fifteen miles per hour, and then the vapor trails of two RPGs streaked low across the plain and detonated to their right. Fella surged forward and sped to a gallop, the horses behind matching her speed, rifles cracking and the noise of low concussions echoing as the building drew closer and the air stung his eyes, watering now from the cold.

He seized a tighter grip on the reins and stretched himself along Fella's neck, speaking to her, telling her she was doing very good. Something tugged very hard on the cargo pocket of his left pants leg, but he didn't look to see what. The rattle of machine-gun fire grew distant, and then they were on the other side of the building, the structure now between them and the enemy, the rifles growing instantly muffled. The ground began to rise, and he slowed Fella to a canter and went uphill along the trail, steeper and steeper, bunch grass waving in the breeze. He dropped to a walk and felt the bellows of the horse's lungs fill and empty, fill and empty, glanced behind him, and saw the others. No one seemed to have been hit and, inexplicably, no one had been thrown. Ziza was leading the captain's stallion, and the scouts were bringing up the remuda. Russell wiped his eyes and halted Fella up on the hillside, turned and looked back and saw that the building looked very small from this height.

When Bixby reached him the first thing Russell said was, "Captain Wynne."

The sergeant's radio was already out, pressed against the side of his face. He was saying, "Underchild Actual, this is Underchild Four; how copy?" repeating the transmission again and again, his voice growing louder and more panicked until all protocol was dropped and he was screaming, "Carson, are you there? Carson?"

"Motherfucker," said Rosa and he'd just gotten the word out when an explosion shook the earth and the horses seemed to scream with once voice. The gelding Perkins rode stood back on its hind legs, pawing air. Perkins hit the ground and the horse whinnied and then went surging up the trail. No one followed. Their eyes were on the building and the enormous tongue of flame erupting out its rear wall. They watched the structure smoke and totter and they watched as it began to collapse: the roof dropping and the walls exploding outward and a huge cloud of white mushrooming into the clear, faultless sky. Several of the men cried out, and Bixby got his horse under control and turned to take it downhill toward the plain, Ox and Rosa just behind.

Only Lieutenant Billings seemed to have figured the calculus of the situation, and he placed his fingers into the corners of his mouth and gave a shrill whistle that froze all of them in place.

They turned to look at him.

"Get back here," he said.

Bixby just stared. He whispered what sounded like the captain's name.

"He's gone," said Billings.

"Fuck you," Rosa said.

Billings turned his horse a full revolution and swept his eyes over each of them, then touched his heels to the palomino's ribs, snapped the reins, and began ascending the trail. One by one the men fell in behind, silent, stunned. The path took them higher, and they passed into a grove of evergreen, and the valley behind them was obscured by trees. Russell understood that he was now riding under the lieutenant's command, and he knew like he knew his own heartbeat that this man would abort the mission and lead them back to the outpost under the shadow of Firebase Dodge.

He thought that he should be grateful but found he was in despair.

The trail rose and then descended, and the trees fell away, and they emerged into a shallow sandstone trough where, several hundred meters to their left, was the valley where the collapsed building lay in a smoking ruins. None of them could look at it for long, and when Russell glanced over, his throat tightened. They traveled down the ridgeline, went past a jagged rock formation in the shape of a whale, and then defiled down a slope and then along a field where green grape fields twisted in the sunlight.

When they rounded the bend on the far side, the captain was seated on a low rock wall that ran beside the trail, elbows braced against his thighs, sipping from the hydration tube in his pack. Lieutenant Billings slowed his horse, and the others dropped their mounts to a walk. Wynne looked up to regard each of them in turn, his blue eyes dimmer in the gold light of morning, his blond hair dusted gray with talc and his uniform almost white with it. He wasn't carrying Rosa's rifle, but other than the missing weapon or the powder that covered him head to foot, there was no indication he'd been anywhere near a fight.

The men began to dismount and walk up to him—Bixby and Ox and Ziza, Russell trailing right behind—reaching to touch their captain on the arms or back or shoulders. Russell's eyes were hot and wet, and he was backhanding tears from his cheeks. He felt as though they were enacting a ritual for which he had no name, something lying dormant inside him all these years, asleep and swimming in his blood. They filed past him like pilgrims at a shrine and then stood with baffled expressions. Russell glanced over and saw that Billings and Rosa were standing a ways back, Billings with rage burning in his eyes, and Rosa with his head lowered, studying the ground. The captain walked toward them, approaching the lieutenant first. Billings had already started to back away—it occurred to Russell that Wynne might strike him—and when the captain reached him, he seized the man's head in both hands, drew him close, and planted a kiss on his cheek: more terrifying, somehow, than any blow. Billings blanched, and when the captain released him, he stumbled backward several steps and looked as though he'd fall. He murmured something Russell couldn't hear and then went silent, Wynne already moving toward Sergeant Rosa.

The man was kneeling there in the dirt, and when he glanced up, Russell could see his eyes were wet. Wynne came up and extended a hand, and Rosa stared at it, shaking his head. Then he took it. The captain pulled him to his feet and embraced him, and the sergeant began to weep. He was saying something over and over, a note of desolation in his voice. Wynne held him very tightly, a sound coming from his lips that sounded like *shhhhhhhhhhh.*

Evening of the following day the men were camped in a sandstone wash beside a dry riverbed when the scouts rode in at dusk and reined their horses out beyond the firelight. The two of them spoke in hurried Pashto whispers and then approached Wynne where he sat between Ox and Ziza, stopping a few feet from the captain and performing a sort of martial bow. There was a series of exchanges between the scouts and Ziza, and then Ziza turned and told Wynne that the compound they'd been seeking was only a two-day ride.

Wynne stared at him a moment. He sunk his plastic spoon inside the packet of rations he'd been eating, wiped the corners of his mouth, and stood.

"Two days," Wynne repeated, but you couldn't tell if it was a question. The captain's shadow moved back and forth in the firelight. Ziza asked the scouts if they'd seen the enemy.

The taller of the two men inclined his head toward the other, they spoke several sentences, and the shorter man began to shake his head.

"No enemy," the tall scout said. He swept a hand in front of his chest, the gesture like a vague salute.

Rosa had walked over to join the discussion, and Bixby soon followed. An informal meeting broke out among the sergeants, and Russell rose, dusted the seat of his pants, and found Wheels in his sleeping bag with his jacket covering his chest. His eyes were open.

"You can really see the stars," he said.

Russell looked up. They blazed brilliantly, and there was even a sense of warmth.

Wheels said, "ATMs."

"What's that?"

"I was laying here and I realized I'd forgotten ATMs. It took me awhile to remember what they even looked like."

Russell took a seat beside Wheels on the cold ground.

"Banks for that matter," Wheels continued. "It ever occur to you we're getting paid for this?"

"Yeah," said Russell. "Hazard pay."

"Hazard pay," Wheels said.

"Stop signs," said Russell.

"How's that?"

"I forgot about stop signs."

"Car washes," Wheels said.

"Yeah. Car washes." Russell was silent a moment. He said, "I've still got my pickup in Smadge's garage."

"That tight bastard," said Wheels. "You get back, he'll charge you a storage fee. See if he don't."

There were several quiet minutes. Russell could hear the murmur of the men talking, but he couldn't make out what they were saying. He told Wheels they were getting ready to go in.

"I figured that," Wheels said.

"You scared?" said Russell.

"Pretty scared," Wheels said.

Russell watched him for a moment, his face silver in the light of the low moon. His mouth slightly open. He blinked.

"We almost died today," Wheels said. "You thought about that?"

"Trying not to," Russell said.

"I been thinking about it quite a bit."

Russell studied his friend. He looked pensive, a little sad.

"I don't even know why we're doing this," Wheels continued.

"You do know," Russell told him: "POWs."

"It's not any POWs," Wheels said.

"That's what we're trying to figure out," Russell explained. "You heard the lieutenant: if there are prisoners, we can't just—"

"If there are prisoners, this sure as hell ain't the way to go about getting them. End up prisoners ourselves. This is Whac-A-Mole."

"It's what?" said Russell.

"We kill one Talib, another pops up over here. We send guys after him, our guys get captured and we have to send more. Then more Talibs join to fight them. It just keeps going."

Russell sat there a moment. He'd never heard Wheels talk this way. He asked him how he'd go about it.

Wheels didn't answer at first. Then he said, "How much you think the necklace Ziza pulled out of that sandbox today is worth?"

"I wouldn't have any idea," Russell said.

"Hundred thousand? Two hundred thousand?"

Russell lifted his hands and shook his head. "What's this got to do with anything?"

"I don't know," Wheels said.

"I don't either," said Russell, "and I believe all this kind of talk does is take our heads out of the game when—"

"Somebody drank the Kool-Aid," Wheels said.

"What Kool-Aid?"

"The captain's," said Wheels. "You used to have a little sketchticism."

"I don't think we can afford 'sketchticism,'" Russell said. "And what the hell good does it do us? In our situation right now?"

Wheels looked over at him and then back up at the stars.

"Yeah," he said, "you're probably right. I'm a little shook up, is all."

"I think everybody's shook up."

"Everybody but the captain," Wheels said.

They rose the next morning and rode out of camp. No one spoke. The captain had sent the scouts out on recon, and the plan was to take the days slowly, carefully, conserve their energy, try to conserve their horses'. Wynne didn't want them assaulting after a full day's ride, and he didn't want one of the men getting a mechanical injury before they reached their destination. Russell watched him at the head of the column, sitting the golden stallion with his shoulders squared, the reins gripped in his left hand as though he'd done it all his life. He tried to picture what the captain would've been without this conflict, but his imagination failed him. He couldn't conceive of Wynne without the war or the war without Wynne. They seemed to have been designed for one other, and Russell wondered, if that were the case, what scenario had been devised for himself?

They made camp that evening in the sheltered basin of a pine-covered hillside and waited for the scouts. The captain had told them no more fires, so they kept stand-to in the twilight and then in the dusk, and when night fell they sat on their saddle blankets with their sleeping bags around their shoulders. It was cold without a fire and so black Russell could barely make out the forms of the men silhouetted against the stars. Wheels was seated there beside him.

He leaned closer and said, "The hell are our scouts s'posed to find us in this?"

Russell didn't know. He said maybe they were accustomed to it. Maybe they had faculties the Americans didn't.

"I hope to Christ they got faculties," said Wheels. "Faculties and a spotlight."

When they woke the next morning, the scouts had yet to return. Wynne conferred with Ziza, then Bixby, then ordered the men to mount up and break camp. The sun rose and the day was hot and bright, the hillsides steaming around them, the trees shimmering in the heat. Russell pulled his ball cap out of his right rear saddlebag and snugged it over his head. He wished he'd brought another pair of sunglasses, but mid-afternoon clouds rolled in from the east and the air smelled suddenly of rain. The goat trail they followed grew steep, and as they ascended a wooded slope, the horses began to nicker and blow. Fella dropped to a slow walk, stepping nervously, and then she just stopped. Russell started to touch his heels and put her forward, but the muscles along her neck had gone tense; he reached to stroke a palm along her neck. He leaned and spoke to her, chucked up and started her walking. The riders crested the rise and went winding among the pines.

They descended the far side of the hill and rode down into a stand of plum trees and cedar, and it was there they found their scouts.

Ziza was riding just behind the captain, and he was the first one to see. He called out in his native tongue, his voice rising from its usual gruff baritone to a high-pitched wail. He leapt from his mount and went sprinting forward, the captain shouting to him, the horses beginning to sidle and lurch. Russell glanced up and saw two bodies suspended upside down from the limbs of an enormous oak, naked except for the *taqiyah* caps on the crown of their heads. The corpses were maybe twenty yards away, but he could see that their throats had been slit in gaping red smiles, their genitals cut away. There were cuts and bruises along their legs and torsos, the skin in places almost black. Ziza had reached the tree, and he knelt there below them in the dirt. He'd vouched for these Afghans, had bullied and berated them every day of their journey, and now he wept inconsolably. Some of the riders were starting to dismount and grab their weapons, and others sat their horses, pale as if seasick, their faces drained of blood. Billings had begun to ride toward the scouts, but Russell raised his voice.

"Keep the horses back," he said. "They don't need to see this."

Wheels was just behind him. He said none of them did.

"He's right," Rosa said. "You don't want to walk the rest of the way, I'd get the animals as far back as possible."

"We might need to hood them," said Russell.

"We should absolutely hood them," Rosa said.

The captain had turned his stallion to listen.

"Robbie," he said, "you and Russ take them over to that shelf. At least you'll be upwind."

Russell pulled the reins softly and began to lead the others away, ducking limbs, monitoring the ground for sinks. They reached the moss-covered shelf on the hillside, strung the picket line, and began to tie off, Russell talking to Fella the entire time, telling her she'd be all right.

When they walked back down the hill, the captain had tethered his stallion to the slender trunk of a plum tree and was kneeling beside Ziza, speaking to him in hushed tones, nothing that Russell could hear. The men had their rifles at the ready, and Ox had taken Morgan and Perkins to set up a perimeter. Russell went slowly toward the hanging bodies, the hairs on his arms electric. He cradled his carbine close to his chest and glanced around at the trees, but it was all a blur of branches and trunks, nothing distinct; he couldn't seem to frame anything, couldn't seem to keep the world from trembling. He leaned against a cedar and stared at the scouts.

He'd been briefed on what would happen if he was captured by the Talibs, what they called "the Afghan way": castration or disembowelment, followed by decapitation. Whoever had tortured their scouts had decided against the latter, but on closer inspection, Russell saw that these men had been scalped. Flies swarmed their bare skulls and crawled over the ropes from which they dangled. It was like watching a movie, with sight the only sensation, no sound or smell. Then the wind shifted and there was that sharp metallic scent, the noise of Ziza weeping. Everything rushed in on him, and Russell bent forward and vomited.

Then Wheels was there beside him.

"Russ," he said very softly, "c'mon." He kept his eyes lowered, and Russell wondered if he'd even looked. He glanced toward Wynne and Ziza and saw that Billings was standing there behind them, staring up at the scouts with detached, academic interest.

He pointed at the bodies.

"How long you think it took them to give up everything they knew?"

Wynne turned to regard him, still kneeling, one hand on Ziza's shoulder.

"Francis," he said.

"Don't 'Francis' me," said Billings. "Don't even start. Those men were tortured. You can bet they spilled their fucking guts. Assume the Talibs know who we are, how many we are. Assume they know where we're—"

He was interrupted mid-sentence. One moment Ziza was genuflecting beneath the bodies of his countrymen with his back to Billings, and the next he'd turned and sprung at the lieutenant, driving his head into Billing's stomach, capturing the lieutenant's legs and locking his arms around the backs of Billings's knees, knocking him to the ground, then passing to Billings's right side, throwing a leg over and straddling the larger man's chest. The entire maneuver took maybe two seconds, and now Ziza sat mounted on the lieutenant, striking him with elbows. He'd gotten in three or four solid hits before the captain managed to wrangle him off Billings, grabbing the short Afghan and pulling him away. The men stood watching. They didn't seem to know whether or not to intervene and likely felt the same as Russell, that, if anything, the lieutenant had gotten off easy. He lay there on the ground staring up at the tree limbs, the scouts' desecrated bodies dangling like nightmare ornaments. The lieutenant blinked several times and tried to raise himself on an elbow, then seemed to think better of it and collapsed back against the dirt. He was cut just below the left eye and high on his forehead, Ziza's sharp elbows having split the skin. Wynne handed the Afghan off to Rosa, who'd come up to try to lend a hand and now led Ziza off into the trees, the commando cursing in Dari or Pashto, they sounded much the same to Russell. The captain walked up and stood over Billings.

"You all right?" he asked.

Billings didn't answer. He lay there feeling the bridge of his nose, testing it with his fingers, first one side, then the other.

Wynne watched. Then he toed him with his boot. "Can you get up?"

Billings nodded.

"Then get up," Wynne said. He reached and extended a hand, but Billings didn't accept it.

He said, "I suppose you think I had it coming."

"What do you think?" the captain asked.

The men buried their scouts in a common grave and built a sandstone cairn against wolves and wild dogs. Ziza said a prayer in Pashto, hands at waist level, palms toward the darkening sky. They withdrew half a kilometer into the hills to make a cold, fireless camp, and when they woke the next morning, Billings and his horse were gone. The men gathered around the captain in the half-light of dawn and tried to determine how to proceed.

"They know we're out here," said Wynne. "If the lieutenant was right about anything, he was right about that."

"Fuck the lieutenant," said Ox, and Rosa wanted to know what Billings thought he was doing.

"He thinks we're poor company," said Rosa, "wait'll the fuckknuckles that strung Haashim and Abdullah get ahold of him."

Wynne watched Rosa a moment. He admitted he and the lieutenant had their disagreements, but he didn't want him falling into enemy hands.

"No shit," said Rosa. "Francis would give up his own mother if he thought it'd save a hair on his head."

"My concern," said Wynne, "is the mission. We always knew the risk. We never had any guarantees. I'd like to hear where everyone is with this."

The men sat staring for several moments, some at the captain, some at the ground.

Then Bixby said, "In terms of whether we ought to continue?"

"In whatever terms you want," Wynne said. He motioned toward Rosa.

"Given our situation," said the young sergeant, "I think it's just as likely we get in contact doubling back as going on ahead. I'd rather do what we came to do."

"Or give it a fucking try," said Ox.

"Exactly," said Perkins.

Morgan spoke next, said he felt the same way, and then Ziza asked if they were willing to consign American POWs to the same fate as that of their scouts.

The men seemed to consider this. Wynne looked over at Wheels and Russell where they sat on their saddle blankets.

"What's your opinion?" he said.

Russell hadn't expected to be included in the discussion, and glancing at Wheels, he could tell that neither had his friend.

"Captain," he told him, "I don't have one."

"Why's that?" said Wynne.

Russell shook his head. "I don't feel qualified. I don't know the ins and outs."

Wynne turned his attention to Wheels.

"What about you, Corporal?"

Wheels didn't answer. He just pointed at Russell as if to say he was with his friend.

Bixby cleared his throat. He said, "Captain, we've lost our scouts. We've lost Lieutenant Billings."

"What's your point?" said Wynne.

"Just playing devil's advocate."

"How about playing mine?"

"When haven't I?" Bixby said.

"Sir," said Russell.

The captain turned to look at him. He told him to go ahead.

"Can I ask your opinion?"

"Of what?" Wynne asked.

Russell cleared his throat. He stroked the palm of one hand across his beard.

"I know you can't say whether or not they got our prisoners in this place we're headed, but let's say that they do. What are the chances of us getting them out?"

The captain glanced up at the paling sky and examined the sliver of moon that sat on the horizon's edge, growing fainter with each passing moment. Then he looked back at Russell.

"I don't think in terms of chances," he said.

They rode along a loose talus trail between crumbling slopes that went towering on either side of them. Mid-morning, the trail narrowed and the rock rose sheer on both sides, so that they traveled an alley of sandstone, red layers of frozen sediment, white layers of passing seasons, centuries of them marbled there, and the face of the rock smooth as if polished by hand. Perhaps at one time this had been a river, or perhaps it was merely the wind that, for millennia, had scoured the surface with grains of quartz and feldspar. Russell rode past and, reaching, trailed his fingers against the rock wall, cold as ice to the touch and almost as slick. The clop of the horses' hooves echoed in the pass, and the sound bounced from wall to wall. There was no breeze and the air smelled very clean, and Russell thought this was a story that ought to be handed from father to son, but he couldn't see how that would be possible, and he couldn't help thinking of Sara. He'd grown used to pushing these thoughts away, but now they wouldn't leave: Sara and a farmhouse. Sara and children and a porch. Sara at a table with steam rising from dishes and a sense that there were others and all of them were his. She was his and the children were his, and he knew this daydream was distant as the stars.

The walls fell away and they emerged into bright sunlight, a low range of mountains to the north like an enormous shadow. The slope started at the horses' feet, and in the distance there were holes in the mountainside that Russell studied for several seconds. Then he lifted his binoculars and stared through the right eyepiece. What had looked like holes were actual entryways, and he could see a flight of steps cut into the rock, leading to black arches. He reined Fella to a stop and his stomach fell. He opened his mouth to say something, but the other riders had already seen. Wynne sat his horse with the rifle scope to his eye, and if he was concerned about seeing what Russell saw, he didn't say it. Wheels was about thirty meters behind, both hands shading his eyes and looking very gravely at the mountains. Russell turned the horse and put her forward. He'd gone a little giddy. The air smelled of cotton and straw.

To the south there was a small solitary hill covered in pine trees, and the horsemen made for it, Wynne riding in advance of the others, his golden stallion held to a fast trot and his carbine braced upright upon his thigh. The riders reached the hill's far side—an island in this field of panic grass and nettle—dismounted in a grove of evergreen and began tethering the horses, tying off on stakes. They gathered and knelt around Wynne, and the captain addressed them in a calm voice.

Wheels and Russell, he said, would stay with the horses and pull security. Rosa would climb the hill to provide overwatch. Wynne and Bixby would lead the rest of them to the entrance in the mountainside—Ziza and Ox, Perkins, Hallum, and Morgan—and they'd see if this was, in fact, an enemy stronghold, and if there were, in fact, prisoners of war.

The captain turned and glanced at something on the hillside above him. He stared several moments and bit his lower lip.

"Hallum," he said, "you stay back with Corporal Grimes. Russell comes with us."

Hallum opened his mouth as if to protest this change, but Wynne snapped him a look that ended it. He glanced at Russell.

"That all right with you?"

"Yessir," Russell said.

Wynne nodded. Then he stopped and stood several moments, and they all grew quiet. Russell could hear the horses swishing their tails. The breeze moved the evergreen limbs on the hillside, branches squeaking against each another, a low rustle of pine needles. He motioned them to their respective duties, and they began to cross-level ammunition and ready magazines.

Russell knelt a moment. Then he rose and moved down toward the horses, turned, and looked back over his shoulder. The men were bustling about. He snaked a hand down inside his pants pocket and removed the silver dollar, flipped it spinning into the air, caught it in his palm, and slapped it onto the back of his hand. It was tails and he decided it would have to be three out of five. He flipped a second time and it was tails, and when he flipped a third time, slapped it down, and removed his hand, there was the eagle once again holding the arrows and the branch, wings spread, winking in the sunlight.

The men went up the slope at a shuffle, the seven soldiers traveling single file—bootlaces double-knotted, flashlights fixed to the rails of their carbines, the jostle of ammo and harnesses, and the sound of their huffing breath.

They reached the rock-cut stair that Russell had seen from the valley floor and went running up it, Ox in front of him, his thighs straining the fabric of his fatigues. The steps were carved from sandstone, surprisingly even, though the edges were chipped and he had to take care not to lose his footing. The staircase had been set in a vertical line, but after fifty meters, it angled to the right. They were all sucking wind and Russell's legs burned, and when they finally ascended the last several steps, they emerged gasping onto a level shelf, and there before them sat the cave.

They moved up quickly and stacked at either side of its entrance. There was a sandstone lintel etched at right angles, and Russell knelt there, studying marks in the rockface made by what looked to be hammer and chisel, hundreds of marks, thousands. He put his gloved hand to the stone, a strange warmth to it even though it lay in shadow, and then breathed deeply to recover his wind. He glanced at the captain crouching on the other side of this doorway into the mountains, eight feet high, three feet wide, perfectly edged and sanded smooth by the weather. Wynne looked back at him and nodded, and then he nodded at Ox. The two of them stood and started in, the others filing in behind.

Twenty meters and they were in absolute darkness. The men began switching on their flashlights, the beams moving along the walls, illuminating the stone floor beneath their feet, a powdered texture against the soles of Russell's boots. Russell glanced back over his shoulder to see the horseshoe shape of the entryway grow small and smaller, and then the tunnel made a gradual turn and the light of the world was lost entirely.

They went another sixty meters. The corridor had the blank scent of sediment, and then there was a rich, fecund smell. It grew stronger, and Russell could feel a slight breeze waft across his ears. The ground shifted from stone to something else, and his boots made a sticky sound, sucking away from the floor. He lifted his rifle and pointed it above him and saw, in the beam of the flashlight, that the ceiling had risen fifteen, twenty feet and was covered with brown leathery forms, slightly furred. They quivered when struck by the light, and Russell stopped and stood studying them. He blinked and looked down at the floor and then he lifted his rifle and looked again.

Thousands of bats hung from the ceiling with their thin wings closed over their bodies. Russell shrank against the wall and took a knee on the guano-covered floor. He tried to shake the smell out of his head and then looked to see the lights of the men receding down the passageway. He coughed into his shoulder, rose, and hurried to catch up.

The tunnel veered, then veered again, and he heard the captain call "Stairs," each of the men whispering the word to the one behind. The floor fell away, and Russell pointed the rifle at his feet and began to descend. They went down a flight of steps until they reached a chamber below. Wynne halted the column and they formed up around him. Russell could feel his heart beating against his body armor. He raised his rifle and scanned the ceiling, but there were no more bats. He could still smell them, though he wasn't sure if this was sense memory or scent. He glanced over at Wynne, whom he could just make out in the glow of the rifle lights.

The captain pulled his radio from his belt and thumbed the talk button.

"Underchild Five, this is Underchild Actual."

He lowered the radio and waited several seconds.

"Underchild Five, this is Underchild Actual; how copy?"

They waited, but there was no response.

Ox pointed at the ceiling. "Might be the rock."

The captain nodded.

"Try it again," Bixby said.

Wynne pressed the talk, but when he did, the radio clicked and he released the button. His brow furrowed. He eyed the men around him. He pressed the button and released it, and the radio clicked again. Then something else clicked from the far side of the room and the men turned in unison toward the noise, beams of light flashing against the rock.

Russell went prone on his stomach. "The fuck?" said someone, but Wynne shushed him.

They lay there or they squatted. Wynne had merely taken a knee. He had his carbine to his shoulder, scanning the walls. Russell watched as the white spheres of light played along the rock, crossing and recrossing one another, merging. He turned off his flashlight and began pushing himself backward, back and to the left, dragging his knees and stomach over the damp stone floor. The others began turning off their lights as well, their beams winking out one by one. The captain's was the last to go, and when he switched it off, the darkness enveloped them like a shroud.

There were a few moments where all Russell could hear was the blood rushing in his head, and then he heard the captain's radio click and an answering click came from the utter black ahead of them. Wynne switched on his flashlight, and illuminated against the wall on the far side of the room was the thin form of a man, naked to the waist, gripping a rifle. He raised a hand to his eyes to fend away the light, and as he did, one of the carbines hissed twice through its suppressor and two dime-sized marks blossomed on the figure's chest, just below his sternum, and a red mist spattered the cave wall. The captain called for them to hold their fire, and the figure came lurching forward, dragging the rifle behind him, eyes luminous. The man made it maybe six or seven steps and then he pitched to one side and lay there, heaving. Russell switched on his flashlight, and then a muzzle flashed about twenty yards to the right and suddenly all was chaos.

The men began returning fire, and another rifle opened up from across the chamber, to their left this time, the noise like a can of spray paint, that dull metallic rattle. Russell thumbed his weapon's safety and squeezed off a shot, scooted several feet farther back, then rose to a knee and fired again. Rounds were sparking off the rocks and ricocheting inside the hall, and gun smoke drifted in and out of the flashlights. One of the men yelled that he was hit and another was saying "Cease fire, cease fire"—*Bixby,* Russell thought.

When the shooting stopped, several of the soldiers moved toward the first man they'd killed, and Morgan walked toward the one who'd been firing from their right. Russell watched him kneel there in the darkness for a moment and then turn.

"He's down," Morgan said.

"Motherfucker," said a voice from beside the captain.

It was Perkins. Russell moved up and watched as Bixby helped the man onto his back and began to remove his IBA. He swept his flashlight across the man's legs and up his torso and stopped when he got to the blood oozing from his neck. Bixby had his trauma kit out and was pressing gauze to the wound, but the gauze soaked through almost immediately and Perkins face was the color of ash. Wynne looked at the man and then he looked over at Ox.

"Make sure we're all clear," he said.

Bixby was sprawled over Perkins with his ear to the man's chest. Russell watched him tilt back Perkins's head and pinch shut his nostrils and begin to blow into his mouth. Watched the medic's breath expand Perkins's chest. Watched the chest collapse.

"We got another tunnel here," Morgan called.

"Blood trail," added Ox.

Wynne placed a hand on Bixby's shoulder.

"He's done, Mother."

Bixby shook his head.

"Let him go," Wynne said.

The sergeant sat back on his heels and placed his bloody palms on his thighs. His moustache and beard were frothed with red. Then he reached forward and closed the man's eyes with his thumb and middle finger, like easing shut the eyes of a doll. Wynne tore the blood-type patch from the strip on Perkins's shoulder, that unnerving noise of Velcro, the nylon hooks and loops. He slid it into his pocket.

The four of them moved over to the passageway where Ox and Morgan crouched, a narrower passage, low ceiling; they'd have to stoop as they went. Ox flashed the light on his rifle down the mouth of the tunnel. He turned and looked at Wynne.

"How you want to do this?" he whispered.

Wynne shook his head.

"Fatal funnel," said Morgan.

"Let's just go," said Bixby, and the men turned to look at him. "Let's get it the hell over with."

"Man of action," muttered Morgan.

"Gentlemen," said the captain, and everyone went silent.

A few moments passed.

"There's something glowing down there," Russell said.

One by one, they switched off their lights. Russell had thought he'd seen the glare of something, a blush along the tunnel walls. They sat in the dark waiting for their night vision to return, the rods and cones adjusting in their eyes, and Russell had decided he'd only imagined it when he detected, once again, the faintest glow, a flicker of red light.

"See it?" he whispered.

"I see it," Wynne said.

"What do you want to do?" Morgan asked.

No one answered for several moments.

Then the captain switched on his flashlight, rose, and started down the tunnel. Ox turned on his flashlight and followed. Then Ziza. Then Morgan and Bixby.

Russell crouched, watching their lights move farther down the narrow passage. Terror seized his stomach. He tried to hold it down, but some things couldn't be held, and he thought, inexplicably, of Sara. The feel of her palm, cool against his head. He thought that she was the opposite of all this, the opposite of squatting inside the mouth of a tunnel in the bowels of a mountain range with your teammate's blood still wet on your cheeks and fear like an imp on your back. Then he turned on his flashlight and started to move.

They emerged from the tunnel into a long low-ceilinged room. Firelight flickered from pinecone torches wedged into cracks along the sandstone walls. Russell counted eight of them. He counted nine. There were piles of ammo boxes and rows of wooden crates stacked three and four high. Several cots sat in one corner, blankets on the cots, and in the opposite corner, a crude iron cage.

The six of them entered the chamber and came slowly forward with rifles shouldered. Sand ground beneath their boots. The beams of their flashlights moved along the walls and ceiling, among the crannies and nooks, but there were no SEALs here, no prisoners of any kind. There might have been at one time, but there was nothing now except crates and stone.

In the room's center lay one of the Talibs that they'd shot. He was sprawled on his stomach heaving his final breaths against the floor, fingers dug into the thin layer of grit as though clawing his way across it. His *pakol* cap lay a few feet behind him, and he wore baggy olive fatigues and black dress shoes, no socks. His shirt was missing, and when the captain stepped up and toed him onto his back, Russell saw two dime-sized holes beneath the man's left nipple, his rib cage covered in a thick arterial blood. With every breath he exhaled, it welled brightly from his wounds. His eyes were dark and wet. He lay on his back staring up at them.

The captain motioned Ziza over, and the two of them knelt above the man. Wynne told Ziza to ask him where it was.

Ziza nodded. He cleared his throat and addressed the dying man in Pashto. Russell thought he'd speak harshly, but Ziza's voice was very quiet, very soft.

You couldn't tell whether the Talib understood him. He closed his eyes and then he opened them. He began mumbling words, or perhaps merely sounds, and Ziza bent closer and put his ear to the man's lips.

"What's he saying?" Wynne asked.

"Nothing," Ziza told him. "Just prayers."

"No," said Wynne. He reached across and drew the knife from the sheath on Ziza's back and showed the Talib its long gleaming edge.

"Do you see this?" he asked the man. "You need to pray to me."

He motioned for Ziza to translate.

The commando turned and began to speak to the Talib, but suddenly, the Talib coughed. Then he coughed again and blood appeared on his lips. He leaned up on an elbow, grabbed Ziza's hand, and clutched it tightly. A vein stood out on his forehead. He spoke urgently in his native tongue, panting between the words, then let go of Ziza and lay back against the ground. His face relaxed. He exhaled slowly and there was a rattle from deep within his chest. Ziza reached and placed his hand to one side of the man's throat. He stayed like that for several moments. Then he looked at Wynne and shook his head.

The captain knelt there. When he rose, he still had Ziza's knife in hand.

"All right," he said, turning to face the men, and then his radio sputtered and clicked. Hallum's voice came through the speaker.

It said, "Underchild Actual, do you copy?"

The men glanced at each other. Wynne raised the radio to his lips.

"Roger, Underchild, proceed with transmission."

"You've got company. Over."

"Say again," Wynne told him.

"I say again, you've got dismounts moving in from your six. Fifteen, sixteen in number. AKs and RPGs."

Wynne asked if they were headed to the horses.

"Negative," said Hallum. "They're headed to you."

"Outstanding," Morgan said.

They stood there in the torchlight.

"Copy that," said Wynne, and he had just said it when the radio coughed once again and they heard the transmitted noise of automatic-weapons fire. Wynne's brows furrowed and he keyed the talk.

"Underchild, are you in contact? Over."

They heard the cackling of rifles. They heard men shouting. One sounded like Wheels, but Russell wasn't sure.

"He's got his thumb on the button," Bixby said.

Wynne glanced at the radio in his hand and he glanced over at Russell. Rifles firing. Men screaming. Static.

Then they were moving, the six of them crouching down the tunnel, then back into the hall where they'd first taken fire, past the body of Perkins, the lights on their carbines flashing the marbled rock walls. When they reached the stone staircase that led up to the passageway, the captain halted. The chamber here was wide enough for three of them to walk abreast and Wynne squatted beside the steps and keyed his radio.

"Underchild Five, how copy?"

"Roger, Underchild. Go ahead."

"What's happening out there? Over."

The voice belonged to Sergeant Rosa. It said, "They're in contact down below me, Grimes and Hallum. I count three Talibs with RPGs and half a dozen with small arms coming to you."

Wynne asked him how far out.

"Just started up the slope," Rosa said.

The captain looked over at Ox, his face lit from beneath like a jack-o'-lantern's.

"What do you think?" he asked.

"Can't let them get their rockets off," said Ox. "They'll suck out the oxygen and suffocate us."

"Or burn us out," said Bixby.

"Or burn us," Ox agreed.

Wynne nodded. He said he was open to suggestions.

Ox said, "We need to hit them while we got gravity working for us. I'd sooner be throwing rounds downhill than up."

"Plunging fire," said Ziza.

"Exactly," Ox said.

"We won't have any cover," said Morgan. "Not out on that shelf."

"They get up the slope with those launchers and we're fucked," Ox told him. "Bottom line."

Wynne seemed to consider all of this. He keyed his radio.

"Five," he said, "we're moving to engage from up top. Can you get line of sight on our Tangos? Over."

Rosa told him he could.

"Execute to follow," said the captain.

"Wilco," Rosa said.

Wynne slid the radio back in its pouch, turned, and stood. He motioned for Ox to lead the way up the stairs, then fell in behind. Morgan followed, then Ziza and Bixby. Russell went trailing after, gripping his rifle so tightly he couldn't feel his hands.

They emerged from the cave into afternoon sunlight, taking knees on the sandstone ledge and then proning out on their stomachs to peer over the edge of the shelf. Russell knelt behind Ziza and then duck-walked toward the rock-cut stairs they'd ascended earlier. Wynne and Ox lay of the very brink of the ledge, staring down through their rifle scopes. Russell shouldered his carbine and looked downhill where the stairs angled across the slope's final stretch, the hillside very steep and, except for the stairs, impassable. He could hear the rustle and clink of gear as Bixby and Morgan got into position. He couldn't see the Talibs and was reaching for the binoculars in the cargo pocket of his fatigues when he heard the captain unsafe his rifle. Then he heard Ox and Ziza doing the same. He squinted through his carbine's optic and saw two black turbans come into view. Faces beneath the turbans, then shoulders and torsos.

The captain keyed his radio.

"Execute," he said.

The lead Talib was completely visible now, running the stairs with his rifle at port arms, about fifty meters out. Russell heard the crack of Rosa's rifle, and a second later a cavity opened in the center of the man's chest and he was propelled several feet forward, pitching onto his face. The man behind him turned to look in the direction of the rifle shot, and Russell heard another crack, and this man's head vanished in a bright burst of red. His body tipped backward and then slid from sight.

Everything went instantly quiet. He breathed in and out. He heard Wynne key the talk button and ask Rosa what the other Talibs were doing. Russell snugged the stock of his carbine tighter into his shoulder, relaxed his hand on the grip, opened and closed it several times to get the blood moving. His scalp was tingling and a warm breeze stirred the damp hairs on the back of his neck. Ziza was just to his right, and Russell glanced quickly at the commando lying there beside him with the scope to his eye. He wondered if the man saw something he didn't. He wondered if they'd have to fight their way back to the horses. It occurred to him that the horses might've been killed in the exchange earlier, and then it occurred to him that perhaps Wheels had been as well.

Then they were taking fire, the rounds buzzing in low and sparking off the rocks. Russell couldn't see the shooters, but he hated them instantly. It always surprised him—men you didn't know, never spoke to, never laid eyes on. As soon as that first shot cracked over your head, bile rose from your gut and you loathed whomever would aim the weapon and pull its trigger. You knew they loathed you as well, and you were bound together until one or both of you died and the hatred turned to sadness or rage, something else to carry inside you like a tumor. Russell pressed his chin against the deck, tried to remember to keep his heels down. Ox was releasing controlled bursts from his machine gun, and Ziza had begun to fire as well—spacing the shots carefully, conserving ammo, Russell thought. He shifted his weight and peeked out through his gunsight at the staircase below. There were no Talibs trying the steps, and Rosa's voice came barking over the radio in a metallic stutter:

"Right flank! Right flank! Right flank!"

Russell was just processing the words when he heard the *whoosh* of a launcher and then the low hiss of the rocket traveling toward them. He glanced over in time to see a vapor trail climbing the steep slope to their right, and then he palmed the back of his head with both hands and tucked his chin between his elbows. He'd just done this when there was a loud explosion and debris began falling from the cliff face above. Sand and small clods of dirt rained all around, and there was a fog of dust so thick he couldn't see. He began to hack and cough, and there was dirt in his eyes. He wished for his sunglasses that he'd lost during the assault on the building where they'd been ambushed, and it occurred to him that they'd been ambushed a second time, only this was a trap they'd expected and the captain had led them into it. He coughed again, cleared his throat and spat, then tried to blink the dust from his eyes. He heard Rosa's rifle crack once, twice, and then his voice over the radio telling them to fall back. The dust began to settle and Russell saw what he could hardly believe: Talibs traveling up the hillside.

This slope was impossible to traverse—as unstable as it was steep—but the three forms came up it regardless, spaced twenty meters apart and sprinting. They wore black turbans and black man-shirts, and as they came they hip-fired their rifles. They were about a hundred yards below Russell, maybe a little less. Ziza already had his gun in the fight, and Ox had moved up to kneel beside him, firing on these men moving up the incline, one dropping and sliding backward, two more appearing in the distance to take his place. The captain had crawled up beside Russell—so had Sergeant Bixby—and he glanced to his left and saw Morgan had pulled the pin on a grenade. He rose to lob it, and then his head whipped violently to one side and he fell back and disappeared over the lip of the shelf. Russell called the man's name, but he couldn't hear his own voice, and it wasn't until the sound of the grenade came from the hillside below that the others turned. Bixby shot Russell a confused look, but Wynne's expression indicated he understood almost immediately, and the captain turned back to the enemies approaching from their right and continued to fire.

Then Rosa's voice was loud on the radio. He said they were under fire themselves. He said they were pinned down. He said the captain's position was about to be overrun, and then the radio went suddenly silent and Russell could hear the man's rifle cracking down below. There was the tight staccato chatter of carbines and then the dull, loose rattling of enemy AKs. Another RPG came *whoosh*ing over the shelf and exploded above them, closer this time. Russell's ears were ringing and fragments of rock peppered the backs of his legs. Smoke everywhere. All of them coughing. The Talibs couldn't get a rocket directly on them, but they were using the explosions to provide cover as they moved, and Russell knew in another few minutes they'd be fighting them hand to hand. The dust started to drift, and the smell of gunpowder was back behind his eyes, sharp as needles, and then he heard the captain's voice:

"No one fire," it was saying. "Everybody on the deck."

Russell didn't know what they'd possibly fire at—none of them could even see—and they were all pressed to the earth anyway, awaiting their deaths.

But Wynne was crawling backward, inching toward the left side of the shelf, hissing for the others to do the same. Russell thought he was directing them toward the cave—which would certainly be the end, boxed in and buried—but that wasn't the captain's plan.

The four of them followed Wynne, belly-crawling, ten yards, twenty, dragging their bodies across the sand backward until their boots touched the rock wall on the far side of the ledge and they could go no farther. Russell was up against the edge of the shelf, the toe of his left boot hanging out over empty space, Ziza beside him, the captain to Ziza's right. Then Sergeant Bixby. Then Ox. Wynne addressed them in a loud whisper. He pointed toward the far side of the shelf, the lip they'd been firing from and over which, at any moment, the Talibs would appear.

"Make them think they've killed us," he said. "Make them think they pushed us back inside. They'll be forming up down below us. They'll come at us in a line. Don't squeeze off a single round until you can see them from the knees up. You need to reload, do it now. Work your way from the outside in. Roger that?"

"Roger," they all said.

Russell ejected his magazine. He had, from the weight of it, maybe ten or eleven more rounds, and he tossed the clip in his dump pouch, pulled a fresh one from his hip, and inserted it in the mag well, giving it a tap with the heel of his hand. He drew back the charging handle and canted his rifle to the left to make sure there was brass in the chamber, then released the handle and let it slam home, careful not to ride it, pressing the forward assist several times to make certain the round had seated. He tightened his grip on the rifle and pressed his heels against the ground, got his spine into alignment, inhaled and exhaled a few quick breaths. Then he stared through his gunsight at the far end of the shelf, holding the red dot about three feet off the ground, aiming for what would be center mass. He thumbed off the safety and rested the pad of his index finger very lightly against the trigger. He thought these would be the last bullets he'd ever fire from a gun, and then there was a shrill cry from the slope below them, a strange alien yawp like a dozen voices screaming the same unintelligible curse, and Russell felt his bladder give way and the crotch of his pants go warm. Wynne was whispering to them, the captain's voice like a narrow bridge onto which he was walking—step by step by step—only the words allowing him to move forward while everything else urged him to close his eyes and collapse. The captain said to stay tight, stay focused, not to break their shots until they could see their targets from the knees up, and Russell managed to step out on Wynne's promptings, a little bit farther, a little farther still. Each word was a brick beneath his feet, and Russell inhaled very deeply and blinked. One moment he was staring through his optic at an empty expanse of sky, and the next there were four men in their long shirts and turbans. Five men. Six. They seemed to appear on the shelf out of nothing—eight of them now—moving at a sprint. They wore the cheap high-top sneakers Americans called "Cheetahs" and carried their rifles very low. Russell watched their expressions shift from resolve to bafflement, eyes visibly widening. He realized they were close enough that he could see their eyes, maybe fifteen yards, and then these men were coming suddenly apart. He'd snapped off half a dozen shots in quick succession, as had Ziza and the captain, while Ox let go his machine gun in a long uninterrupted burst. The men rushing them seemed to have struck an actual wall, bodies moving back as their legs continued to carry them forward, garments shredding, a black-sleeved limb separating from its torso and turning end over end in the dry desert air. And then just as quickly as the Talibs had appeared, they were lying on their backs with legs bent underneath them, Wynne already up on a knee with his rifle shouldered, then Ox, then Ziza, the three of them standing and moving forward, hips locked, walking from the knees down, snapping additional rounds into the dead and dying Talibs as they went past, kicking rifles away from their hands. Russell cast a quick glance over to Bixby, who was still proned out on the ground himself, then looked back toward the captain and Ziza and Ox, who'd reached the far end of the shelf and were now firing over its edge.

And then the engagement was over. Wynne was walking back toward them, keying the radio to raise Hallum or Rosa, Ox behind him laughing contentedly, a warm light in his eyes, joyful as a boy. Ziza began to laugh, and Russell found that he was smiling as well—he couldn't help it—adrenaline coursing, the euphoria like something that could split your chest. He could hear gunfire from across the valley, the long rattle of an AK, and then two quick shots in answer. Then nothing.

He stood and followed Bixby over to the mouth of the cave, where Ox stood beside the captain. He glanced at Ziza. The Afghan was still standing at the far end of the ledge. He looked at

Russell and smiled, ejected the magazine from his rifle, and let the mag fall to the ground. He'd reached to the mag pouch on his belt when a Talib clambered over the lip of the shelf with an AK to his shoulder. Ziza turned to see him just as he appeared—the two of them less than a meter away—and the commando dropped his rifle and reached behind his neck to draw the enormous knife from its sheath. He raised it and stepped forward to make a pass at his enemy, but the Talib emptied his clip into Ziza and sent him sprawling back. Ox and the captain had their backs to the men, but Bixby lifted his weapon and fired, missing each shot. The Talib pointed his rifle, but he was either out of ammunition or his gun malfunctioned, and Russell drove his gun forward and put two rounds into the man's midsection.

The Talib went down hard, rifle in his lap and his hands pressed against the bright blood spreading across the front of his shirt. The captain turned and began firing, and the Talib jerked backward and then lay still.

The four of them moved up and knelt around Ziza. He'd fallen onto a clump of broken sandstone, and there were bullet wounds across his groin, bullet holes in his throat and face. His mouth was open, the front teeth shattered, and his brown eyes stared up at nothing. Wynne put his hand to the commando's chest and Ox began to curse. The captain tore the Velcro patch from Ziza's shoulder—A POS—and held it a moment. Then he rose, slid it in a cargo pocket, and started back toward the mouth of the cave. As he went he keyed the radio, calling once again for Rosa.

"What are you thinking?" Bixby asked.

"I don't know," the captain said.

"You think their radios are down?"

"I said I don't know," Wynne told him.

He tried the radio again: "Underchild, this is Underchild Actual, how copy?"

He stood waiting for a response, with the breeze stirring his hair, blue eyes very bright. He turned and looked back toward the valley where they'd left the others. Then he turned and looked at Bixby and Russell.

"Take Russ and go see what the deal is," he said to Bixby. Stay in radio contact. You get eyes on, grab Wheels and beat feet back up here."

"You're going back?" Bixby said.

"Me and Ox," the captain told him. "Get moving. I want to be back on the trail in an hour."

"How about we get back on the trail now?" said Russell.

The captain's brows tightened and his eyes seemed to narrow.

"Get moving," he said.

Russell and Bixby came down the slope, skidding through the talus, raising a gray dust. They made the flat floor of the plain and went toward the grove of evergreen saplings at a sprint. It was about a hundred yards out, and then it was seventy-five yards, fifty, twenty-five, and then they were jogging among the leaves and limbs. They came crashing through the underbrush and branches, and when they entered the clearing where the horses had been tied, the first thing Russell saw was Hallum on his back with his body armor stacked beside him; the second thing was Wheels sitting beside him with the radio propped on his knee. He had his back to a tree and a tourniquet wrapping his left thigh, and Russell walked up and saw that Hallum was dead. Wheels looked up at Russell. He'd been shot through his right thigh. His eyes quivered.

"We've been sort of busy," he said.

Bixby began examining the wound, cutting off Wheels's pants leg with a pair of medical shears, pressing the skin around the wound with his fingers. Russell didn't think it looked that bad, but the sergeant's face was grave.

"Where's Rosa?" Russell asked.

"Still in his perch," said Wheels. "You had to've heard his rifle."

"We heard it," Bixby said.

Wheels shook his head. "He's been racking them up. He'll be pissed no one's here to confirm."

"Morgan and Perkins are gone," said Bixby.

"Zero too," Russell added.

"Talibs?" Wheels asked.

Russell nodded.

"They got Ziza?" said Wheels.

"Yeah."

"Perkins too?"

"Perkins too," said Russell.

"Where's the captain?"

Russell was about to tell him, when the radio crackled to life.

"Underchild Five, how copy?"

Wheels glanced down at the radio, then picked it up and keyed the talk.

"I read you," he said, "go ahead."

"What's your situation? Over."

"We lost Hallum," said Wheels. "I took one in the leg. We don't have eyes on Rosa. His radio isn't working."

"Have you seen Corporal Russell?"

"He's sitting right here beside me," Wheels told him.

"Put him on."

"Wilco," said Wheels and passed the radio.

"How do things look out there?" the captain asked.

"Terrible," Russell told him.

"Are you in contact?"

Russell told him not at present.

"We need some help in here," said Wynne, and right as he said it, they heard Rosa's rifle from the hill up above them.

"Sergeant Rosa's engaging targets."

"That's good," said Wynne. "We're going to need some help."

Russell was silent a moment. He told the captain they needed help themselves.

Wynne didn't respond to this. He said, "Put Mother on."

Russell passed the radio to Sergeant Bixby.

"Get back up here," Wynne said. "You and the corporal."

"Captain, I've got a patient," Bixby told him. "It's a through-and-through, but the round just missed his femoral. He could turn into a category highest."

"Not up for discussion," the captain said.

Bixby sat there several moments. Russell could see the struggle on his face. He watched it move from his mouth to his eyes and then back to his mouth again.

"Now?" he asked.

"Right now," the captain said.

Bixby stood and brushed at his pants. Another gunshot came from the hill—still Rosa's—and then another that wasn't. They waited a few seconds and heard Rosa answer the shot. Then everything was quiet.

"Roger that," said Bixby, and then handed the radio back to Wheels.

Russell had reloaded and charged his friend's carbine, then stacked spare magazines beside him on the ground. He squatted there, studying Wheels's face. He was frightened for him and frightened for himself if something should happen to the man. A great cavity of need seemed to yawn inside him, and he knew that he'd only been able to keep it together because Wheels had somehow propped him up. It wasn't the kind of thing you ever said, and he didn't say it now.

What he said was, "You going to be all right? Down here, I mean?"

"Be better down here than you'll be up there," said Wheels.

Russell said he had a point. He gestured toward the man's rifle. "That enough ammo? I can get a few more mags from your saddle."

Wheels glanced at the magazines laid out along his leg. His lips mumbled, counting.

"No," he said.

"You need water?"

"Not thirsty."

"Keep sipping from your tube anyway," Bixby said. The sergeant pointed at the tourniquet around his thigh. "Especially with that."

The cave was cold and quiet, and Bixby and Russell went along shoulder to shoulder, their carbine lights flashing over the dead rock walls.

When they passed down the narrow tunnel and emerged into the torch-lit chamber, they saw that Ox and the captain had removed the lids from dozens of crates, overturned them and spilled their contents on the talc-covered floor. Countless rounds of ammunition, hundreds of Soviet-era grenades. American MREs and new American uniforms and a number of brick-sized packets of plastic explosive, wrapped in wax paper like sticks of butter. There was a small pile of detonators and blasting caps. Another pile of toe-popper mines. Russell and Sergeant Bixby stepped farther into the room, lowering their rifles, glancing around. Bixby called for the captain, and then Russell looked over and saw him. He and Ox were on the far side of the chamber, bent over what looked like a metal footlocker—about two feet long, a foot wide, another foot in depth. He had no idea what was in the chest, but as soon as he saw it, something seemed to yaw inside him and his hands started to shake. The captain turned to look at them, then motioned them over.

Russell went toward the captain. He felt like he was floating. His head seemed to drift through the clove-scented air. He stepped up to the locker, bent down, raised the lid, and let it fall back on its rusted hinge. Then he squatted there in the torchlight, staring down.

It was gold. Gold coins and gold bracelets and medallions of gold the size of your fist, faces in profile on the medallions, none that he recognized. Necklaces. Earrings and pendants. A perfect golden cup. There were steel handles on either end of the chest, and Russell closed his hand around one and pulled. Nothing. Like trying to lift the floor.

He put a hand to his sternum, massaged it, and then he gripped his temples with his middle finger and thumb. He felt his world dissolving, and he thought he was going to be sick. He rose unsteadily to his feet.

"Easy," Bixby said.

Wynne was staring at him, those blue eyes searching his face. Scanning. Assessing.

"We have to get this out," he said. "Use some of these ammo

crates, divide it so it's lighter, try and carry it down two at a time. You and Ox on one. Me and Bixby on the other. We're looking at a few thousand pounds, probably. It's going to take us several trips."

Russell started to speak, but his mouth was so dry nothing came at first.

"You knew," he tried to say.

Wynne continued staring.

"You knew the whole time."

Wynne didn't respond. He heard Ox clear his throat.

Bixby said, "We're burning daylight."

"Were there ever any prisoners?" Russell asked.

"We didn't know what there was," said Wynne.

"Perkins and Sergeant Morgan," said Russell.

"All right," said Ox.

"Ziza," said Russell. "Sergeant Hallum."

"That's enough," Ox said.

Russell had started to back away. He went slowly, palms out in front of him. Like the victim of a robbery.

Wynne watched. He said there'd be time for questions later. He said to give them a hand.

Russell kept stepping backward.

He said, "Wheels is out there with a bullet through his leg."

"I understand that," Wynne said.

"No, sir," said Russell. "I don't believe that you do."

"The captain gave you an order," Ox told him.

"We're not going to get out of here with that," Russell said, pointing at the chest.

"Calm down," Wynne told him.

"If we move Wheels now, he might could have a chance."

"Goddamnit," said Ox. "You will get your ass over here and help move this crate. Do you have any idea what this will buy these fuckers?"

Russell was still moving toward the tunnel, inch by excruciating inch.

Wynne said, "Our enemy will use this to murder thousands. Think about that for a second: men and women and children.

It's not about any one of us. What do you think your grandfather would say if—"

Russell raised the rifle and trained the red dot on the captain's face. His ears were humming and blood seemed to rush to the base of his brain. He could feel himself separating. He was twenty feet away from the captain, and compensating for the height of his optic over the barrel, the rounds would strike Wynne in the throat. When he thumbed off the safety, he could hear the smooth click of the selector snapping into place. He could hear the sound of the torches burning along the walls. He wouldn't have heard this unless it was very, very quiet.

The captain stared at him for several moments.

He said, "You plan to shoot me?"

Russell kept backing toward the tunnel, boot soles scraping across the floor.

"Corporal," said Ox, "have you lost your fucking mind?"

"It ain't me that's the crazy one."

"You better lower that weapon," Ox said, "and you better do it now."

The captain said, "I'm willing to take your service into consideration. I'm willing to make some allowances. First, put down the rifle."

"You say another word," Russell told him, "so help me God."

The captain said, "You're heading down a treacherous road."

"*Put. Your weapon. On. The deck,*" Ox said.

Russell felt his back collide with the wall. The opening to the tunnel was just to his right, but he wasn't going to take his eyes off the captain to look. He stepped sideways, then sideways again, squatted down and started crawling backward. He was a few feet inside the tunnel, his left palm touching the ground, holding the rifle to his shoulder by the grip, the red dot swaying over the captain's chest.

Wynne said, "You realize what you're doing?"

"I should've realized a lot sooner," Russell said.

"This is willful disobedience of a superior officer," said Wynne. "Add to that, desertion."

"You can go to hell, sir."

"They can execute you for this, son. You understand that, right?"

Russell shook his head. He wasn't disagreeing with the captain. He was trying to shake the man's voice out of his brain.

Wynne stared at him another moment. His face was very solemn, almost sad. Then his expression seemed to soften. He nodded at Russell and gave the slightest smile.

"You can go," he told him.

Then Russell was retreating, the arc of torchlight receding in front of him, scooting into the blackness at his back. He'd already decided to empty his magazine into anything that appeared in the tunnel. His arm ached from holding up his rifle, and after several meters he clutched the weapon against his body and focused on getting away. He was halfway through the passage, then a little farther, and then the walls fell away and he emerged into the chamber, crouched for a moment, and stood. He stepped to one side and turned on his carbine light. He waited for a grenade to come rolling down the tunnel. He waited for the flashbang that would detonate and knock him senseless.

He backed across the floor, watching the tunnel's entrance, weapon shouldered and his flashlight casting its circle across the rock. His breath came to him in ragged gasps.

He passed the body of Sergeant Perkins. His light illuminated the brass of a dozen shell casings. Blood dried on the slick stone floor.

He moved several more meters.

Inhaled and exhaled.

Then he turned and ran.

When Russell made it back to Wheels, the sky was shading into evening and clouds trailed toward the mountains to the east. Russell knelt there beside his friend, studying the entry wound on his thigh, studying the flesh on either side of the tourniquet. He looked at him and said, "The captain's gone completely batshit."

Wheels said, "You're just figuring that out?"

He told Wheels about the gold, but Wheels just nodded, as if it didn't surprise him in the least.

"Can you walk?" asked Russell.

"I ain't tried," Wheels said.

Russell squatted there a moment. He told Wheels he'd be right back, rose and went across the clearing, and then down to where the horses were tied. He walked over to Fella, tethered to the picket line by her lead. When he ran a hand over the horse's neck, her skin rippled like water.

"It's all right," he told her.

He heard Rosa fire his rifle from the hillside above, and then the noise of automatic weapons came from the distance. He waited for Rosa's answering shot, but the shot never came.

He walked through the trees, threading his way back to the clearing. Wheels was leaning against a poplar and holding his left foot a few inches off the ground, his jaw clenched and his teeth gritted together.

"Can you ride?" Russell asked him.

"'Course," said Wheels, and then he placed his foot against the earth and his eyes rolled into his head, and Russell thought Wheels was going to faint. He went over and steadied him, then bent to study the wounds. A clear serum was leaking from them.

"I think they got Sergeant Rosa," said Wheels.

"I think they did, too," Russell said.

"What do you want to do?"

"How about we skedaddle?"

"Captain ain't going to like that," said Wheels.

"Captain can kiss my Sooner ass," Russell said.

He went back to where the horses were tethered, untied Fella, mounted her, and then rode over to the other picket line and untied Wheels's horse. The stallion was nervous, but he led just fine, and Russell walked them up through the trees and back into the clearing. He rode over beside Wheels and then he brought both horses to a stop and swung down from the saddle.

They managed to get Wheels to the horse, and he took the horn in one hand and the cantle in the other and tried to pull himself up. He turned back and looked at Russell.

"I'm going to need a little boost," he said.

Russell nodded. He interlaced his fingers, made a stirrup of his hands, bent, and slid them underneath Wheels's left boot heel.

"Count of three," said Russell. "One. Two. Three."

Russell was bent from the waist, and he jerked up, lifting Wheels's boot. He felt Wheels rising and then he felt something give way in his back, and a white hot pain shot down his legs. Then Wheels was in the saddle and Russell staggered and leaned against a tree. He thought for a moment he'd been shot.

Wheels was asking if he was all right. Russell didn't answer. He staggered to his horse, put his foot in the stirrup, and swung himself up. When he got seated in the saddle, he knew something was very wrong, and he bit down so hard he was afraid he'd crack a tooth. His entire lower back felt as if the bones had been sucked out and stuffed with cotton, and a sharp electric pain was traveling down his legs, an ice cream headache in the nerves.

Russell flipped the reins and put the horse forward, and they went across the clearing, through the trees, past the other horses, past the captain's perfect stallion, gunshots ringing out behind them as they chucked up and went riding down the trail.

THEY RODE UNTIL just after dark, the horses stepping along the trail between the high sandstone walls. Every hoof fall and bounce in the saddle sent the pain shooting down the backs of Russell's legs, and he tried to lean forward to take the weight from his spine, but if he was going to ride, he was stuck with it. Wheels had begun to drift in the saddle, and when they stopped in a sycamore grove a few hundred yards from the trail, his leg started bleeding again and Russell couldn't get it to stop.

Russell climbed down from Fella and leaned against her several moments. He could feel the horse's heartbeat syncing with his own, his own with the horse's, and he tried to decide how he'd get Wheels out of the saddle. Then he tried to figure out how he'd get him back on it when it was time to move on. He stepped back and looked at his horse. She had bent her neck and was cropping tufts of grass. He petted her several seconds.

"Let's get you some water," he said.

When he walked over to Wheels, his friend's eyes were closed and Russell thought he'd passed out. He was about to place his palm on Wheels's thigh, when he said, "What do we got to eat?"

"You hungry?"

"Starving," Wheels said.

"Let's get you down."

"How you want to do it?"

"I'm open to suggestions," Russell told him, and Wheels sat there, staring at the ground like it was something he'd build a bridge to. He looked at Russell.

"We're about a pair."

"Yeah," said Russell.

"How's your back?"

"Hurts," Russell said.

"What do you reckon you did to it?"

Russell didn't know.

"What if I just climb down on the right side here, sort of use you for balance."

"Can you do it that way?" Russell asked.

"Yeah," said Wheels. "I think."

It ended up being much easier than he thought, and Russell helped Wheels down and then a few feet over into the trees, and they made their camp, Russell spreading their saddle blankets and sleeping bags and then going back to the horses for their MREs.

When he ducked under the limbs, Wheels was seated against the trunk of a sycamore with his leg crooked up, studying the wound. He looked over and saw Russell.

"What are your thoughts on a campfire?" he asked.

"I wouldn't risk it," said Russell, and Wheels said that was probably for the best.

He walked down to a stream and found a cloudy pool into which he sunk his canteen. He squatted there watching the moon reflect off the water's surface and then he lifted the canteen and stood. He thought the odds were against them living through the night.

They sat mixing creek water into their MRE packets—beef ravioli, potato cheddar soup, cocoa beverage powder—stirring the concoctions into various pastes and slimes. Russell had treated the water with purification tablets, strained it through a T-shirt, and still the mixtures tasted foul. They ate every bite and then ran their fingers along the inside of the packages and licked them clean. They'd decided to make a third meal and split it between them when an immense explosion echoed down the valley and a low rumble shook the ground. Flocks of birds went scattering from the trees. They sat frozen with their hearts hammering.

"The fuck was that?" Wheels said.

Russell's mouth was full of chocolate pudding. He swallowed painfully and stared up at the stars.

"Artillery?" said Wheels.

"Wasn't artillery," Russell told him. "We'd have heard the round."

"Then what was it?"

Russell shook his head.

"Should we get out of here?"

"Probably."

"Are we?"

Russell thought about it for several moments. Then he said if something was going to get them, it would have to get them.

When Russell woke the next morning in the gray light before dawn, Wheels was sitting up against the tree, eating another MRE. Russell brightened when he saw him seated like that, but when Wheels passed him the canteen he'd been drinking from, his hand felt like he'd just removed it from a fire; Russell set the canteen aside and pressed the back of his hand against his friend's forehead.

"You've got a fever," he told him.

"Tell me something I don't know," Wheels said.

They were on the trail all day long. Around noon, Russell's back began to hurt so badly that he removed everything from his Molle pouches and stowed the various items in his saddlebags. Then he began to strip off the body armor. The vest weighed just under thirty pounds, and he felt lighter after dropping it, but not much. Wheels, sick as he was with blood loss and fever, turned in the saddle and looked back toward the sound of Russell's IBA hitting the dirt. He stared at Russell a moment.

"You're bulletproof now?" he asked.

Russell didn't answer, and after a while Wheels faced forward and they rode on.

That evening, they made camp in a narrow draw beneath an

overhang in the rock, and it began to sprinkle and then to rain. Russell was lying face-up on his sleeping bag when the drops started, and he watched them slant in the twilight. His back was to the point that he had to breathe very shallowly in order to stand it. The electricity pulsed down the backs of his legs, and the toes of his right foot were completely numb. He had two fentanyl lollipops in his kit, but he was saving them, he didn't know for what. He rolled to his side, made it to his feet, and walked over to where he had the horses hobbled, removed the poncho from his saddlebags, and then went to get Wheels's. When he came back, the man's fever was gone but his breath was very shallow and he stared at Russell as if from some great distance. His eyes had calmed and the pupils were motionless.

"Don't you even think about it," Russell said. "You hear me, Brett?"

Wheels gestured down at his leg. The bandage was soaked through with blood.

"Only got so much of that in me," he said.

"You stay with me," said Russell. "Don't leave me out here like this."

Wheels shook his head, closed his eyes for several moments. Then he wet his lips again and looked up at Russell.

"They're going to ask you about him. Tell them the truth."

"Tell them yourself," said Russell.

"Promise me something," Wheels said.

Russell nodded.

"Don't try and take a bullet for the man."

"I don't know what you're talking about," said Russell.

"Yeah, you do. When they ask about him, you tell them everything you saw. Tell all of it. Don't leave nothing out. Don't try and make him look no better than what he is."

"You don't need to worry about me making him look good," said Russell. "I get the chance, I'm going to give somebody an earful."

"Just tell them the truth," said Wheels.

"When have you known me not to?"

"That's what I'm saying," Wheels said. "Don't start now. Don't try and cover for the man. I don't care that he was a Ranger."

"He ain't no Ranger to me," Russell said.

Wheels smiled.

"Good," he said. "That's good." He reached and patted Russell on the arm. "Now quit bugging me and let me sleep."

Russell prayed that night. He couldn't remember the last time he had. He always pictured God as some amalgam of his grandfather and an old face in the sky, and he lay on his back staring up at the sandstone overhang, asking that they make it out alive. He said he didn't want to die out here and he didn't want his friend to die, and he asked that he'd be able to see Sara again, and he asked for a good night's rest. He thought of praying for his back, but he figured he'd already asked enough of God, and he drifted off to sleep listening to the sound of rain against the rocks and the snuffling of the horses.

When he awoke, the sun was already up and the sky had cleared, and it had turned cool and his breath fogged. His sleeping bag was wet, and he rose stiffly and stretched and then went to check on Wheels.

The man had propped himself up in the night, leaning back against the rock, knees pulled to his chest. His eyes were open and he was very still, and Russell knew before he even checked his pulse. He walked out onto the trail and stood there in the morning light. Birds were chirping from the trees and the stream alongside the trail was swollen with water, and Russell stood with his face in his hands, the sobs coming to him in spasms.

He was back on the trail before noon, Wheels's horse tethered to Fella and his friend doubled over the saddle, wrists bound to ankles and the body wrapped in the man's blankets and tied at either end. The day had grown warm in the space of several hours, and Russell went along the trail, his back in agony and his mind numb as his feet. He didn't care whether or not he made it, but he did care about the horses. He was traveling the same path they'd taken to the compound, but he didn't recall the terrain. He found himself talking to Wheels. It didn't occur to him that this was strange.

"We get lost out here, they'll be finding the both of us dried out like locusts."

He turned and glanced back at the corpse of his friend and saw swarms of flies at either end of the blanket. He stopped Fella, then doubled back along the ten feet of lead line and began to swat furiously at the insects. The flies would disperse for several moments and then immediately return. He felt his throat growing tight and the tears starting to come, but he knuckled them away, turned his horse, and rode back down the trail.

He rode for the next several days, the hours bleeding into one another, the days merging into nights. His watch had stopped at some point. He didn't know when. On the evening of the fifth day, he counted rations and found he had two meals left and half of another. He'd no idea how much farther he had to ride or how much longer he'd even be able to, and the horses had six boxes of oats left between them. He'd been lucky, so far, when it came to water, but he couldn't count on his luck to hold. He made a cold camp in a high pass on the mountainside, inspected the horses' hooves. Their coats were in need of grooming and their tails had started to grow out, but other than that, they were better than could be expected.

He slept fitfully that night and woke bleary-eyed before dawn and sipped water from his canteen. The numbness had traveled farther up his legs and he sat there kneading the muscles with his fingers, but it wasn't the muscles that were the problem. He glanced over to Wheels's body, which he'd left on the horse for fear he wouldn't be able to get it back on.

He laughed to himself, and it was as if he were laughing for Wheels, laughing where his friend would have laughed. Then he came to himself.

"C'mon," he said. "Keep it together."

He rode all that morning and afternoon and when evening came, he didn't stop to make camp, just continued along in moonlight, staring distractedly at the stars.

Morning found him descending a narrow path that wound down from a low mountain, and he watched the sun breach the horizon and illuminate the cragged range of peaks to the east. He reined Fella to a stop and sat watching. Wheels's horse continued forward several feet behind him and then it stopped as well. He'd run out of water in the night, and his tongue felt swollen inside his mouth and his head felt like it would split. He'd almost learned to ignore the ache in his back, but the sharp electric pain down his right leg couldn't be ignored and the numbness had traveled to his knee. Russell turned and glanced back at Wheels's horse and the corpse of his friend tied over the saddle, and he looked again at the sky. Very high, a carrion bird circled.

By noon, others would join, six vultures wheeling against the bright blue sky. In the early evening, he paused among a stand of dry and splintered acacia, climbed down from the saddle, then tottered and fell. He sat there with his legs bent beneath him. He lifted his hands and pressed his palms against his eyes and then he looked up at Fella. The horse was standing there above him. She took several steps forward, bumped Russell's shoulder with her nose. Russell reached up and ran his hand back and forth under her jaw.

"I don't know," he told her, shaking his head. "I just don't know."

He glanced past Fella at the dead man's horse, the stallion beginning to bow under the weight of his friend's body. He had been going to do something about that, but now he just sat. It occurred to him he might have difficulty getting up and then it occurred to him he might not be able to get up at all. The sensation of pins and needles ran up and down his legs. He leaned over and lay on his side. He didn't bother with his sleeping bag or blanket and he didn't bother to hobble the horses. If he were to pass in the night, he wanted them to have some chance at escape. Dusk fell around him and then the moonless dark, and he lay curled in on himself, sleeping fitfully and awakening to the howling of wolves, though whether real or imagined, he could never have said.

• • •

He would have died if it hadn't been for the patrol. They found him early the next morning hunched against a lightning-splintered tree trunk, the Afghan militia emerging from the mist like apparitions, with their leader, Bari Gul, striding at the head of the column. Russell watched these men and he watched Bari, recalling that the last time he'd seen this man, he'd poured five gallons of gasoline down the severed neck of a corpse and set the body ablaze.

The Afghans constructed a makeshift litter from pine saplings they'd hacked to length with their machetes, folding a blanket between. Bari directed four of his men to lift Russell and bear him toward the American camp. Russell was in a delirium of pain and dehydration, and when he glanced over, he saw that several of the Afghans were snatching at Fella's reins and trying to lead her away. He watched Fella dig her hoofs into the earth, snorting and shaking her head, fighting a short man who tugged at her bridle. The man pulled until sweat stood out on his forehead, and then he doubled his grip on the lead line, took a switch from the ground, and began swatting the horse on the flank. Fella whinnied and reared, and then Russell was off the stretcher, tottering forward, screaming for the man to leave her alone, if he touched his horse again, he'd kill him. The Afghans surrounded him and tried to usher him back, but Russell struggled, striking one man in the face, knocking down another. He'd almost reached Fella when motes began to swarm before his eyes. The world seemed to shift on its axis, and the ground rushed up to meet him. He lay there, passing in and out of consciousness. Bari Gul leaned over him.

"It is not to worry," he said. "The animal will be provided."

He smiled and swept a hand between them.

"Everything," Bari said.

When Russell came to, he was in the infirmary tent at Firebase Dodge. The first thing he asked about was his horse, and the next was the body of his friend. The doctors who tended him didn't know anything about horses, but they said Corporal Grimes was being prepped for flight, and the following evening Russell was loaded onto a Black Hawk next to a body bag containing Wheel's remains. The helicopter lifted, circled the spur of the mountain, and then headed southwest toward Kabul.

He was in the hospital at Bagram Airfield for just over a week—hooked to saline IVs and dosed with Dilaudid—and then one afternoon, two orderlies pushed him down a hallway and out onto the tarmac, where he was placed aboard a C-130 outfitted to transport casualties from Kabul to Riyadh. He asked one of the men where he was being taken, and the man said "Germany," locked his stretcher into the fuselage, and injected something into his catheter.

He vomited twice on the plane ride, and when they put down at Ramstein Airbase, he was carried out and loaded onto a truck, driven some distance, and then placed onto a gurney and wheeled into a building. Fluorescent lights in the ceiling. Hospital rooms passing on his left and right. Men on beds and men limping down the hallway on crutches and men seated in chairs wearing thin paper gowns.

They took x-rays. They did a CAT scan and an MRI. The surgeon who came to visit said Russell had ruptured a disk in his lower back, herniated it on both sides, split the annulus. As he spoke, he had pictures that he pointed to with his pen. He said that the procedure they'd perform was called a laminectomy. They'd suck out the disk at L5, S1, fuse that part of his spine, and graft bone between the vertebrae. Russell listened to the doctor very intently, and when he was finished speaking he asked the man if it would hurt.

"You'll be out," the man told him. "It's a ten-hour procedure."

"I mean after," said Russell. "How will I feel after it's done?"

"Like you've been worked over with a baseball bat."

"But I'll heal?" Russell asked. "I'll be able to ride?"

"What do you ride?"

"Horses," said Russell.

The doctor straightened his glasses.

"Let's take it one step at a time," he said.

• • •

Russell was awake, but the anesthesia was so strong he could barely open his eyes and what little he could see was bright and blurry. Around him, the beeping of machines, monitors, groaning from men on the beds to either side. He lay there, time passing at unfamiliar speeds, and then there was a woman standing at the foot of his bed.

"How are you feeling?" she asked him.

"Mmmmmmm," he said.

She pulled back the sheets and touched his right foot. She asked if he could feel her hand.

"Cold," he said.

"That's good. Are you starting to hurt?"

"Yes, ma'am."

"Hold on just a second."

He didn't know where it was she thought he'd go. He was beginning to feel his spine, less painful than strange, and then the nurse was back, this time at his side.

"I'm going to put a little something in your IV."

He wondered what exactly 'something' was, and then a warm feeling suffused his body and it felt as though he might actually lift off the mattress.

"Does that feel better?"

He tried to tell her yes, it felt wonderful, but he couldn't operate his mouth.

Then he was being wheeled down a hallway. His mouth suddenly began working, and he spoke to people whom he couldn't open his eyes wide enough to see, and then he was in an elevator with an orderly and they were going up.

"No hard feelings," Russell told the man. "You were one of the good ones."

"Thanks," the orderly said.

In the room he was assigned, a figure came to hover at his bedside, and he knew by the smell of the cologne it was his grandfather. Russell tried to open his eyes, but now they wouldn't open at all, and he thought, *This is happening, I am not dreaming this.* He reached to touch the man, and there was no feeling in his fingers, no feeling in his face. His hand was like something connected to him by string.

"How'd you find me?"

"I know how to find you," his grandfather said.

Russell lay there. There was a low hum in the room. He didn't know what from. He went to reach for his grandfather once more, but his arm didn't seem to be with him anymore and he ended up exhaling a long breath, a sound like a deflating tire. It seemed to keep going and going. Then he inhaled. He could feel a burning sensation in his lungs, not unpleasant. He told his grandfather he'd done something bad.

"What is it that you did?"

"I don't know if I should tell you."

His grandfather didn't respond for a moment. The sheet felt cool against the tops of his thighs. The light was bright and very warm, and he had the notion if he could just unseam his eyes he'd be granted a rare and radiant vision.

Russell lay there—the humming from something just to his left and the cool of the sheets on his legs and the light pulsing red through his eyelids.

"I disobeyed," said Russell. "I didn't follow my orders."

His grandfather asked how come him to do that.

"How come me not to follow?"

"How come you not to follow."

"My orders?"

"Your orders," his grandfather said.

Russell thought about this. He said it was because they were wrong.

"Well," said his grandfather.

"I'm just not going to do whatever. There's things I've decided I'm just not going to do."

"Well," his grandfather said.

Russell lay there in the warm humming light. He felt like he should just go ahead and get it over with. He started weeping at some point, but there was no sound. His face was wet. Then his neck.

"They're going to kick me out," he whispered. "They're going to give me the boot for sure."

"Ohhhhhhhhhhhhh," said his grandfather, "I don't know about that."

"They'll do it," said Russell.

"Ohhhhhhhhhhhhh," the man said.

He went on to say other things. He seemed to be somehow younger. Russell hoped the man would tell him he was proud, but that wasn't what he said.

The man said that the world was spinning faster, things moving more quickly. You hoped they'd stay the same, but of course they couldn't. He said none of this really mattered, because he'd always known Russell would be all right. From the time he was a little boy, his grandfather could already tell.

"It don't matter how your momma turned out. It don't matter about your dad."

Finally he said that Russell was getting older and soldiering was a young man's burden. He said he'd like to see Russell put his hands to others things. He didn't say what those other things were.

"What am I supposed to do?" he asked, but the man didn't answer.

Russell lay there. He drew a breath from deep in his stomach and managed to force open his eyes. There was an IV stand and the heart monitor, a clear tube running from under the sheets filled with yellow liquid, another running alongside it filled with red. There was a tray with a pitcher of water on it, a plastic vase of flowers, but his grandfather was gone.

When Russell woke the next morning, there were two men seated in folding chairs on the other side of the room: one bald and bearded in military dress, the other clean-shaven with wire-rimmed glasses, white shirt, gray slacks, and black patent shoes. The bald man wore the Class-A service uniform—dark green, the rank insignia of a major on his epaulets—and the black flash on the beret in his lap denoted 5th Special Forces. The men noticed he was awake, turned to regard each other, then rose, carried their chairs across the bright tile floor, and placed them next to Russell's bed. They stood for several seconds. The spectacled man was the taller of the two but he also looked softer, like he spent his days behind a desk.

He pointed at the bald man and said, "This is Major Serra. My name is Fisk."

Russell cleared his throat. Something traveled down it, hard and sharp. He asked them who they were.

"I'm Major Serra," said the shorter man. "This is Special Agent Fisk."

Russell stared at him.

"Agent of what?" he said.

Fisk stood looking down at him. He smiled. Or he seemed to smile. The light behind Russell's bed reflected off the lenses of his glasses. From this angle, you couldn't really see his eyes.

He hitched his slacks and sat. Russell could see his eyes now—very dark brown eyes that were almost the color of his pupils.

Russell tried to lean forward, prop himself up in the bed, but he saw that wasn't going to be possible. His mouth was dry. He ran his tongue between his cheek and gums.

"I'd like to speak with a JAG officer," he said.

"You don't need a JAG officer," said Fisk.

"I'd like an attorney," said Russell.

"This isn't court," Fisk said.

Russell asked him what it was, and the man glanced around the room, a little too theatrically.

"Looks like a hospital," Fisk said.

"We're just here to talk," the major told him.

"Talk," Russell said.

Now Fisk did smile. The corners of his mouth rose, and his lips parted to reveal a row of very straight teeth. He'd had braces at some point. There was no way he hadn't.

He said, "How are you feeling?"

"How do I look like I'm feeling?"

"Like shit," the major said.

Fisk said, "We have some questions about your captain."

"He ain't my captain," Russell said.

"You know what he means," said the major.

"He ain't no kind of officer," Russell told them.

"We have some questions," Major Serra said.

Russell turned and looked toward the door that could open into the room and saw that it was closed. The nurses had been coming in every fifteen minutes or so, but no nurse had been in for a while.

He lay there. He thought that if they smothered him with his pillow or drowned him with a washcloth and the small pitcher of water on the tray beside his bed, there would be nothing he could do.

"Ask," he told them.

The men sat staring a moment.

Then the taller man, Fisk, said, "We understand you were involved in an assault on an enemy compound."

"I was involved in a lot of things," Russell said.

"We understand you crossed into Pakistan with Carson Wynne's ODA and took casualties."

Russell was suddenly very angry.

He said, "Mister, you ain't got no idea what I took."

"Calm down," Serra told him.

"You got no idea."

"Calm down," Serra said.

Agent Fisk was the closer of the two men, and Russell would have struck him, but he could barely lift his arms. His back had started to ache, but he was afraid if he hit the button on the pain pump, he'd say something he'd regret.

"The captain was after something in that compound," said Fisk. "We'd like you to tell us exactly what."

"What compound?" said Russell.

"Corporal," said Serra, closing his eyes momentarily and giving a brief shake of his head.

"There's no need to make this hard," said Fisk.

"Yeah," said Russell, "I'll just bet."

"What did the captain find in the compound?"

"Why do you think he found anything?" Russell asked.

"We don't 'think.' We *know.*"

"You don't know shit," said Russell. "You wouldn't be here if you knew."

"We know more than you might think we know," Fisk told him.

"What are you—CIA?"

"You don't need to concern yourself with that," the major said.

"NSA?"

Serra shook his head.

"ISA?"

"You're turning this into something it doesn't need to be. We're just here to talk."

"Then talk," Russell said.

"Listen." Fisk told him. "We know the captain led a team into the compound. We know—"

"What compound?"

"You know what compound," Fisk said. "We believe he exited the compound. We—"

"I never saw him exit nothing," said Russell, and he was sorry as soon as he did.

The men looked at each other. They looked at Russell. The one called Agent Fisk—who might have been neither an agent nor a Fisk—gripped his chin between his forefinger and thumb.

"Is that true?"

Russell looked back toward the door.

"Is that true, Corporal?"

"It's what I said, ain't it?"

"You never saw him leave the compound?"

"What'd I say?"

Fisk said, "What's the last thing you saw? Before you left?"

Russell drew a breath and released it. He drew another. He thought if they were going to clap the cuffs on him, they should just go ahead and do it. He shook his head.

"Where were you?" asked Major Serra.

"Where was I when?"

"During the assault, Corporal. Where were you during the assault?"

"I grabbed Brett and left."

Fisk said, "Corporal Grimes?"

Russell nodded.

"Why'd you leave?"

"He was shot. I was trying to get him out."

"You didn't leave with the captain," Serra said, his voice almost a whisper. It wasn't a question, and Russell looked back over at the man.

"Did you see the captain exit the compound?" Fisk asked. "Did you have eyes on?"

"It was more like a cave," said Russell.

"Did you see him exit the cave?" Serra asked.

Russell stared at him a moment. He shook his head.

"Is that a *no*?" Fisk said.

"No."

Fisk's face darkened. He said, "'No' you didn't see the captain exit, or 'no' that isn't a *no*?"

"I didn't see him," said Russell. "Captain Wynne."

"Didn't see him leave," Serra clarified.

"Affirmative," Russell said.

"What was the item?" Fisk asked. "In the compound—"

"Cave," said Serra.

"Cave," Fisk said. "What was the captain trying to get out?"

Russell lay there. The pain in his back was hot and sharp. He felt it travel up from his tailbone, creeping along the muscles at either side of his spine, up into his shoulders and neck. The pain pump was lying over the rail next to his hand, a beige length of plastic like the handle of a jump rope, a button on one end, a slender tube threading out the other, running up to a box on his IV stand. He went to reach for it, but he caught himself and curled his hand into a fist.

"I don't know what you're talking about," he said.

"You don't need to protect him," said Serra.

"What is it you're trying to protect?" Fisk said.

Russell thought at this point he was trying protect himself, but it certainly wasn't working.

"Why don't you just go ahead and tell us?" said Fisk.

"Why don't you kiss my ass?" Russell said.

Fisk didn't flinch. His face remained impassive, pale and bloodless.

"Corporal," said Major Serra, "we're just here to determine what happened. People are dead. Your friend is dead. Your commanding officer ordered you to take part in an unsanctioned operation on the soil of a country that is supposed to be an ally."

"Unsanctioned," said Russell, trying the word.

"*Illegal* is more like it," Fisk said.

"Somebody sanctioned it," said Russell. "We went out with thirteen men. We had support from a Bravo team out of Third Group's shop, and there was an entire platoon from the 82nd providing security. They had Afghan spotters and scouts. If you're trying to convince me this was some kind of audible, you're full of it."

Serra leaned back in his chair. He nodded a few times.

"Some of this is debatable," he said.

"I hope to God it's debatable," Russell told him. "I hope we didn't get sent into Pakistan just because someone got a wild hair up their ass."

"Not what we're saying," Fisk told him. "I think what the major is suggesting is that while this mission might have received approval at some level, it's currently what you might call *under review.*"

"So why're you here?"

"We're reviewing it," Serra said.

Russell looked back toward the door. He looked at the pain pump. His eyes were beginning to water, but he didn't want these men to think they'd broken him. He told them if they wanted to charge him with something, to just go ahead and do it.

"Charge you?" said Fisk.

Serra regarded him a moment through narrowed eyes.

He said, "Are you under the impression you're in some kind of trouble?"

"Ain't I?"

The men looked at each other and then they looked back at him.

"Corporal," said Serra, "I'm going to make a recommendation that you be promoted."

Russell felt his world shiver. It seemed to have actually moved, and he placed his palms on the rails to either side of the bed.

"Promoted," he said.

"He's prepared to make that recommendation," Fisk told him.

Recommendation, Russell tried to say, but the word came out "Recadation."

The men sat staring at him.

"Listen," Serra said, "we need you to tell us what the captain took out of that compound."

"Cave," Fisk corrected.

"Cave," Serra said.

"I don't know he took out anything."

"What was he trying to take out?"

"It was a chest," said Russell.

"Chest," Fisk said.

"What was in it?" asked Serra.

"Gold was in it," Russell said.

"And you saw this?" said Serra. "This is something that you saw?"

"What kind of gold?" Fisk asked.

Russell closed his eyes. When he opened them, Fisk had stood from his chair and was gripping the bed rail, knuckles white like he was gripping the rail of a balcony.

"Listen," the man said, "I don't think you fully understand the importance of this."

"I think I understand plenty," Russell said.

Fisk studied him. His face was red now. His cheeks and his neck and the backs of his hands. His entire body had flushed.

"It's not what you're thinking," he said.

"Tell me what I'm thinking," Russell said.

Serra cleared his throat. "We're getting off track," he said.

"He needs to tell us," said Fisk.

"He *is* telling us," Serra said. He gestured to the chair his partner had just vacated. "Why don't you have a seat."

Fisk turned to look at the major, but the major was no longer looking at him. The pain in Russell's spine was like a presence. An actual second person. He slipped his right hand under his thigh and pinned it against the mattress.

He said, "Why don't you just tell me what you want. If it's the gold, I ain't got it on me."

"What we want," said Fisk, "is to know exactly what you saw. Did you see it?"

"The gold?"

"The gold," Fisk said.

Russell lay there. He heard himself say, "It wasn't, like, in blocks."

"Bricks?" asked Serra.

"Ingots," corrected Fisk.

"Jesus," said Serra and gave Fisk a look.

Russell studied Fisk. He wondered why, if they were going to send someone, would they send someone like him? Then he remembered they'd sent Wynne as well.

Serra told him to continue.

"There were all these coins," said Russell. "Bracelets and things."

"And this was where?" asked Fisk. "The cave?"

Russell nodded.

"You went *inside?*" Serra asked.

"Yes."

"With the captain?"

"With the captain," Russell said.

Serra said, "Then what happened?"

"All hell broke loose," Russell said.

"Tell us," Fisk said.

"The Talibs," Russell told him. "They waited until we got inside. Then they came up behind us. We laid up on this sort of ledge and engaged them. They killed our terp and they killed Sergeant Morgan. We'd already lost Sergeant Perkins. There was a gunfight back over where we'd left the horses, and that's where Wheels took one through the leg. We went down to check on them, and Sergeant Hallum was dead. Then the captain ordered me and Sergeant Bixby back inside and we had a disagreement. I guess that's what you'd call it."

"What was it about?" Fisk asked. "The disagreement."

"I said we needed to get Wheels out while we still could, get *ourselves* out for that matter, but all's the captain cared about was the goddamned—"

"I want to show you something," Fisk said. He reached inside his shirt pocket and pulled out two photographs, each the size of playing cards. He handed the first to Russell. It was black and white and he stared at it for several moments, blinking.

"What is this?" he asked.

"Satellite photo," said Fisk. "The mountains where this took place. That one was taken six months ago. You see that small black area?"

Russell lifted the photograph closer to his face and squinted.

"This right here?"

Fisk nodded. "That's the entrance to your cave."

"If you say so," Russell said.

Fisk passed him the second picture. "This one was taken yesterday."

Russell studied it. It looked the same as the first.

"What am I supposed to be seeing?" he asked.

"The entrance is missing," Fisk said.

Russell looked again. So it was. He looked at the first photograph, then back to the second. Same shot or almost the same. The only difference was the lack of the black speck that Fisk claimed was the opening to the tunnel. How he could know that for certain, Russell didn't ask.

He said, "I don't get how that's possible."

"We're not concerned with that. What we're trying to figure out is what the captain did with the package. I need you to see the importance of all this, Corporal. This is treasure we're talking about. It belongs to the people of Afghanistan. It belongs to their government. If Captain Wynne thinks he can waltz out the door with millions of dollars, then he's—"

"No way he waltzed anywhere," Russell said.

"Why do you say that?" Fisk asked.

"It just ain't no way. He and Ox—"

Serra said, "Sergeant Boyle?"

"Sergeant Boyle," said Russell, nodding. "I doubt four of us could've gotten it back up the tunnel, much less down the side of that mountain, and there was only the captain and Ox and Sergeant Bixby." He looked back and forth at the pictures. "I don't know what else—"

Then the hairs on the back of his neck rose and a chill ran up his spine. Something welled up inside him, and he began suddenly to laugh. It was excruciating, but he couldn't stop. He gripped the photographs in his left hand and the bed rail in his right.

"What is it?" Fisk said.

Serra said, "Corporal, what the hell?"

"He blew it," Russell said, tears beginning to run from his eyes.

"Blew what?" Fisk asked. "What are you talking about?"

"The gold," said Russell. "He blew it all to hell."

Fisk and Serra looked at each other. The major told him to explain himself.

"Me and Wheels heard an explosion, but we didn't know what it was. We were down the trail a few klicks, and we thought maybe it was mortars, but it didn't sound like mortars, and we—" He broke off and started coughing. His stomach felt like it was on fire.

"This doesn't make any sense," Fisk said.

"Makes perfect sense," said Russell. "He wanted to keep it out of the Talibs' hands. He couldn't get it out, so he went with the next best option."

"I don't buy it," said Fisk.

"Buy it or don't buy it," Russell told him, chuckling.

Serra said, "What—C-4?"

"Sure," Russell said.

"He had enough to do that?"

"Had more than enough," said Russell. "Just what Sergeant Perkins carried could've blown that cave. And there were crates of demo stacked yay high. Artillery shells. They could've brought down the whole mountain. That's why your photo's all wrong."

Fisk looked ill. The blood had drained from his face.

"Let me get this straight," he said. "You're saying that the captain, instead of moving a chest full of Afghan treasure that was worth mill—that was basically *priceless*—you're saying he wired it with C-4 and blew it up?"

"That's exactly what I'm saying."

"You don't think it's a lot more likely that they got it out?"

"Nope," said Russell. "I think it's a lot more likely that he blew it the fuck up."

"It's lunacy," Fisk said.

Russell shook his head. "Did you not have any idea who it was you sent?"

Fisk sat for several moments studying his lap. Then he looked up at Russell. The nauseated expression had turned to fury. He said, "Corporal, you're being awfully cavalier about this."

"I don't even know what that word means," Russell told him.

"It means this operation was of vital importance to our coalition. It was meant to—"

"Well, which one is it?" Russell said.

Fisk just stared. "Which one is what?"

"When you thought the captain ran off with your gold, the operation was 'illegal,' but now that he blew it up, it's of 'vital importance'?"

"Listen, you hayseed. Do you have any idea the kind of shitstorm that's about to hit? We've got a Special Forces officer unaccounted for and the better part of an ODA missing or dead. Not to mention the whole reason for this clusterfuck is, according to your expert opinion, blown to smithereens."

Russell looked at Major Serra, lifted a finger, and pointed at Fisk.

"Can you get him the hell away from me?"

"Corporal," said Fisk, "I don't think you realize what's—"

"Mr. Fisk," said Serra, "I'd like for you to wait outside."

Fisk turned and stared at the major. He opened his mouth to speak. Then his lips tightened into a small red button, and he rose soundlessly from his chair and walked across the room. He turned at the door and studied the two of them. Then he opened it and went out into the hall and closed the door behind him.

"What's his deal?" Russell said.

"His deal," said Serra, "is he's an asshole."

"Are you for real about the promotion?"

Serra nodded. "How much time you have left?"

"On my contract?"

"Your contract," Serra said.

Russell did some calculations, but his back hurt and his head was foggy and he was likely doing them wrong.

"I would've been stop-lossed sometime in March. I'd need to sign on for another go."

"Then you sign on for another go," Serra said.

Russell pointed down at his legs, as though that was where he was wounded. "Depends on all this."

"No, it doesn't."

Russell felt his brow crinkle. Even that hurt.

"I mean," said Serra, "you wouldn't exactly be running and gunning."

Russell asked what exactly he'd be doing.

"Training for us."

"What—" said Russell, "Fifth Group?"

The major nodded.

"What would I be training?"

"Horses," Serra told him. "We'd like to implement the model you helped establish."

"Model," Russell said.

Serra nodded.

"I can't see this was much of a model for anything."

"We disagree," Serra said. "Regardless of what our friends at the Agency might think. I think that what we're really looking at is an operation that was flawed in its execution, but conceptually speaking, it was very sound. Think about it for a second."

"I done thought about it," Russell said. He realized he'd yet to call him "sir."

The man said, "You're looking at a way of transporting our operators across some pretty impossible terrain. You don't have to worry about engines or mechanical parts or even mechanics. You don't have to worry about fuel. Or gasoline, anyway. You're able to maintain noise discipline. You can carry more equipment than you ever could on an ATV. And there's a psychological effect on the locals. They're way more likely to be sympathetic. They know horses. They use horses. It's our gear and technology they don't understand."

"I heard all of this before," Russell said.

The major sat there looking at him, a thoughtful expression on his face. Then he stood and squared the beret on his head and extended his hand. Russell wasn't sure, at first, what he was doing. Then he lifted his own hand and took the major's, and the major gave it a gentle pump.

"Think about it," said Serra. "You get back stateside, we'll drop your SF packet and you head up to Fort Campbell."

He released Russell's hand, then walked across the room, opened the door, and stepped out into the hallway, closing the door quietly behind him.

Russell lay there for several moments. He'd heard folks talk about the fog of war, the uncertainty of combat, but they didn't seem to understand that there was something beyond the confusion, out beyond the gray, occasions where the universe narrowed to black and white, to either/or, and the equations you solved were zero-sum. Recognizing those occasions was the real challenge, and Russell thought that, for the captain, such choices came down to principles or people. That day in the cave, Wynne had picked the former, Russell the latter. Run the scenario a thousand times, they'd end up making the exact same selection.

At the time, all Russell had been able to think about was Wheels, and the captain was a thing that had finally been unmasked. Now that he knew Wynne had blown the gold, Russell felt differently. He didn't want to like this man, but he couldn't help admiring him—his purity, his drive—and then the gray reached and tugged at him, and he was back inside the fog. He still blamed the captain for Wheels's death, but he knew the principle Wynne fought for was noble. Furthermore, in that final moment, Wynne had let him go.

Russell lay there. His back hurt, but he wasn't thinking about his back. He was thinking about the captain, his blue eyes burning, that smile playing across his lips as though the world turned on its axis because he'd given it a push. And through the pain, he felt once again the pull of this man, a gravity strong as any planet. He closed his eyes and tried to shove him away. Drew a breath and released it. When he opened his eyes, the captain was still with him, another ghost to carry through his days. Russell reached over, took the plastic handle off the rail, and pushed the button.

He waited several moments.

Then he pushed it again.

Russell was in the hospital at Ramstein Airbase for the rest of April, and then two weeks into May, walking in the shallow end of an Olympic-sized swimming pool, lifting three-pound weights while balancing on a Swiss ball, lying prone on a low table while a German masseuse kneaded the muscles at either side of the surgical site. The scar, when he glanced in a mirror, was still a bright jagged red. You wouldn't think surgeons would make so uneven an incision. And after the exercises, after the massage, lying on ice packs, staring at the ceiling, home another lifetime away and the war still very close.

His final week on base, he limped down to the building's Internet café. He wore black sweatpants and a gray sweatshirt with ARMY printed in black across the chest, and he carried a cane in his left hand. They'd dug into his right hip to get a bone graft for the fusion, and the pain was very sharp. The doctors said he wouldn't need the cane forever, but he certainly needed it now, every step its own separate struggle. There was a guard behind a table at the call center, but the man didn't ask for Russell's ID, just looked at his face, looked at his cane, and nodded him through. He went to the nearest computer terminal, sat, and brought up a browser. The person before him had been on Facebook, and Russell typed in his e-mail address and password. Then he sat several moments, staring at the screen.

He had 3,342 friend requests and another 2,000-and-some-odd updates. He scrolled and clicked, trying to figure out how to deactivate his account, but it was completely beyond him, and he ended up logging out and bringing up CNN's homepage. Didn't care about the headlines, just wanted to make Facebook go away. He couldn't remember why he'd wanted to get online in the first place and was about to close the browser and get up when he went to akologin.us.army.mil, slid his CAC/PIV into the card reader, and signed in.

There were the standard government e-mails he used to read and delete and now didn't bother reading at all, several spam messages that had managed to make it through the server, an e-mail from a "Sergeant Dime," another from "B. Stafford Storm," and then three in a row from sdavidovich@mail.mil. The first was titled "Testing" and the second "Is This You?" and when he opened them they both read: "This is Sara. E-mail back so I know this is the right address." Russell felt his throat tighten and his pulse begin to race, and when he clicked on the last e-mail, there was a longer message. It read:

Elijah,

I don't know if you're going to get this, but I decided to write it anyway. I wrote a couple of times before—maybe you don't do e-mail? I have to say, you don't seem like the e-mail type. I'm not either. (This is an exception, so feel special, okay?) If you get this, please send something back pretty soon, because I don't know how long this address will be good for. I'm guessing not long.

They kicked me out—you might've already heard. That little incident with the Xanax and the loony bin that I thought my aunt was able to "fix?" Well, not so much. "The wheels of justice grind slow in this big green machine, but they do grind." (A warrant officer actually told me that. He outta be in pictures). The MPs arrested me at Kandahar Airfield last month, week after you left with your guys. They didn't tell me what the charges were until we'd landed at JFK. "Lying on my application," they said. I thought they were too desperate to worry about that kind of thing, but turns out they're just desperate enough. Go figure. They were threatening to bring charges, but my aunt (same one who was supposed to have "fixed" my situation to begin with) has a good attorney, so I ended up with a dishonorable discharge instead.

So now I'm back in Reno. Living here in this apartment with my mother, working at the Panera down the street. "Would you like an apple or a baguette as your side?" That's my life now. I thought with my time over there I might be able to get my old job at the hospital, but the dishonorable discharge put the kibosh on that. I'm thinking about going back to school for my RN. Not a lot of motivation these days, though, so I don't really know.

Geez. I didn't mean to go off on a thing, but it looks like I went off on a thing. You're the one in a war, and here I am trying to depress you, apparently. It's actually not that bad (that's what I tell myself). At least I don't have any Xanax.

Joking, of course.

I have TONS!!!

That was another joke. (Would you like a baguette with that?)

I actually went out for a run after writing that last sentence. Nothing I've said so far is what I wanted to say. Trying to build up the courage, I suppose, but it's not working. So I'll just go ahead and come out with it. You probably won't get this anyway. And I'll confess to having had a post-run glass of wine.

Meeting you, Elijah, and spending time together, and our talks, and that one night that I'm not going to say any more about . . . I can't quit thinking about all of that. I know I'm being such a girl right now, but . . . I actually can't think of any way to finish that sentence. BUT. That says it all.

I'll be making plans to do this thing, or thinking I'm going to do that thing, and then I'm thinking of you. Wondering if you're all right. Actually praying for you. And I don't even know if I believe in God, for christsakes!

So what do I expect? I have no idea. I guess if you decided not to answer this I'd totally understand, since both my family AND the army think I'm crazy and I'm sure, by this point, you agree. I have these fantasies of us going out on an actual date (do people go on those anymore?), and I have fantasies of us owning a dog together (yeah: I have no idea). I have other fantasies, but I think I've embarrassed myself enough for now, so suffice to say, I really, really hope you get in touch. (Really.) Please write me back soon. If you get this, that is.

Love,
Sara

PS: Tell your buddy I said hi. (Is it terrible that I can't remember his name?)

Russell finished the message and then he read it again very slowly. He hit the reply button, hunted and pecked on the keyboard with the index fingers of both hands, told her he'd received the message, told her he'd thought about her a lot, told her he'd been injured but was fine and would be back in the states in a week. He sat there reading over what he'd written. Then he asked for a phone number where he could reach her and hit "send."

A message came up in his inbox immediately. It looked like it was from Sara's address but "Delivery Error" was in the heading, and Russell glanced over at the guard behind the desk and asked if he could help.

The man rose, walked up, and leaned over Russell's shoulder. He had a slight German accent.

"What is the problem?" he said.

"I just sent this e-mail to a friend and then I got this back," Russell said, trying to keep the panic out of his voice.

"It's a delivery error," said the man.

"What's that mean?"

"You just hit 'reply'?"

"Yeah," said Russell.

"And then this came immediately back?"

"Exactly."

"The address is no good."

Russell stared at the screen. He turned and stared at the man.

"No good?"

"It has likely expired," the man said.

Russell nodded. He thanked the guard and fetched his cane, stood, and started walking. The man asked if he wanted to log out, but Russell told him he never should have logged in.

He touched down at JFK a week later. An hour layover and then a connecting flight to Raleigh. He wore a brand-new uniform with his Airborne and Ranger tabs on his left shoulder, the 3rd Ranger Battalion Scroll on his right. A man in first class tried to give up his seat and swap with him, but Russell told him that was all right, then shuffled past him down the aisle.

In Raleigh, a staff sergeant named Kirby was waiting to take him to Fayetteville, about an hour's drive, and they barely spoke the entire way. The radio was tuned to a country station, and at one point Sergeant Kirby asked if he'd like to listen to something else. Russell told him the music was fine, and that was their last exchange until they pulled through the gates and into the motor pool at Fort Bragg.

He filled out some forms in the office, spoke for a while to a lieutenant who brought up his file on a computer and informed Russell he was past due on his contract. Russell told him he was supposed to head up to Fort Campbell for reassignment, and the lieutenant told him he could take care of all of this up there.

Then he asked Russell what things were like in Afghanistan. He was just out of Ranger School, getting ready to deploy that summer with his own platoon. He asked Russell if he had any advice.

Russell sat for a moment. His back was tightening, and he reached into his ruck, pulled out his bottle of hydrocodone, and took one with the cup of coffee he'd been sipping.

"Listen to your platoon sergeant," he finally said. "And don't take off your helmet."

He spent the night off base with a friend who'd been in the 3rd Rangers before transferring to the 82nd Airborne here at Bragg. He was now a sergeant major, and Russell had left his pickup parked in the man's garage, stored several cardboard boxes in his attic. Two boxes of clothes. Another box of CDs and tools and a coffeemaker his aunt had sent him as a present. He and Travis stayed up most the night on the back porch talking, Travis drinking bourbon, Russell pretending to drink.

"They want me up at Fort Campbell," said Russell.

"When?"

"Yesterday," Russell said.

Travis cocked an eyebrow and stared at him over his glass. "You aren't AWOL, are you?"

"No," said Russell. "Contract expired. I'll renew when I get there."

"So, as of right this minute, you're basically a civilian?"

"Basically," Russell said.

"Fort fucking Campbell."

Russell nodded.

"What—you joining Fifth Group?"

"They want me training horses."

"Horses?"

"Yeah," Russell said.

Travis finished his drink and poured himself another.

"Greenies," he snorted. "What a bunch of psychos."

Russell told him he had no idea.

Russell was on the road before nine the next morning. He reached I-85, then traveled up until he came to the I-40 junction and turned and headed west. The day was clear and a little cool, and Russell drove with the windows down and the wind wings cracked to funnel the breeze. It was a seven-hour drive to Nashville, and he started the climb up into the Smoky Mountains a little after noon, the blue Carolina sky against the evergreen ridges, his pickup laboring around the bends. It was an old Ford F-150, a '74 model—his grandfather had bought it off the showroom in Cleveland, Oklahoma, in the fall of '73. It was Russell's first and only vehicle, and over the years he'd rebuilt the engine and installed a new transmission, replaced the shocks twice and brake pads three times. In high school, he'd sanded down the entire body by hand, repainted the truck, and had the bumpers rechromed. The interior, however, looked how it'd always looked: rubber dash, cracked plastic steering wheel, steel glove box and doors, and a bench seat over which Russell had thrown a saddle blanket much like the one he'd used on Fella. He couldn't think about the horse without getting emotional. You spend so many hours on an animal's back, and with every bump and bounce you are jarring some part of yourself into the horse and the horse into you, a transfer of the spirit through violent osmosis, convection by impact, collision.

He reached Nashville early that evening. Here I-40 met up with 24, and you could take 24 all the way to Fort Campbell. Traffic was beginning to clog the interstate, but he made good time, and soon a sign told him that the exit for I-24 was coming up in a mile and a half. Then he passed another sign that said he'd turn off in three-quarters of a mile. When he topped a hill and saw the actual fork in the interstate, he put on his blinker, slowed the truck and pulled onto the shoulder. He sat there several moments with the truck idling and the traffic hurdling past, semis passing in a roar that rocked the pickup on its springs and shook the cab. He scooted across the bench seat, opened the passenger door, and got out. There was a guardrail and a grassy hill on the other side that descended to an access road, and Russell left his cane behind, stepped over the rail, and started down the slope. He stopped halfway and sat with his elbows on his knees, looking toward the lights shining from the buildings downtown. Chet Atkins. Merle Travis. Patsy Cline. All these names from records his grandfather kept in his office: they'd sung and played and died in this town. He sat there thinking about his grandfather, what the man had told him when he'd visited the hospital room. That was either a trance or narcotic hallucination, but it was his grandfather's voice and his grandfather's smell, and the words his grandfather had for him were the words his grandfather might have used. Which meant it was both real and it wasn't. It was his grandfather and it was a dream.

When he stood and started back up the hill, the air was cold on his cheeks, and truckers passing, seeing this lone American soldier, tugged at their horns, but Russell was done with soldiering. He reached his truck, opened the passenger door, unzipped and removed his jacket, bent down and pulled a flannel-lined Carhartt coat from one of the cardboard boxes, threaded his arms through it, then climbed up into the cab.

Russell stood in line at the restaurant during the lunchtime rush. Men seated around the dining area in business suits. Women in skirts and blouses, hose and high heels. Russell turned and saw his reflection in the tinted window alongside the front doors. He wore a new pair of Tony Lamas he'd picked out at a western store in Amarillo. A new pair of Levi's and a dark denim shirt with pearlized snaps. His brown leather belt was also new, but he'd fastened it to his grandfather's old buckle and replaced the silver dollar in its center. He'd cut off his beard at the hotel that morning, then shaved for the first time in months. He stood in the mirror examining that smooth alien face, the skin pale on his cheeks and chin, dark on his forehead and temples. Then he dressed and hobbled along the streets until he found a barbershop. The man cut it short, smeared it with gel, then parted and combed it to the side. In his reflection, it still looked a little wet.

The Nevada sun came slanting through the blinds, terrain out the windows like what he imagined he'd left behind. Low mountains in the distance, blue in the noon light. The line moved and he took a step forward. Two women in front of him, clicking the buttons on their phones. A large man in front of them doing the same. Another man at the counter, staring up at the menu on the wall, and behind the register, Sara. She wore a black visor on her head with the store's logo embroidered on the front, a black polo with the logo above her left breast. She'd yet to notice him. She looked flustered, and her green eyes went from the customer standing in front of her, down to the register, back to the customer again. There was another woman working the register at her right and another to her far right on the other side of a glass case of pastries. She handed the customer what looked like a plastic coaster with red flashing lights, handed him a clear plastic cup and a receipt. The next man in line moved up, and Russell took another step forward behind the two women.

She wore a bit more makeup than she had at the outpost, a bit more eye shadow and rouge. She was more slender than he remembered. A little more slight. She'd let her hair grow longer, and it was gathered in a ponytail behind her head. He could just read her name tag from where he was, and he saw that whomever had made it had added an *H* to the end. He imagined a manager giving her the tag and Sara standing there a moment, a smirk playing across her lips. Perhaps she liked the idea that she wasn't exactly herself.

She passed the man his cup and coaster, and he walked toward the soda machine set up in a nook against the far wall. She said she could help whomever was next. She still hadn't seen him. The two women moved up together and began to give their orders. Russell was maybe six feet from her now. His heart began to race and he felt his throat tighten. A sweat broke out on the back of his neck. And of all things he thought of Captain Wynne, their conversation in the predawn before they'd assaulted the tower, sitting there sipping coffee, only time they'd ever been alone. No, that wasn't right: they'd been alone at the corral that first time they'd met. So they'd been alone exactly twice, and that second time the captain had questioned him about his father and mother, about his decision to join the Rangers, and after listening to Russell, he'd sat there a moment. And it wasn't what the captain said that stayed with him. It was the look on his face, his entire demeanor, as if what had happened to Russell's parents clarified a number of things. And Russell had sensed something strange. He could tell that the captain pitied him. He could tell Wynne thought he'd been broken, as roughly and thoroughly as any horse. Russell hadn't liked it, and now he liked it even less.

Because, what if he had been broken? What if he still was? The phrase Wynne had used was *children of adversity,* but what he was really saying was that Russell had ended up in his particular set of circumstances because he'd been abandoned. Or damaged. Or wrecked. And maybe what bothered him most was that he suspected the captain was right. He'd thought of Sara in that way. It was one of the things that drew him. You see someone like that—a woman like that—and something inside you reaches out. At least it did in him. And standing there, just feet away from her, it occurred to Russell she might feel exactly the same.

One of the women reached into her purse and handed over her credit card. Sara swiped it and handed it back. Russell tried to calm his thoughts, and he had a strong urge to turn around and bolt. She still hadn't seen him. She wouldn't even know. He had a life waiting at Fort Campbell if he wanted it. Something he knew about. Something he could do. A place and a purpose and a people he understood. The girl in front of him was unknown territory. She was what he'd never actually tried. And she could be what actually destroyed him, worse than any bullet or bomb. He thought about all of that. He could still turn away and walk. A few thousand miles on his truck, several nights of hotel bills, a dozen or so tanks of gas. Call it a detour, an early summer break. The women got their cups and coasters. Sara was staring down at her register. He still had a few final seconds.

The women moved off toward the soda fountain, and Russell stepped forward, put his hands on the counter to steady himself, drew a deep breath inside his lungs, and with it, her perfume. His mind went instantly quiet and the fear seemed to subside. He exhaled the turmoil and panic.

Sara's eyes were on the register. She pressed a button and it made a beeping sound, then it made another. Her face relaxed, and she put a hand to her mouth and cleared her throat.

"Can I help you?" she asked him, and then she raised her eyes.

THEY CAME DOWN the trail in the early morning light, three horses, three riders, the horses so haggard you could see every rib. Their saddlebags were gone, but still they stumbled beneath their riders' weight, the riders themselves stripped of packs and pouches, their uniforms dusted the same color as the mountains, their lean faces powdered with talc and their beards chalked white. A gray company. A cavalry of ghosts. The blue eyes of the man riding at the head of the column were all that marked them among the living. He had a rifle slung across his back and a pistol holstered on his thigh. The men behind him were likewise armed, blood dried in black splotches on their vests. The sky in the east was a pale shade of rose, and when the sun crested the horizon, it stained the riders and their horses with a deep crimson light. The stallion at the head of the column shook its massive head and began to sidle, but the blue-eyed rider spoke to him and reined him to a halt. The horses behind him stopped as well and then stood there, steaming. The stallion snorted and shook his head, muscles rippling beneath his perfect golden coat. He lifted his front leg and pawed the earth. His breath fogged in the morning cold. The rider reached to stroke his neck and the stallion went motionless. The man sat the horse, staring. Then he raised his hand and gestured toward the rising sun, chucked up the horse, and they continued eastward into the strange country below.

Acknowledgments

I'd like to express my deepest gratitude to my agent, Nat Sobel, and my editor, Eamon Dolan. Both saw something in my manuscript better than what was on the page. Then they helped me see it. Thanks also to the A-team at Sobel Weber Associates: Judith Weber, Julie Stevenson, and Adia Wright. More thanks to the tier-one operators at Eamon Dolan Books/HMH, Ben Hyman in particular. And to Kate Davis: commando of copyeditors.

My three best friends were instrumental in keeping me going on this project: Clint Stewart, Mark Walling, Adam Schnier. I wouldn't have done it without you.

(Or you, Skeeter—you continue to draw my blood.)

Special thanks to Sergeant Chip Herrin of the 509th Airborne; to Sheldon Kelly, cowboy extraordinaire: you saw the elephant and went back for another gander. Much respect and appreciation to the Rangers and Special Forces operators who answered question after question: wish I was able to mention you by name.

Lastly, I want to thank Robbie Rosas, Nick Long, and Jerry Redman: baddest gunfighters walking. *Nous defions,* my brothers. *Nous defions.*